The Guilty Woman

M.L. Lexi

Coming Soon

THE UNFAITHFUL WOMAN
THE COMPLETE WOMAN
THE DETERMINED WOMAN
THE FORGIVING WOMAN
THE NOBLE WOMAN

"The Guilty Woman" Paperback Edition
Published by M.L. Lexi

Cover design by M.L. Lexi.
ISBN: 978-1-7752956-6-2
The Guilty Woman Copyright © 2020 by M.L. Lexi
All rights reserved.
Visit our website at mllexi.com
Visit our blog at mllexi.blog

For Albert, who has made this journey through life a memorable one. And to my family, here and long gone, who have made me who I am today.

Authors Note

As a novice, self-published writer, I'm flying solo, and mistakes will be made.

My first mistake was the initial release of this novel.

There were more errors throughout the manuscript than I care to admit because I relied on an editor—I deemed a professional—instead of myself, to check my work before publishing.

The second mistake was to put my novice-writer ego over sound judgment.

I trustingly allowed my editor to skew my judgment by eagerly accepting her overly complementary, three-paragraph manuscript evaluation to pass for expert criticism. My swelled ego clouded my judgment and led me to accept her explanation that she'd made so few edits to the manuscript because my writing had considerably improved. Reading the novel one year later, I'm finding zero revisions made.

The third mistake was to rely on someone other than myself.

I hastily accepted my editor's assessment of the manuscript was good to publish as-is and proceeded to upload without thoroughly checking it. The novel was riddled with mistakes: spelling, punctuation, character names, and their descriptions were inconsistent, to name a few. All errors I relied on a professional—I paid well—to correct.

As the saying goes, "Live and learn."

It's possible my manuscript wasn't worthy of her editing services, but this is my dream she willingly toyed with. Not to mention the fact I didn't need to pay someone thousands of dollars to read my book, which I believe is all she did, and contribute to my embarrassment in the process. I can embarrass myself just fine on my own.

From here on, I'll be triple checking my work and rely only on me, myself, and I. As a result the prose may not be as perfect as I would like, but not only will I save a ton of money, but I'll avoid the needless aggravation and possibly put out a better product.

I think I have a nice story to tell. I hope you enjoy this second edition, written, edited, cover-designed, and published by me, myself and I.

I can now cross out the bullet point off my bucket list.

No one can leave your past behind unless you do.

—M.L. Lexi

Prologue

March 1948

THE AIR WAS raw and thick with death.

A river of blood, still red and fresh, flowed from the man's smashed skull soaking and spreading on the ivory carpet like a Rorschach inkblot. Sofas, chairs, tables, and walls were splashed red. Pearl buttons from Francesca's silk blouse lay scattered in the pool of red, looking up like lifeless eyes, staring, judging, condemning. The coffee table Francesca had fallen back on when she'd managed to escape his grip lay upturned. Shards of crystal and glass from shattered tumblers and bottle sparkled like diamonds on polished wood.

The scene before her belonged in a horror movie, not in her living room, Francesca thought as she violently threw up her dinner.

For Francesca's sake, when the sickening smell of warm blood slammed into Father Matthew's gut, he didn't let emotion slip into his eyes or his voice. He'd keep the nerves kicking in his gut like sharp fists making the sour waves of nausea rise in his stomach at bay. With a calm, Father Matthew didn't feel he set the blood-covered candleholder in his hand on the end table before lowering two fingers to the man's neck.

"He's dead," Father Matthew, confirmed when he didn't feel a pulse and wiping his bloodstained hands on his cassock, reached into his pocket for his stole. Kissing it, he draped it around his neck. "*In Nomine Patris*," Father

Matthew said, piously crossing himself and launching into prayer.

Watching the ritual performed over the lifeless body, made the taste of sickness claw at Francesca's throat again. She swallowed hard to prevent herself from heaving whatever she had left in her stomach as she stared at her bloody, trembling hands.

"*Deus animae meae miserere.*" Father Matthew begged God to have mercy on his soul before blessing the body and rising to his feet. "It'll be all right, Francesca."

Reeling from the violence she had endured moments ago under the dead man's hands, Francesca's voice trembled when she said, "How's this going to be all right? This is never going to be all right. He's dead on my living room floor." Francesca's eyes shifted to the lifeless body, willing it to come to life. When it didn't, she was glad he lay face down. As much as she believed his demise was the outcome he deserved, Francesca couldn't look into the eyes of death. "What am I going to do?" She let her head drop weakly and let the tears flow.

"It'll be all right, Francesca. I'll be right by your side." Shock flew into Father Matthew's eyes when the face that carried the night's violence rose to meet his. Her face was swollen and raw. Her left eye was puffed shut. There was a deep gash on her cheek where the ringed hand-delivered the fisted punches, and her lip was split open. Blood ran down from both. "You're hurt."

"I'm fine." Francesca pushed away the hand Father Matthew raised to her face with the defiance of a humiliated woman. "What am I going to do?" she asked again, this time her voice sounded defeated.

"Don't worry. I'll sort it." Father Matthew crossed to the telephone. The blood-soaked hem of his cassock painted the floor like a Pollock painting. "Leave everything to me. I'm going to call the police now."

Bolting to her feet, Francesca stepped over the body and crossed to Father Matthew. "You're not calling anyone," she said, tearing the handset from his hand and setting it back in its cradle.

"We need to call the police Francesca." Father Matthew tried to reason.

"No, we don't. We'll take care of it ourselves." The smell of warm blood all at once filled Francesca's lungs, and she began to tremble.

Father Matthew walked a shaky Francesca back to the only unstained chair in the room. When he'd coaxed her into it, he sank to his knees beside her. "Take a deep, calming breath. Do it. Now," he ordered. He watched her breathe in deep, exhale, and repeat when his rolling hand encouraged her to do so. "We can't take care of this ourselves. We have to get the police involved."

Feeling steadier, Francesca forced herself to set emotion aside and set her lawyerly, logical mind to think. Mulling the facts in her head, she said, "Go ahead and call the police, but I don't want you here when they show up. I'm going to plead self-defense, and I don't want you involved in any of this."

"No, Francesca, I'll admit to the attack. I'll confess my sins to the police." Father Matthew looked down at the motionless body. The gouge in the back of his skull had welled with blood. Father Matthew couldn't begin to imagine the blades of pain the blows to the head inflicted. "God forgive me," he murmured under his breath.

"But…"

"You will say nothing. Do you hear me, Francesca?" Father Matthew firmed his lips in determination. "Nothing."

"I have to. It's my house. It's my husband lying dead on the floor."

"You don't have to say a word. I'll confess, turn myself in. I'll tell them exactly what happened. He was viciously beating you, and I jumped in to stop him. And…" He raised a hand to silence her when she started to speak. "I need to confess, Francesca. Understood?"

The initial shakes had passed, and Francesca laid her throbbing head back against the chair for a moment to let herself think. "All right, but as your lawyer, you do as I say. Understood?"

Nodding Father Matthew murmured *Deus animae meae miserere.*

One

May 1939

SETTLING INTO THE lounge chair after her swim to dry up under the rays of a bright sun, Francesca caught sight of him. Sliding her sunglasses down her nose to get a better view of the gorgeous specimen working on the gardens hemming the pool, she fixed hazel eyes on him.

He was tall, six-plus by her estimation. His long, black hair billowed in the unseasonably warm wind. The white T-shirt he wore was tacked down to his lean body with sweat like a second skin. Francesca could see the chord of arm muscle tighten as he dug the shovel deep into the dark earth.

He looked nothing like the boys she met at the country club. Those boys were all so perfect: perfect hair, perfect wardrobe, perfect education, and ideal lineage. Francesca hated perfect. Too often, perfect was used to mask a moral code that shook you down to the foundation.

Francesca's eyes locked on the tight butt straining against faded jeans when he bent over to set the purple catmint into turned soil. Intently, Francesca watched as he pressed earth around the plant with boots that had seen many foot miles, and then mulched it. Francesca didn't know who the gardening Adonis was, but she set her mind on finding out.

TOMMY HAD SEEN FRANCESCA MINUTES BEFORE she saw him. He'd watched her since she dove into the pool, and followed her when she stepped out after swimming fifteen laps—he'd counted it off. Her body and hair glistened from the dampness. Tommy's eyes never left Francesca as she finger-combed the long, chestnut ropes of wet hair back from her face. When Francesca stretched her long, wet body on the lounge chair to let the sun paint her dark, Tommy became spellbound. She was perfect. He appreciated perfect.

From that moment, Tommy's probing eyes switched to full-on staring. How could he not? The way the tiny bikini hugged the curvy body oiled in cocoa butter warranted admiration and appreciation.

Tommy had worshiped the female body since his sixteenth birthday when he got his first sexual experience compliments of Backseat-Becky Burnett. Two years his senior, Backseat-Becky in the backseat of her VW bug showed Tommy how gratifying the female body could be. It had been a tight squeeze in the small car for the five-eleven Tommy, but Becky's flexible cheerleading body was accommodating that night and to his delight for the rest of the summer.

Francesca wasn't the Backseat-Becky type, not by any stretch of the imagination, and he was definitely diving into unknown waters with her. Still, Tommy determined to get to know her.

FRANCESCA SET HER SUNGLASSES BACK ON her nose and sank to the depths of the lounge chair. "I see you hired new help, Mr. Scott."

"Not new help, Miss Thompson. It's my son Tommy. He normally manages the garden center for me, but today I'm short-handed." Mr. Scott wielded the garden shears like a swordsman over the box hedges. "Hard to find dedicated gardeners nowadays. Kids don't want to dig their hands into worm riddled earth…"

While Mr. Scott rambled on about the lazy youth of today, Francesca mulled the name in her head. Tommy was such an understated name for the hell-with-you looking rebel, Francesca decided. No matter, because whether he was named Tommy or Blaze, what woman didn't appreciative a rebellious looking man? The fact he was gorgeous was the icing on the cake.

"It's hot today, don't you agree, Mr. Scott?" Francesca watched him rake the trimmings into a green pile.

"Can't disagree with you there, Miss Thompson."

"Would you and your son like a cold glass of lemonade? Mrs. O'Sullivan made a fresh pitcher this morning."

Mr. Scott removed the plaid flat-cap and wiped the film of sweat from the sun-weathered face with his sleeve. "If it's no trouble, I wouldn't say no to that, Miss Thompson, and I'm sure Tommy wouldn't either."

"No trouble at all, Mr. Scott. I'll be right back." Francesca bolted to her feet and slipping into her cover-up, dashed up the flagstone path, across the terrace, and into the kitchen. Moments later, she returned with a tray stocked with a pitcher of ice-cold lemonade, two glasses, and a plate of Mrs. O'Sullivan's oatmeal cookies. Setting the tray on the teak table, she poured into two glasses, handed one to Mr. Scott. "Feel free to enjoy Mrs. O's cookies."

"I wouldn't say no to one of Mrs. O'Sullivan's cookies. They're the best I've tasted." Mr. Scott flicked love-struck eyes toward the kitchen window.

If only Mrs. O'Sullivan could see how enamored the man was with her, Francesca thought. "You should tell her, Mr. Scott. She never tires of being told what a good baker she is. In the meantime, I'm going to take a glass of lemonade and cookies to your son." Francesca called over her shoulder, dashing across the lawn.

Wet blades of grass glinted in an emerald carpet that stretched to the grove of pines, maples, and linden trees fanning out for miles on the south side of the property. The smell of damp earth lingering from last night's rain hung in the air along with the scents of summer.

Francesca cleared her throat. "Umm ... I, ah, thought you could use something cold to drink." Up close, Francesca could see Tommy Scott's eyes were the color of a stormy sea. He had a scar along his jawline, which she romanticized as the mark of a bar fight he'd started and won hands-down. Damp, black hair stuck to his forehead and neck. Gorgeous with a touch of rugged and danger, Francesca thought. "It's umm ... lemonade, and ah, these are oatmeal cookies. Freshly made. This morning. By Mrs. O'Sullivan," she stammered. She never stammered, but the smell of sweat, earth, and man slid into her and scrambled her brain. Take deep, relaxed breaths, Francesca.

"How did you know lemonade and oatmeal cookies were my favorites?"

"I didn't."

Accepting the glass, Tommy raised it to her before tipping it back. "And who are you, princess?"

The cockiness in his voice was meant to set Francesca's teeth on edge, but instead, Francesca curved her mouth into an alluring smile that arrowed to Tommy's groin. "My name is Francesca Thompson. My family and friends call me, Frankie."

Tommy speared the shovel deep into the soil and reached for a couple of cookies. "Francesca suits better."

She gave him a side-eye look. "Why?"

Tommy bit into one cookie and crumpling the rest sprinkled it on the grass. Within seconds, a flock of starlings swooped down from the trees to feast. "Francesca sounds exotic, European, sexy."

Pecking at every morsel of the crumbled cookie, the starlings set off in flight, and the sound of the gurgling creek, which meandered across the Thompson Estate, replaced their tweets.

"I am all that." Francesca's smiling brandy-colored eyes met Tommy's.

She had the look of money, lady-of-the-manor appearance, Tommy thought. Her long, chestnut hair, dry now, fluttered in the wind around a delicate face, with high cheekbones, a pert nose and a wide mouth with lips meant to be kissed. Francesca smelled of chlorine, and Tommy thought it was the best scent going.

"Do you eat, princess?"

"Of course, I eat. What type of simple question is that, Mr. Scott?" Francesca's voice flowed with the graceful sound of wealth.

Blue eyes steady on brown eyes, Tommy pulled out the pack of cigarettes from his T-shirt sleeve and plugged one into his mouth. "It's Tommy, Mr. Scott is my father," he corrected automatically. "Girls like you rarely eat. It's all about the figure and looks," he said although he couldn't help but appreciate both on her.

The wind took Francesca's hair then, and Tommy thought she looked like a siren surfacing from the ocean water. "Well, Tommy, I'll have you know I do eat. Substantial amounts of food," she added as an afterthought.

With a cocked brow, Tommy scanned the long, lithe body beneath the sheer cover-up. "Sure, you do."

"I do. I've been blessed with a good metabolism, and when it doesn't kick in, I run and swim. I was also a cheerleader in school."

Her long, muscular legs had the lean lines of a runner, Tommy concluded exhaling a thick plume of smoke. "Of course you were, princess."

"You look like you played football in school."

"I would have if they hadn't expelled me senior year."

"Hmm, so you are a bad-boy." Francesca turned to walk toward the creek's bank hemmed in tall, willowy cattails. She didn't bother to gesture Tommy to follow. Francesca knew he would. Men, in her opinion, weren't difficult to figure out. They were what she categorized as visual-thinkers. Showing, rather than telling, got them to do what you wanted.

"I think of myself more as misguided." Drawing in smoke, Tommy expelled it in a thin white cloud as he trailed her. "You have quite the spread here." Tommy's eyes roved across the twenty-acre estate.

A thick green carpet of rolling hills hemmed the long stretch of hundred-year-old trees. To the east, the colonial home with its pillared entrance, whitewashed walls, and the vast expanse of windows wrapped in wrought iron balconies stood tall against a blue sky. The estate boasted comforts Tommy could only dream of: a pool, a gazebo, a tennis court, a paddock, and stables that came complete with the best riding horses.

"I like it. I prefer the isolation and quiet to the frenzied downtown life. My father is the total opposite. He prefers the choked streets and the hustle and bustle of city life. During the week, because he works long hours, and because I figure he 'entertains,'" Francesca air quoted the word, "He stays at our downtown condo. He's been doing so since shortly after my mom passed away five years ago," she said, unsure why she'd told him so much.

"I'm sorry about your mom. Does it bother you that your father 'entertains'?"

"It used to." Francesca tilted her face to the burning sun and went silent, and Tommy deduced they'd exhausted the topic. "Do you ride? Horses, I mean." She sat on the nurse log of a red maple next to the creek, picked at its bark.

"Do I look like the horse riding type, princess?" Tommy picked at the bark along with her.

Francesca shook her head. "I can teach you if you like."

Tommy breathed out smoke. "Maybe I'll let you."

"You know your father's smitten with our Mrs. O'Sullivan." From the surprised look on Tommy's face, Francesca surmised this was news to him. "I think it's adorable. The only problem is Mrs. O is oblivious to how he feels. I think she needs a bit of nudging. You don't mind if I nudge, do you?"

Tommy wasn't sure how to react to that piece of information, and mulling the thought over, he remained silent. His mother had passed eleven years ago. Tommy was ten, since then, there had been no woman in his father's life or their home, and he wasn't ready for anyone to step in anytime soon. Francesca left him pondering the notion that maybe his father was ready to embrace a companion.

Tommy had kept his father busy since his mother's death. In his rebellious youth, Tommy had caused his father many sleepless nights. He'd only come to his senses a couple of years ago when he'd spent five days in a juvenile detention center. His time there had been a rude awakening for Tommy, but not more than when his father showed up to pick him up on his release, and all he said was: I've missed you, son. Let's get you home.

That was a turning point for Tommy, and from that day, he set off to change his ways. He voluntarily worked at his father's garden center dedicating long hours to learn the business from the ground up. To his father's surprise and delight, Tommy did everything and anything asked, never giving lip or attitude—a rarity for Tommy.

"I think they'd make a cute couple."

"Yes, they would, and you should nudge. I want Dad to be happy," Tommy said, surprising himself.

"Good. I will." Francesca watched him tap cigarette ash. "You know those things will kill you."

Drawing in a mouthful of smoke, Tommy said, "I've heard. So, how about dinner, princess?" In an unexpected gesture, Tommy played with the ends of her hair and was pleased when she let him. It was as soft as rose petals. "I can't afford Winston's. Nick's Burgers is more in my budget, and I won't be picking you up in the sporty Beemer you're accustomed to, but in my work pick up. The words Scott's Garden Center emblazoned on the door and the bed dirty from hauling soil."

Francesca felt a twinge of guilt Tommy thought her to be such a snob and a tug of attraction at his sincerity. A quality so rare in the titled boys she'd grown up with, and whom her father looked to as prospective husbands.

"I love Nick's," Francesca said, although she'd never been, and looking over her shoulder as she walked away added, "Pick me up at seven."

Two

NICK'S BURGERS, A greasy diner housed in a streetcar, which Nick Papadopoulos decided to rescue from the scrap yard teemed with the usual Saturday crowd looking for a great, greasy burger. Lively swing music pumped from the speakers hanging off the awning hemmed in colorful lights.

"How about this table?" At Francesca nod, Tommy held her hand as she maneuvered herself over the seat board of the picnic table. "I'll go place our order."

"You mean there are no servers." Francesca laughed when Tommy's brow winged high. "Jesus ease up, Scott."

"Sure, okay. I'll be right back," Tommy said, and Francesca followed his tight butt, which looked even better tonight in freshly pressed jeans, to the order window.

Francesca's eyes never leaving Tommy, she watched him place the order and push away from the counter to wait for his number to be called. She smiled when his eyes skirted the two strawberry-blonde haired beauties prancing their assets for his attention to her. Looking past them, Tommy gave Francesca a wink as he plucked a cigarette, and touched flared lighter to its tip.

Female satisfaction came over Francesca at seeing the many female roving eyes on Tommy and knowing he was there with her. She found the feeling oddly empowering.

"Looks tasty and heart-clogging." Francesca eyed the meal Tommy spread before them.

"It is, and it will. It's why it's so good." Setting the tray aside, Tommy took his seat across from her. "By the way, you look great tonight." Tommy's gaze swept over the cotton sundress as bright as sunshine. He liked the way the chestnut waves spilled around the unpainted face. She was way out of his league, Tommy thought. What a rich, well-bred, educated girl who had the pick of any boy was doing with someone like him, eating a burger at a dive like Nick's perplexed him?

"And you look just as good in a dry T-shirt as you do in a sweat-drenched one." Francesca flashed a dimpled grin that gut-punched Tommy and he couldn't take his eyes off her.

"You should see me in my Italian silks." Tommy watched Francesca replace half of his onion rings with French fries.

"Gucci or Fendi?" At his cocked brow, Francesca said, "I know you're screwing with me, and I told you I like to eat. Also, you're sharing your chocolate milkshake unless you want to exchange it for my soda."

"I'll get you a milkshake and your own onion rings." Tommy was halfway out of his seat when Francesca gestured him back down.

"We can share. Next time ask me what I want to eat. Okay?"

Tommy mulled the words "next time" with an inward smile. "All right."

With the scent of grilled meat, and the buzz of loud chatter from the packed patio, Francesca and Tommy talked like friends who'd known each other for a lifetime.

The fact they were from opposite sides of the track couldn't have been more obvious as Tommy told her about his wild and reckless past, and Francesca told him about her orderly life. The one thing Tommy and Francesca had in common was that their fathers raised them. Their mother's taken from them at a young age, Tommy and Francesca, knew the feeling of loss. Understanding what their mother's death had ripped out of them, Tommy and Francesca shared a bond children affected by the loss of a mother could.

"I was only twelve when she died. It took me a while to get over it, but you have to, don't you?" Francesca absently dipped an onion ring into ketchup.

Tommy nodded. "My mom used to say life is full of interruptions and complications, but the determined never give up." Tommy picked up a curl of her hair, pulled it out straight then let it go. The gesture sent an unexpected tingle skittering up and down Francesca's spine. "Would you like dessert?"

"Tempting, but I'm stuffed."

"All right, then let's go."

"Where to?"

"It's a surprise."

TOMMY DROVE TO THE VACANT FIELD adjacent to Scott's Garden Center. Parking on grass, Tommy left the truck radio swelling with the melody of *Dream a Little Dream of Me* and helped Francesca onto the truck's hood. Then, climbing up next to her, Tommy handed Francesca a bottle of beer.

The night air carried the pungent aroma of earth and fertilizer from the garden center, and the land rolled under a gray sheen like a thin layer of fog. Fireflies floated, speckling the darkness, an owl's hoot echoed from the trees as crickets burst in song.

"From me to you, the stars and the moon." Tommy pointed to the sky where a round moon floated white in a dark sky sprinkled with stars.

No one had said more perfect words or reached her as deeply as Tommy did just then. "It's the best present anyone has given me. Thank you."

"You're welcome." Tommy sipped beer. "My father owns a piece of this land. Someday, I want to fill it with greenhouses. Lots of greenhouses. I want to grow everything we sell and market it under Scott's Garden. I want to grow the business into a franchise. Picture it, Scott's Garden Centers all across North America." His words tumbled out of him in excitement.

An admirable smile played across Francesca's face. "Ambitious dream."

"Until a year ago, I wanted no part of the business. I wanted nothing to do with it."

"What changed your mind?" Francesca took a sip of beer, cringed at the taste.

"Not a beer fan?"

"No, and it's not because this little-rich-girl is used to drinking Kristal as that tiny brain of yours is thinking. I just don't like the taste. Never have." Francesca shot back with a flash of irritation.

"What's Kristal?" Tommy asked with a playful smirk.

"Now you're teasing me."

Tommy shook his head. "Well, maybe a little."

"Anyone tell you, you could be infuriating."

"It's one of the qualities you like about me. Anyway, to answer your earlier question of what changed my mind," he jumped in when Francesca started to speak and told her about his short incarceration, which smartened him up. "The experience opened my eyes, and my life suddenly didn't seem as shadowed or pitted, and I thought my dad deserved better."

"That jail stint led you to find your path and purpose. We end up where we are meant to be."

"Profound. Who said that?"

"Francesca Thompson."

"You're not a seventy-year-old woman in the body of a seventeen-year-old?" Smiling, Tommy stared at her. Her eyes were as brown as topaz. "You don't mind hanging out with a felon? I mean, you are the daughter of the top criminal lawyer in Canada, and appearance is everything."

"That depends." Francesca liked the way the strands of hair curled around his face.

"On?"

"The reason you were taken in."

"A fight. I used to be a beacon for them."

Francesca watched Tommy light the cigarette. "Does it mean you're not anymore?"

"I told you I'm a changed man."

"Well, then, that settles it. Besides, I think you were acting out in response to your mom's death. There was anger and emptiness in you, and you expressed those feeling with your fists. It's a guy thing. Girls cry themselves dry. We're smarter." Francesca watched Tommy mull her psychological analysis over. From the expression on his face, until then, it hadn't dawned on him. "It's why, in my opinion, boys and men should try to be more emotional. A good cry can solve the world's problems. It can prevent wars. The bottom line is I have nothing to worry about except for your smoking."

At that, Tommy inhaled deeply and flicked the cigarette onto grass, watched it bounce and sputter. "Satisfied?"

"Yes." Francesca felt the cool balm of a soft breeze, and she wrapped her arms around her body for warmth.

"What are you going to do now you've graduated?" Tommy shrugged out of his jacket and set it on Francesca's shoulders. It smelled, of Old Spice, of him and a pleasant, exhilarating shock of arousal shot through Francesca's system. She'd never felt anything like it before. She liked it.

"I'm waiting to hear from a few universities. I'm planning to study criminal law like my father," Francesca said as Virginia Bruce's breathy voice flowed from the radio, claiming she had him under her skin. Francesca smiled, thinking how those words suddenly made sense to her. Tommy Scott had slid under Francesca's skin, and she wanted him to stay there.

She imagined how her father would react to Tommy, and the thought rattled her. Peter Thompson was a staunch live-by-the-rules authoritarian. He wouldn't be as understanding as she was about Tommy's reckless past. Peter would forbid her to see Tommy, and if Francesca refused, he'd ground her until she was thirty.

If their relationship progressed past tonight, Francesca decided she'd keep Tommy her secret. What Peter

Thompson didn't know wouldn't hurt him. Francesca decided she'd keep Tommy from Mrs. O'Sullivan too.

"So you'll one day take over your father's practice," Tommy said simply although her father's firm was anything but simple.

Peter Thompson ran one of the most prestigious and well-respected legal firms in Canada. Thompson and Associates was one of the largest with the best legal minds—or so he'd read in the newspapers. Peter Thompson had made a name for himself for defending celebrities, politicians, and the innocent presumed guilty in the public eye before their day in court.

"Something like that." Francesca rested her chin on her knees. Like it or not, a career in law was mapped in her future since the day she took in her first breath, and Francesca didn't dare defy her father.

"Are you going away to study?" Tommy's blue eyes were sober at the question.

Francesca inched her head back, looked him in the eye. "Maybe. Why do you ask?"

"Just wondering." Tommy swilled back the rest of his beer and took her bottle when she offered it.

"I'd rather not leave, but I'll have to see which university accepts me. My dad wants me to study at Stanford—his alma mater. My dad's brother is a professor there, and I can stay with him while I go to school."

A soft breeze whiffled, and the sweet smell of Francesca's perfume, the kind that crept into a man's senses and lingered there forever, slid into Tommy. All he wanted to do was kiss her. "I hope they reject you."

Francesca's mouth twisted into a grimace. "Tommy Scott, that's not a very nice thing to say."

Tommy needed a good pull of his beer before he spoke what was on his mind. "I don't want you to go."

The words arrowed into Francesca's heart and, with emotion mirrored in her eyes, said, "I don't want to either. Not anymore."

Tommy gently tucked a strand of her hair behind her ear. "I'd like to get to know you better."

Putting on a smile, Francesca shifted to face Tommy. "Me too," she said, falling into the circle of his arms. "There goes a falling star. Make a wish."

"Already did." Tommy tightened his arms around Francesca as he willed it to come true.

Three

MRS. O'SULLIVAN WATCHED Francesca slather mayonnaise on the fifth BLT sandwich she'd assembled on her own. Mrs. O'Sullivan was impressed by the fact Francesca had grilled the bacon herself. She didn't think Francesca knew how to turn the oven on.

As her only child, Katherine Thompson spoiled Francesca. Then, on Katherine's death, when Mrs. O'Sullivan stepped in as a surrogate mother to a hurting twelve-year-old hurting and craving love, she couldn't help but pick up where Katherine left off. Francesca was lost and broken, and Mrs. O'Sullivan couldn't help but spoil and love the girl she'd considered a daughter since birth.

Mrs. O'Sullivan studied the girl who, in the past few days, donned the expression of young love on her face. She'd seen the exchanged looks between Francesca and Tommy. A new phase of womanhood was dawning in Francesca's life, and Mrs. O'Sullivan felt the tugs of anxiety. She was out of her depth. Motherhood certainly had its challenges.

Peter Thompson wasn't going to be pleased, and he'd blame Mrs. O'Sullivan for Francesca cozying up to Tommy. He was Francesca's father but left the parenting to Mrs. O'Sullivan. The moment Peter found out his daughter was associating with a known felon he was bound to overreact. Optics was everything for Peter Thompson, who put his firm, his reputation over Francesca's interest.

It hadn't always been that way. When Katherine died, Peter became as lost and broken as Francesca. Instead of turning to his daughter for comfort, he turned to his work. Working eighty-hour weeks, kept Peter from dealing with the hole in his heart left by Katherine's death and made him drift further away from Francesca.

That Francesca was looking for a male influence in Tommy was obvious to Mrs. O'Sullivan, but at seventeen, Francesca's relationship with the older Tommy was bound to cross boundaries she hadn't before, and Mrs. O'Sullivan wasn't sure how to handle it. Mrs. O'Sullivan was entering uncharted waters and where the heart was involved— especially a young heart—the outcome was unpredictable.

"Would you mind taking these sandwiches to Mr. Scott, Mrs. O? I'll take these to his son. He's somewhere out there," Francesca tilted her chin toward the grove, "Cutting down dead trees."

"I don't know what you're up to with the boy, my girl, but you best be careful. He has a tainted past." Not to mention his sexual expertise rivaled Francesca's naiveté, Mrs. O'Sullivan thought. "And you know how your father is about you taking up with boys from ... outside your circles."

"Unless you tell him he won't find out. Daddy's never home. He's either working, traveling for work, or entertaining. You won't tell Daddy, will you, Mrs. O? Please don't. If he finds out about me seeing Tommy, he'll put a stop to it."

Mrs. O'Sullivan wiped her hands dry on the apron tied around her thick waist. Long, thick lashes haloed eyes that were coal-black and aware. Mrs. O'Sullivan was, as she often said, older than Methuselah, but her face bore none of the marks of a sixty-year-old. She had a delicate, fine-bone face with a small mouth and upturned nose.

"I won't tell your father—for now—if you tell me what you're up to with the lad." Mrs. O'Sullivan let Francesca squirm for a moment. "If you don't want me talking to your father, you will tell me everything, young lady."

Francesca stared into the wide, dark eyes of the woman who'd stepped in as a surrogate mother the day her own was buried. Francesca loved Mrs. O'Sullivan, turned to her for motherly comfort and advice, but in matters of the heart, she doubted the older woman would be helpful. Mrs. O'Sullivan had been single for too long, and Francesca doubted she knew what the love of a man felt like anymore. The proof was in the fact Mrs. O'Sullivan couldn't see Mr. Scott's deep-seated affection for her. If Mrs. O'Sullivan was blind to that Francesca didn't think she'd be able to understand how she felt for Tommy. Francesca believed Mrs. O'Sullivan would dismiss her feelings for Tommy as naïve infatuation, but it wasn't like that for her and Tommy.

"What are you up to with the lad? I'm waiting, missy." Missy meant you fessed up and told nothing but the truth— or else.

Francesca drew in a deep breath. "Tommy invited me to dinner last week, and since then, I've been helping him on the grounds. That's all. That's all," she repeated when Mrs. O'Sullivan's brow cocked higher above dark eyes.

"And what's Tommy Scott's interpretation of dinner?"

"A burger, onion rings, and the thickest chocolate milkshake I've ever had. We ate at a picnic table, under an awning lit up like a Christmas tree." From the glow in Francesca's eyes, Mrs. O'Sullivan deduced the girl had already stumbled into love with the rebellious Tommy Scott. "Afterwards, he took me to an empty field to…"

"Oh, Jesus, Joseph, and Mary." Shock flew into Mrs. O'Sullivan's eyes as the thoughts flashed in her mind of the wayward Tommy Scott with her sweet girl.

"To watch the stars and talk, Mrs. O." Francesca didn't mention the beer. Although she'd only taken a couple of sips and didn't like it, she was certain Mrs. O'Sullivan wouldn't react kindly to that piece of information. "It was wonderful, Mrs. O. We sat on the hood of his truck and…"

"And what, missy?"

"He held me. We did absolutely nothing, Mrs. O, and it was…"

"Romantic, wonderful, a night you will never forget."

"Yes, that's exactly how it felt."

"Don't sound so shocked, Frankie." Mrs. O'Sullivan reached into the refrigerator for the pitcher of lemonade.

"Who knew doing nothing could be so amazing."

"It's how you do the nothing that counts. Get us two glasses from the cupboard, will you, darling?" Mrs. O'Sullivan walked the pitcher of milk to the table. "Your night with Tommy sounds very similar to the first night my Aidan courted me. My Aidan took me to the shores of the Irish Sea, but the sentiment was the same. We sat there for hours listening to the roll of waves lapping the shore, watching the stars. Strong, cold winds blew inland, making it fierce cold, but my Aidan kept me as warm in the chain of his arms as if we were sitting by a roaring fire. It was the perfect night." Mrs. O'Sullivan's Gaelic accent flowed into the words as she drifted back to memories.

"That's how it felt with Tommy. He made me feel so special and loved, Mrs. O. There were none of the pretenses I've had to endure from the vain, self-important boys from the country club Daddy encourages me to date. Tommy was honest, unpretentious, and caring."

"The boy tell you he loved you?" Mrs. O'Sullivan said, pouring lemonade over ice.

"No, that's just it. Tommy didn't say any of the nonsense the boys say an hour into the date to get into my..." Francesca stopped when Mrs. O'Sullivan's jaw dropped. "Oh, Mrs. O, you know in centuries of evolution, boy's overactive hormones are the only thing that hasn't changed. They've had one thing on their mind since Adam was put on this earth."

Mrs. O'Sullivan fanned herself. "Can't argue with that, but I hope you haven't fulfilled anyone's needs."

"Maybe one or two."

Mrs. O'Sullivan crossed herself. "Jesus, Joseph, and Mary, we haven't had the ... talk yet, Frankie," she said, knowing she never would. Many failed attempts were proof

Mrs. O'Sullivan would never bring herself to discussing the mechanics of baby production with anyone—let alone a young, naïve girl.

Francesca burst into laughter at Mrs. O'Sullivan's saucer wide eyes and beet-red face. "I'm joking, Mrs. O, I haven't done anything of the sort. I'm still a virgin. I'm saving myself for that special someone. I want my first time to stay with me for the rest of my life."

Mrs. O'Sullivan huffed a breath of relief. "I hope it won't happen until you're well into your thirties."

Francesca snorted a giggle. "Tommy said he wanted to get to know me better." Francesca's mind drifted to that night. So clear were her memories of Tommy she could smell him, see the brilliant, smiling, blue eyes, feel his arms chained around her. She felt his presence close to her. She heard the comforting sounds that filled the night as they watched the stars. Francesca was certain for years to come she'd relive that night in her mind with fond memories. "I felt so special when he said that."

A smile creased one corner of Mrs. O'Sullivan's mouth when the wave of memory of her Aidan hit her. "The boy is a romantic."

"He is, Mrs. O. I've never felt more special than I did that night."

Mrs. O'Sullivan rose and crossed to the cupboard to get two plates, then reached into the refrigerator for the cheesecake. "Are you sure it's not his good looks or his bad-boy image, which has you romanticizing the boy?"

"Sounds as if you speak from experience, Mrs. O. Was your Aidan, a bad boy?"

"Never you mind about my Aidan. We're talking about you. Reach into the cutlery drawer for forks and the cake cutter."

"He is gorgeous, and his hell-with-you attitude was what drew me to him, but as I've gotten to know him, I've found him thoughtful, caring, and honest. Many people I know aren't half as honest as he is. Aside from his smoking, he's perfect, Mrs. O. I wouldn't change a thing."

Francesca set a fork on each plate, handed Mrs. O'Sullivan the cake cutter.

Mrs. O'Sullivan cut two slices of cheesecake and set them on Royal Doulton plates. "So, you'll be stepping out with him again?"

"If that means going out on a date, then yes." Francesca hesitated for a moment, debating. "I've been seeing him for longer than one week. It's been two weeks. We've gone for walks in the park and the boardwalk. He even took me fishing a couple of days ago. Can you picture me fishing? I'm sorry I didn't tell you, but I didn't think you'd approve of him. I know Daddy won't, but I like Tommy, Mrs. O," Francesca blurted out in a hurried flow.

Mrs. O'Sullivan could see as clear as day in Francesca's mooning eyes she didn't only like him. Francesca was in love. From personal experience, Mrs. O'Sullivan knew when love struck that hard, nothing anyone said or did would tear a woman away from the man she loved.

Her Ma tried—hard. Jemma O'Rourke desperately tried to keep her daughter away from the rebellious Aidan O'Sullivan. As hard as Ma tried to keep her daughter from falling in love with young Aidan, her misguided efforts only drove them closer together. She loved Aidan more than the stars were bright and made it clear to her Ma she'd have followed Aidan to the depths of the ocean.

Even after they'd married, her Ma tried her best to split them up. Her Ma often told her: He's a useless, lazy git like your father who will only be good at mounting you whenever his hormones demand satisfaction, and drinking ale. But in the end, Aidan proved her Ma wrong. Aidan put food and a roof over her head. Aidan provided for her, showed his love and devotion for her when she couldn't give him the children he wanted.

It took a special man to stick by a woman who wasn't able to give him the brood of boys he wanted. It took a loving, faithful man to tell every woman in the village who questioned Mrs. O'Sullivan's childless existence he was to blame.

God, she missed her Aidan every day since his death twenty years ago.

"When are you stepping out with Tommy again?"

"Tomorrow night. Tommy said he's taking me on a picnic. I'm not sure where. He told me it was a surprise."

The boy knew how to romance a girl. She'd give him that.

Mrs. O'Sullivan took a forkful of cheesecake. "I want to have a talk with Tommy before your date tomorrow." She held a hand up to silence Francesca's refusal. "Either I talk to Tommy or I talk to your father. Your choice, Frankie. I'm not going to give the boy the third degree. I just want to have a chat with him."

"All right, Mrs. O. I'll have Tommy come to see you before he leaves for the day. Right now, I'm taking these sandwiches to him."

"Take him a piece of cheesecake too. After the hard day's work the boy puts in, he needs sustenance. Fill up the thermos with lemonade. There's a basket in the pantry you can use to carry everything."

"I will." Francesca pecked Mrs. O'Sullivan's cheek. "Thank you for understanding and for letting me talk to you like I would with my mom. I love you, Mrs. O."

Mrs. O'Sullivan's eyes misted. "I love you too, you silly girl."

"Mrs. O, you should take Mr. Scott a piece of cheesecake too. He loves your cooking," Francesca said, stocking the basket with food and thermos.

Mrs. O'Sullivan stopped the glass of milk mid-sip. "He does?"

"He does. He loves everything about you." Francesca darted out the kitchen door leaving Mrs. O'Sullivan with a confused look on her face.

Four

AT THE FAR end of Scott's Garden Center, amid the tall linden trees, their thick, green canopies sheltering them from the slow, steady fall of rain, Francesca watched Tommy spread the checkered blanket on the grass. Around them, dozens of candles burned, their yellow flames dancing in the soft wind. Potted flowers, pink, white, and yellow tulips, purple lavender, lilac, and red roses, circled them.

Tommy spread the food on the checkered blanket. There was fried chicken, potato salad, and coleslaw, and for dessert, a Black Forest cake. They were all of Francesca's favorites. How Tommy knew didn't matter to Francesca. The important thing was he'd done if for her.

Closing the distance between them, Francesca skimmed her fingers over Tommy's cheek. Her hair was pulled back in a ponytail, and her unpainted face jumped out to him. Her eyes gleamed under the flicker of candlelight. It was such a beautiful face, Tommy thought.

"Thank you for all this. No one has ever done anything this thoughtful and romantic for me." Francesca linked her hands behind Tommy's neck.

"I'd do this for you every night forever if it makes you happy, but I have a confession to make."

"What's that?"

"Mrs. O made the food. She insisted on it."

"Hmm, guilt food. She must have given you a lashing this afternoon. Spill."

Tommy threw his head back in laughter. "She told me I'm to take care of you and never hurt you. That if I ever made you cry, she'd castrate me with her bare hands."

"Ouch."

"I have a feeling she's had experience there. Then she fed me. Stuffed me like a pig heading for the spit all the while telling me she knows all the foods you liked, and I should stop by the kitchen to pick up the food basket before I picked you up."

Francesca snorted a laugh. "I love that woman. Did she also say you weren't to kiss me?"

"No, she didn't."

"Then, you should." Francesca leaned in, her mouth a whisper from his, Tommy felt her warm breath on his cheek, and his heart began to pound like a jackhammer. Still, Tommy pulled back. Francesca's face warped into a mixture of anger, disappointment, and confusion. "Don't you want to kiss me, Tommy?"

He slipped free from her chained arms and put distance between them. "I do, but..."

"There should be no, but. You should want to." Francesca's temper flared hot. "So everything you've ever said to me was complete bullshit."

Tommy heard the tears in her voice. He'd hurt her, and it wasn't what he intended. "I'm sorry, Francesca. I didn't mean to upset you," he said, reaching for her hand.

"Don't touch me." The pain of rejection was warring with cold, stony rage, and Francesca tore away and sprang toward the falling rain.

Tommy ran after her, his boots sinking into muddy puddles. "Please, Francesca, let me explain." His hand gripped Francesca's wrist when he caught up with her and spun her around so fast her body plowed into him.

"Let go of me, you brute." Francesca tried to tear loose from Tommy's hold, but he was too strong.

"It's why I won't kiss you." Rain and tears mingle on Francesca's face as her brow creased in confusion. "I'm not..."

"Interested." Francesca finished. "Let go of me." There was pain in the words, in the hazel eyes, and weakening, Tommy released his hold.

"You're wrong about that." Tommy ducked when the potted lily came at him like a bullet through the sheet of rain.

"Why would you lead me on this way?"

The unexpected begonia that followed nicked him on the forehead. "Jesus, Francesca, you almost got me full on the head."

"Maybe this time I will." Francesca reached for the closest thing and aimed the trowel straight for his head. A bolt of lightning lit the sky, and she willed it to strike the steel water can that followed and landed at his feet.

"Please stop, Francesca. Let me explain." Tommy ducked to the right to avoid the clay pot that came next.

"I hope Mrs. O does end up castrating you." She covered her face with her hands when the tears came faster. She hadn't known a hurt like that before.

Francesca's heart-wrenching tears ripped Tommy's heart out. She looked so fragile, Tommy thought, and rushing to Francesca's side, he chained arms around her. This time he didn't let her get away.

"I never thought you of all people would hurt me." Francesca sobbed, and even under the drenching rain, Tommy could see her tears.

"I'm sorry. I didn't mean to. It's just … Kissing you is not a simple kiss for me, Francesca. It means so much more to me, and I'm scared…"

"It won't mean anything to me?" Francesca's eyes kindled with shock when Tommy nodded. "Why would you think so lowly of me?"

Tommy brushed tears and rain from her face. "Look at me, Francesca. I am a brute. I'm not high-society like you. I dropped out of high school, and I'm sure as hell, not wealthy. You're going to be taking over a multi-million dollar company. I'm a gardener, the son of a gardener. My hands are deep in manure laced soil every day."

The wall of rain coming down on them, Francesca looked up to Tommy. "Christ! Do you believe me to be so shallow? That all I think about is money and status."

"No, I don't, but look me in the eyes and tell your father would approve of me." Tommy's heart ached at the words, but not more so than when Francesca remained silent. "What you see is what you get with me. We're standing in a mud puddle, drenched in rain, the smell of fertilizer all around us, and you deserve so much more than this, Francesca."

"Why are you deciding what I deserve?" Francesca swallowed rain. "You underestimate yourself. You're honest, kind, and thoughtful. You do things just for me. I've been out with a lot of guys."

"Are you bragging?" There was jealous anger in Tommy's voice.

"As I was saying, I've been out with a lot of guys, blue-blooded, as you call them and none stack up to you. All they ever try to do is to charm their way into my pants. None comes close to being half the man you are. Jesus, we're on our tenth date, and you've done everything perfectly by me, but not once have you tried to kiss me."

Tommy cupped Francesca's face in his hands. "Only because I..."

The pain of rejection went bone-deep. "Don't touch me."

"I love you, Francesca, and if I kiss you, I'll have the taste of you in me. Once I do, I don't think I can live without it. Kissing you means letting my feelings flow, and I'm scared you won't feel the same. I've never felt like this, and I'm just so confused."

Francesca's flush of anger died away, and she rested her forehead against his. "I love you too, Tommy."

"You do?"

Francesca held a steady gaze on Tommy as rain streamed down his face. "I do. I love you, Tommy. I have since the moment you gifted me the moon and the stars. It was my wish on the falling star you'd feel the same way for me."

Tommy's eyes mirrored the explosion of emotions in hers. "Mine too."

Under the wall of rain, Tommy kissed Francesca with such tenderness it reached deep into her heart. Her lips tasted of rain. All Tommy wanted to do was absorb them until Francesca was a part of him. And he did. Tommy kissed Francesca long, passionately, until it soothed every ache, and filled his heart with a love he'd searched for so long.

Five

FRANCESCA'S HAIR TUCKED under a red cap her
sleeves rolled to the elbows she spread mulch on the
flowerbed edging the gazebo as Tommy shoveled it off the
bed of his truck. The day tasted of heat and summer. Trees
dripped in green, and the gardens were in glorious bloom. It
was a perfect day to be lazing around the pool soaking sun,
but there was nowhere else Francesca would rather be.

Since the rainy night when Francesca nicked Tommy's
forehead with the clay pot—requiring three stitches—she'd
spent every waking minute with him. Francesca traded
tennis at the club with helping Tommy at the garden center.
Riding alongside Tommy on deliveries took priority over
lunch and shopping with friends at posh downtown
boutiques. Walks on the boardwalk or stargazing at the
empty lot replaced walking on the white sand beaches of
Saint-Tropez.

Francesca fished for bass with Tommy at Musselman
Lake. She'd done it to make him happy because baiting a
live worm was an experienced best left untried. The
weekends her father was out of town on business,
Francesca, with Mrs. O'Sullivan's blessing, invited Tommy
to laze by the pool with her. Afterward, they'd enjoy a
picnic by the creek, followed by a horseback ride on the
estate. Many weekends she and Tommy sat by the stream,
feet wading in clear water, talking. Other times, under the
shade of a tree, in the circle of his arms, Francesca read
Tommy the classics he'd refused to read in school.

"Am I getting paid for this?" Francesca leaned on the rake and flicked eyes up to Tommy. She'd never tire of seeing the sweat-drenched T-shirt clinging to his chiseled chest.

Tommy jumped off the bed of the truck. Landing inches from her, he pulled her in, crushed his mouth to hers with want, longing, and heat. He nibbled his way down her neck. When her breath hitched, and her body shuddered, Tommy thought there was nothing more potent than a woman reacting to a man's touch.

"That's your payment," Tommy said, forcing himself to pull away. It was getting more difficult to stop himself from wanting all of her.

"I'll settle for that, but only if you promise me there's more of it in store for later," Francesca said, breathing in his rich male scent.

"As much as you want." Tommy kissed her again. This time the kiss was more passionate, and her heart melted like butter. "Have I ever told you how sexy you look when you're all sweaty?"

"Ditto." Francesca rested her hands on the rock-hard chest. She'd fantasized what it would feel like to get her hands over his naked body.

Francesca had dreamed about making love with Tommy, feeling his touch on her. She imagined Tommy would be a great lover, tender, gentle, understanding of her innocence. But as much as Francesca's mind ran wild, she wasn't ready for that type of intimacy yet, and Tommy hadn't pushed her. The fact he hadn't was one of the many reasons she was crazy in love with him.

Francesca had never had to fight him off, as she had to do with Quinn Montgomery II, who diluted himself to think every girl desired him. Or Harper Percy, whose idea of a date was a two hundred dollar meal, then demanding payback afterward. Francesca never felt unsafe with Tommy as she had with Blaise or Asher. Tommy was twice the man those boys—which her father approved of—would ever be.

"I got an acceptance letter this morning from Osgoode Law School."

"Congratulations." Tommy breathed in the scent of her hair. It smelled like a sweet summer day with a touch of sweat and freshly cut wood. It shot a slow burn to his belly.

"Osgoode is here in Toronto, so I don't have to leave town. You hungry?"

"I am." Tommy reached into the cab of the truck for the basket of food and the checkered blanket Mrs. O'Sullivan packed. "It's great news about Osgoode, Francesca, but..."

"But what, Tommy?" Francesca took the basket and waited for Tommy to spread the blanket under the canopy of the weeping willow. "Talk to me." She watched him silently spread the meal of turkey sandwiches, garden salad.

"You were also accepted at Harvard and Columbia, all excellent schools. You need to consider all your options. I don't want you limiting yourself because of me." Tommy poured lemonade into two cups.

"I'm not." From somewhere above, birdsong suddenly flowed along with the pecking of a woodpecker.

"Don't dismiss them because you want to stay close. You need to do what's best for you."

Francesca closed her hand over Tommy's arm when he started to reach into the basket for napkins. "But I don't want to be away from you."

Looking into Francesca's eyes, Tommy tucked a loose strand of hair behind her ear. "I don't want you to pass up on your dream. I don't want you to limit yourself from reaching your full potential. You have excellent grades. You're smart and ambitious with the financial resources to go to the best schools, and you need to take advantage of that."

"Osgoode is an excellent school." Francesca watched the family of squirrels scamper up a tree and perch themselves on its branches patiently waiting for the scraps of food to come.

"And so is Harvard and Columbia. Don't you see, Francesca? You're the type of person who will do great things. You can't deny yourself of that because of me because, in the end, you'll resent me if you do." Tommy looked Francesca straight in the eye to drive his point home.

"I could never resent you."

"You will if you don't do what you want. You need to do what's right for you, not what's right for me," Tommy said, the painful words knowing her moving away would alter the course of their lives forever.

Francesca linked fingers with his. "I'm doing what's right for us."

"And I love you for thinking that way. If you don't do it for yourself, do it for me. Promise me you'll think this through and choose wisely."

"I promise, but you always say life is full of interruptions and complications, and I don't want either of those things to touch us. Besides, if I were to go away to study, it would be to Stanford, and I haven't heard from them. It's already mid-July, too late to be getting good news from them, so my guess is I'll be getting a rejection letter."

Tommy sat back against the trunk of the willow, stretched his legs out, crossing them at the ankles. "They'd be crazy to pass up on you," he said, reaching into his pocket for a cigarette. Francesca only had to lift a brow for Tommy to return the cigarette to the pack.

"I don't want to leave you."

"I don't want you to go away, but I don't want you not to do what you want."

Francesca rested her head on Tommy's shoulder. "Would you wait for me forever?"

Tommy loosened her ponytail, felt her hair flow through his fingers. "I would."

Francesca pulled back, far enough to meet Tommy's eyes. "How come you haven't asked me if I'd wait for you?"

"Because I know you would." The smile that filled Tommy's eyes when Francesca nudged him with her knee was sad.

Tommy knew once Francesca went away, once she was around the type of men he could never be, men she deserved to be with, she'd see the world in a different light and he'd lose her.

"Well, you're right. I'd wait for you, Tommy." Francesca fell into the circle of his arms. "I'd wait for you forever." Her back snug against his chest, Tommy tightened his arms around Francesca, wondering how many more times he'd be able to do it.

PETER THOMPSON STOOD ON THE TERRACE, eyes fixed on the gazebo. There was someone out there with his daughter, but trees and shrubs caped in thick green made it difficult to get a clear view, and he turned to go into the house.

"Who's Frankie out there with, Mrs. O'Sullivan?" Peter asked, stepping into the kitchen. He wore loafers, black pants with perfect knife-edged pleats, a buttoned-down white shirt, sleeves rolled halfway up. At a glance, Peter Thompson passed for a man in his mid-forties rather than fifty-seven.

Mrs. O'Sullivan panicked, debated how to answer. She hadn't expected his return from his London business trip for another day, but there he was making her debate truth over deceit.

"It's the Scott boy, Mr. Thompson." Mrs. O'Sullivan opted for the truth. The man was a criminal lawyer, able to see through your lying eyes.

"Tommy Scott?" Dark eyes went hard in a handsome, unpleated face capped with thick hair silvered at the temples, and fringed with a fashionable stubble.

"I've had Francesca help him around the garden. Mr. Scott's arthritis has been acting up, and I thought it would be good for her to do some work around the house since she's off for the summer. Idle hands an all that."

"Doesn't look as if they're doing much gardening."

"I had Francesca take the boy a sandwich and a cold drink. It's hot today, and the boy has been working since early morning. Tommy works hard, and he's a good lad, Mr. Thompson." Mrs. O'Sullivan rushed to defend, keeping her eyes focused on the dough she was shaping into cinnamon buns.

"He's not, Mrs. O'Sullivan. The boy is bad news." Peter inclined his head to get a better view of the gazebo. "She shouldn't be alone with him out there, behind all the shrubbery."

Mrs. O'Sullivan prayed Peter didn't catch his daughter snogging Tommy as they often did when they thought no one was watching. She could only imagine what Peter would do—to all three of them. "He's not the same boy, Mr. Thompson."

In his misguided way, Peter Thompson loved his daughter. He'd never deny Francesca anything but his attention. As much as a young, impressionable Francesca needed him after her mother's death, Peter was rarely there for her. His first love was his work, his firm. Law was in his blood; all he ever thought of. Everything came second to it, including his daughter.

Since his wife's death, the little time Peter had spent with Francesca was focused on controlling her. Don't do this. Don't do that. Do only as I say. Never an, I love you or let's spend time together. Mrs. O'Sullivan ascribed Peter's domineering way to the pain he carried from losing Katherine. Peter's heart still aching from the loss of his wife, Mrs. O'Sullivan believed, was what kept him from bonding with Francesca. And God knew being a single parent was a challenge, no matter your station in life, but

Francesca was a child when Katherine died, hungry for attention and love, and Peter hadn't stepped up.

Mrs. O'Sullivan did. She became the surrogate parent Francesca needed. Since Katherine's death, Mrs. O'Sullivan was the person Francesca turned to, for emotional support, to talk, to share her life's events, and she was always there for her—not Peter, never Peter. Still, Peter always managed to twist everything to suit his purposes as he was now. Stepping into Francesca's life for the few hours, he was able to spare this weekend and questioning Mrs. O'Sullivan like one of his criminal clients and making her second-guess her decision to let Francesca be with Tommy.

"The boy's had a questionable past, and I don't want his recklessness touching Frankie." Eyes peeled out the window, Peter sipped on black coffee.

"That's in the past, Mr. Thompson. The boy has turned a new leaf." Mrs. O'Sullivan sprinkled sugar over the cinnamon buns. "I'll keep an eye on Francesca and the boy." She opened the oven door and set two pans side by side. One she'd deliver to Mr. Scott, along with the food she'd cooked for him when she'd visit with Francesca later in the day.

Knowing Mrs. O'Sullivan wouldn't deny two helpless men the benefit of her cooking or a helping hand around the house, Francesca talked her into both when Mr. Scott contracted a bad case of the flu. For the past couple of weeks, Mrs. O'Sullivan prepared home-cooked meals and gave a helping hand around the Scott household. Now, with Peter in the way, Mrs. O'Sullivan wondered how she was going to manage the visit.

"How long has Francesca been helping him?" Peter's suspicious eyes stared out the window.

"A couple of weeks." Mrs. O'Sullivan hoped Peter didn't detect the tremble in her lying words.

"How often is the boy here?"

Questions, questions, questions. "Weekly, sometimes twice a week." She had to get to Francesca before Peter did,

Mrs. O'Sullivan thought as she wiped the counter clean with a damp cloth.

"Well, I want it stopped now. We pay Mr. Scott for his gardening services, not to have his son entertain Frankie." Peter walked to the coffee maker, poured himself more coffee.

Mrs. O'Sullivan fisted her hands on the sink lip. The man was home minutes and already disrupting the flow of the house—her serenity. "Of course, Mr. Thompson, I'll speak to Mr. Scott."

"As soon as Frankie gets back, please let her know I want to speak to her." Peter stopped at the door. "I'm her father, Mrs. O'Sullivan. I only need you to watch over her for me, not to make decisions that affect my child's welfare."

"Of course, Mr. Thompson," Mrs. O'Sullivan said, biting back tears.

THE KITCHEN SMELLED OF FRESHLY BREWED coffee and cinnamon when Francesca stormed in and slid onto a stool at the breakfast bar. Mrs. O'Sullivan remained silent, deciding it best to wait it out until Francesca got the anger resulting from her talk with Peter out. Thirty years in the Thompson household had taught Mrs. O'Sullivan a thing or two about the personalities under that roof.

Right now, what Francesca needed was venting time because if Mrs. O'Sullivan knew Peter Thompson, he'd laced into Francesca about canoodling with Tommy Scott behind thick brush. And if she knew Francesca, she'd conceded defeat the moment her father opened his mouth as she always had since she was a child.

Mrs. O'Sullivan watched Francesca get to her feet, pace the room with pent up anger, then plop back down on the stool. Mrs. O'Sullivan counted down from five to one to hear Francesca tell her everything she wished she'd said to her father.

At the count of one, Francesca burst like a geyser. "He told me I couldn't help Tommy anymore. How can he demand that of me when he doesn't even know Tommy?" The anger in her tone meant for Peter came through loud and clear.

Mrs. O'Sullivan packed cinnamon buns, stew, and biscuits she'd made into the basket.

"He says Tommy's a bad influence, and he doesn't want him around me. He doesn't know Tommy well enough to make such a cold, heartless remark." Francesca paced the kitchen floor. "Don't forget the beef pies, Mrs. O."

"Yes, the pies. Thank you for the reminder, darling." Mrs. O'Sullivan reached into the refrigerator.

"Tommy's anything but a bad influence on me. As much as I don't want to leave him, he's encouraging me to do so. He told me to consider all my university options based on what I want, on my future, not our future, even if it means enrolling in a school out of the country, far away from him. Tommy thinks I have the potential to become a top criminal lawyer like Daddy, and he doesn't want me limiting my options. Does that sound like Tommy's a bad influence?" Francesca took the glass of water Mrs. O'Sullivan handed her and sipped to wet her sandpaper dry throat.

No. No, it doesn't Mrs. O'Sullivan wanted to say, but thought it best not to fuel Francesca's anger. "Your father is only thinking of your welfare. Pass me the tea towel, please." Mrs. O'Sullivan spread the white cloth over the food, then closed the basket lid.

"Daddy told me you'd be reporting to him what I do, where I go, so not to think about defying him."

"Yes, he's asked me to do so." Mrs. O'Sullivan set the basket aside and brushed the front of her flowery summer dress. She'd dabbed on a touch of lavender perfume and brushed her hair to a sheen.

"You look great, Mrs. O. Here put some of this pink gloss on your lips." Francesca reached into her jeans pocket for the tube and watched Mrs. O'Sullivan dab it on her lips.

It was the first time she'd seen Mrs. O'Sullivan express concern for her appearance. "You're not going to report me to daddy, are you Mrs. O? You won't tell him if I see Tommy, will you?"

The question caught Mrs. O'Sullivan off guard. What was she to do? What was she to say to the girl that she considered a daughter? How was she to balance years of loyalty to Peter Thompson with betrayal, young love over Peter's skewed standards?

"I love Tommy. I love him so much, Mrs. O. I need to see him." Francesca fell into Mrs. O'Sullivan's arms.

Her girl was hurting. "I know, my darling."

"You do? How long have you known?"

"Since the day we first spoke about him. A blind person can see how you feel about him." Mrs. O'Sullivan brushed her hand over Francesca's hair with a motherly touch.

"I need to be with him, Mrs. O. You won't tell Daddy, will you?"

Nothing Mrs. O'Sullivan could say or do would change a young heart in love. She knew from experience the more she forbade Francesca to see Tommy, the more she'd push her toward defiance. It was what she'd done to her ma. Convention never held up against love, and Francesca's love for Tommy was as real, as his was for her.

Mrs. O'Sullivan debated. What would Katherine do?

After a short contemplative silence, Mrs. O'Sullivan said, "I won't tell your father, but you must promise me you will do as I say or the two of us, and Tommy for that matter, are going to be in deep trouble."

With a nod of her head, Francesca threw her arms around Mrs. O'Sullivan. "I promise. I love you, Mrs. O."

"I love you too, darling. And Frankie, I wouldn't mention the conversation with your father to Tommy." The boy deserved better, Mrs. O'Sullivan thought. "Now, go fetch your car keys. You need to drive me to my friend Brenna's house."

"I thought you were going to visit with Mr. Scott. Tommy's expecting me."

Mrs. O'Sullivan crossed her fingers. "Go grab your keys, and tell your father you're driving me to Brenna's house."

"No, we can't keep Brenna waiting," Francesca said when she caught on and smiling rushed out of the kitchen.

She was already stacking the lies into the feeble house of cards, which would eventually tumble, Mrs. O'Sullivan thought. She only hoped it didn't fall soon because if she'd seen the love in Francesca's eyes for Tommy as clearly as she had, so had Peter, and he'd soon enough put a stop to it.

Mrs. O'Sullivan had an idea of how Peter was going to do it and when, and she could do nothing to stop him. She only hoped Peter would come to the realization his resolve to impose his skewed morality on a young girl in love stood to alienate his daughter—or possibly lose her.

Six

PETER THOMPSON SET the report down on his desk and walked to the unblinded window of his fifteenth floor King Street office. The August sun was bold and bright. Peter could feel the heat beating against the glass pane. On the street below, traffic moved at a snail's pace. Sidewalks teemed with tourists, cameras at the ready. Smartly dressed professionals dashed in and out of buildings. From behind the hot dog cart, Frank served hungry customers.

Peter kept his eyes focused on everything and nothing as he digested the information he'd read in Lamont's report. He hadn't wanted to ask Lamont Jones—the firm's private investigator—to tail Francesca, but he couldn't trust Mrs. O'Sullivan to follow through on his instructions to keep his daughter away from Tommy Scott. The woman couldn't say no to Francesca—even if it were for her own good.

From what Peter had read in the report, and Lamont was nothing if not thorough, he'd made the right decision to have Francesca tailed. Lamont's photographs proved Francesca wasn't just helping Tommy around the Estate. She was letting Tommy help himself to her. The photos of Francesca and Tommy were innocent enough: eating hamburgers at Nick's, walking hand-in-hand down the boardwalk or sitting on Tommy's porch talking. They spent a lot of time talking nonsense, Peter concluded, because what could a seventeen-year-old and an uneducated, felon possibly have to talk about? Francesca was wasting valuable time she should be spending with the well-educated boys with bright futures from respectable homes he chose for her, with a felon with no future.

Peter worked his fingers to the bone to give Francesca the best money could buy so she could associate with a better class of people. Here Francesca was, throwing it all away by spending her time with a known criminal.

Peter's hands fisted at the thought of the gossip Francesca's association with Tommy was generating. He cringed at the idea of the gossip reaching Templeton family ears—particularly those of James Templeton III.

James Templeton III, the only son Bryce Templeton and heir to the Templeton fortune fit Peter's criteria as the perfect mate for Francesca. James was a Stanford law graduate with a notable surname and the right pedigree. Carefully chosen from the handful of candidates Peter had considered, James was the man to carry out Peter's plan.

James would make the perfect son-in-law. More importantly, James was the suitable partner to carry on the business because Thompson and Associates, the firm he'd built from the ground up, would never fall to outside hands. It would remain in the family. Peter had to step in before Francesca's misguided actions jeopardized his plans.

Pressing the intercom button on his telephone, Peter asked his secretary to connect him with his brother William. After a twenty-minute conversation with William, Peter hung up and reached for his car keys.

SCOTT'S GARDEN CENTER WAS BUSIER AND bigger than Peter imagined. They sold the necessary tools to meet your gardening needs: plants, soil, fertilizer, garden tools, outdoor fountains, and statues. That too surprised Peter. Mr. Scott had done well for himself, he thought. Peter's eyes scanned the barn-style building until they landed on Tommy, who was outlining the benefits of sheep versus cow manure laced soil. Peter watched Tommy dip hands into dark soil to display its darkness and consistency to a customer. The boy was knowledgeable and a good salesperson, Peter gave him that.

Seeing past the soil stained hands, jeans, and the white T-shirt, Peter saw the rugged good looks that drew Francesca to Tommy. From the lustful gazes of the women—young and old—aimed Tommy way, it was clear to Peter he could have had any woman he wanted. Yet he chose Francesca.

Peter ventured to guess Tommy was after Francesca's money, and somewhere along the way, Tommy fell in love with her. He'd seen the puppy love in Tommy's eyes in every one of the surveillance photos. No man with the raging hormones of a twenty-one-year-old spent night-after-night holding a woman and gazing at the stars if he wasn't in love.

In the weeks Lamont had tailed them, aside from kissing and holding hands, Tommy made no untoward moves on Francesca. That was the sign either of a man biding his time until he got what he wanted or of one deeply in love. Peter's instinct's told him it was the latter. It was why he was determined to get Tommy out of Francesca's life before it went any further.

The truckload sale of soil for the Thornhill Community Centers' garden overhaul sealed, Tommy approached Peter. "Can I help you?"

"I'm Peter..."

"I know who you are, Mr. Thompson." If Tommy was surprised by Peter's appearance at the garden center, he didn't show it.

"May we speak, Mr. Scott?" Peter's mink-colored eyes bore into Tommy.

"Yes. We can talk in my office. Tim, I'm stepping off the floor for a few minutes." Tommy gestured Peter to follow him when Tim waved his acknowledgment.

"Thank you for seeing me without an appointment, Mr. Scott." Peter, all dignity and class, took the folding guest chair across the beat-up metal desk, and Tommy wondered how the man with the polished hue of respectable wealth felt in the small, messy office.

Invoices and purchase orders were strewn on the desk. A rotary telephone smudged with soil sat in one corner. Two grey cabinets overflowed with paperwork. On top of each, gardening magazines and catalogs were stacked ten high. The pungent smell of fertilizer hung in the air, and dust mites dance in the beam of light spilling from the only window in the room.

"It's Tommy, and you're in a garden center, Mr. Thompson, not a Bay Street office." Tommy reached for the towel hanging off the porcelain sink, dried washed hands. "I'm sorry I didn't shake your hand, but I was handling fertilizer. I didn't think you'd appreciate the aroma on your hands. Can I get you something to drink?"

"No, thank you. I'd like to get right down to the reason I'm here."

Tommy slid into the chair behind the desk. Strips of black masking tape covered the worn armrests and torn seat. "I'd expect nothing less."

"I'm here to talk about Francesca, man-to-man."

"I didn't think you were here to talk about my selection of pruning shears." Tommy's blue eyes didn't betray the waves of nausea sweeping through him.

"Right, well, straight to it. I know you're in love with my daughter, and my guess is she's in love with you." Peter let a stretch of silence pass to allow Tommy to respond. Tommy said nothing. "You do understand at seventeen, Frankie is a child and a neophyte in matters of the heart."

Tommy thought about his response because it was important to him what he said next. "You don't know your daughter, Mr. Thompson. She's far from being a child. She's a mature, intelligent seventeen-year-old woman with a thought process of her own. She has dreams, ambitions, and knows what she wants. There are so many fascinating and interesting layers to her you should make an effort to get to know." Tommy was pleased when Peter's jaw set tightly.

Tommy's remark rattled the mighty Peter Thompson. Tommy, a newcomer to Francesca's life, knew her better than him. Tommy hadn't meant to shoot from the hip so early into the conversation, but he had to make Peter aware how little he knew his daughter.

Tommy would point out that Francesca missed her father and wanted the love and attention of the only parent she had left in her life if it did any good, but it wouldn't. If Peter still hadn't figured out know how much Francesca revered him, how much she wanted to please him, and how much she needed his validation and love, nothing he could say would impact how Peter treated his daughter. Francesca would do anything to please her father, but he wouldn't return the sentiment.

The times Francesca had opened up to Tommy about her father, her heart-wrenching tears had ripped his heart out. Only his mother's death affected him as Francesca's tears had.

"Don't go there, Mr. Scott. Don't inject yourself into my affairs or judge without facts." The small office felt stifling, the guilt suffocating.

"I'm neither injecting myself nor judging, Mr. Thompson. I'm relaying what Francesca's told me with tears in her eyes." Tommy saw anger, and possibly resentment come over Peter's face.

"You've known her for a few weeks, and you presume to know my daughter."

"We've been seeing each other for nearly four months." From the shock, Tommy saw on Peter's face it was news to him. "Would you care for that drink now? It's cheap scotch, but I think it'll do the trick." At Peter's nod, Tommy walked to the filing cabinet and opening the bottom drawer, pulled out the half-empty bottle, and poured into two plastic cups.

Peter took the handed glass and swilled its contents in one swallow. "My daughter is barely out of high school. You're older than Frankie, an experienced man."

"I'm a friend, Mr. Thompson." Tommy poured another three fingers into Peter's cup. "Francesca needed a friend to talk to, and I gladly became that for her."

"She has lots of friends. Why would she need you to talk to?"

Tommy ignored the comment meant to unnerve. "Not one who's lost a mother at a young age." Tommy let the silence hang to let that sink in. "Francesca needed someone who could relate to the life-changing event in her life, and I made myself available to her. I was there for her day and night with a listening ear. I gave her a shoulder to cry on when she needed it." The phone shrilled loudly in the silence Tommy left, but he ignored it.

"Very noble of you, but I was a phone call away. She could have called me anytime." Anger took form deep within and sprang hot from Peter, but Tommy understood it was in reaction to his guilt.

"You're a busy man, rarely home. She feels alone and unloved. She needs her father's physical and emotional presence in her life, Mr. Thompson." Tommy watched Peter stiffen before he pushed to his feet to pace the office.

"I'm not here to talk about my relationship with my daughter. I'm here to talk about yours."

"One you disapprove of because of the mistakes I made as a misguided youth, my lack of wealth, education, and my blue-collar background. I have many more flaws I can point out and, which by the way, I laid out to Francesca." When Peter remained quiet, Tommy pressed on. "Not once did I lead her on or took advantage of her. Nor did I pursue her for her wealth as you've already decided. I can hold my own. I have high regard and complete respect for your daughter." Tommy reached for his glass of scotch to wet the mouth, gone dry as dust. "And yes, I do love her. I didn't mean to fall in love with her, but I did. And yes, as you suspect, I'd like to make a life with her." Affection flowed in Tommy's voice, deep and natural when he said the words.

"Make a life with her? She's seventeen, Mr. Scott."

"And it's why I've encouraged her to pursue her studies at the most suitable university even if it means putting distance between us."

"I wasn't aware you'd done that." There was a tinge of respect for Tommy in Peter's voice.

"I'm not the callous hood you think I am. You need to get past the reckless boy you got out of jail all those years ago."

The image of the terrified imprisoned teenager cloaking his fear behind a cocky façade, Mr. Scott begging for his help, came to Peter with clarity. "Reckless? You attacked a man twice your age with a broken beer bottle. You slashed his face to the tune of fifteen stitches."

"And in your investigation, you found it was self-defense on my part."

"It's how I argued it in court, and it was what I told your father, but the information my investigator uncovered was inconclusive."

Tommy felt a thickness in his throat as he mulled Peter's words. "You used the information to have the charge thrown out of adult court back to juvenile. It was how you managed to expunge my criminal record and ultimately have all charges dismissed." Tommy argued defensively.

"I'm an excellent lawyer, Mr. Scott. It's why your father came to me."

"You may be a good lawyer, and I will forever be grateful to you for what you did for me, for my father, but I wasn't guilty, and you damn well know it. Regardless, it's in my past. I'm not that person anymore. You can't brand me for life for a mistake I made as a kid." Tommy needed a cigarette, and unlocking the top desk drawer reached into the depths of it. He breathed a sigh of relief when he found the only cigarette pack he'd managed to hide from Francesca for moments like these.

"I never said you were."

Tommy lit the cigarette, inhaled deeply, appreciating its calming effect. "No, but you think it. You think I'm not good enough for your daughter. I don't blame you for being protective of Francesca. As a man, I can understand why you're here, but as my own man, I don't need to prove my character to you, nor do I want or need your validation."

The boy didn't lack chutzpah, Peter thought.

"You can erase my criminal record from the legal system, but you can't do the same in your mind. To you, I will forever be colored by my checkered past." Tommy reached out to tap ashes on the tin ashtray and remembered Francesca had tossed it in the garbage. Snatching the glass with a few drops of scotch, he tapped ashes into it. "What is it you really want from me, Mr. Thompson?"

Peter sank back into the depths of the folding chair. The flashy gold Rolex sparkled when his suit sleeve slid up. "Francesca has been accepted to my alma mater. I came here to ask you not to dissuade her from going."

Tommy's gaze cut straight to Peter. "I figured sooner or later you'd intervene to get her posted at Stanford. You think so little of me you feel the need to put three thousand miles between us." The idea of it made Tommy's stomach hurt. When Peter started to speak, Tommy cut him off. "Well, you've wasted a trip. I would never stop Francesca from going. You have my word. I love her too much to stand in the way of her future."

"I appreciate it." Peter reached into his jacket pocket for the envelope, handed it to Tommy.

"What's this?" Tommy asked when he saw the twenty-five thousand dollar cheque.

"For your trouble, Tommy, and for doing what's right for Frankie."

And for keeping away from her, Tommy thought. Reaching for the lighter, Tommy flared it and touched it to the cheque. "It's Mr. Scott to you." Peter turned on his heel and headed for the door, the words, "My father is right. Close mindedness is an affliction that can't be reversed," followed him out.

Seven

AFTER THE ONE-SIDED conversation with her father, Francesca ran straight to Mrs. O'Sullivan's bedroom. She knocked and knocked until she remembered Mrs. O'Sullivan was out with Mr. Scott on their first official date. Alone and confused, Francesca dialed Tommy's number.

"I need to see you, Tommy. I need to talk to you. Now," Francesca said between sobs.

Hearing the tears and anxiety in Francesca's voice, Tommy's stomach clenched. "What's wrong, Francesca?"

"I need to talk to you," Francesca repeated in a whisper.

"Why are you whispering? What's going on?"

"My father's home and… Just come, Tommy."

"I'll be right over."

"Meet me at the mouth of the creek, by the woods. Park your truck on the dirt road," she instructed, deciding to sneak out of the house through the backway so her father wouldn't see her.

"I don't want you traipsing through the grounds in the dark. I'll pick you up at the house."

"I know my land like the back of my hand," Francesca pointed out. "Meet me there."

"All right." The sadness in Francesca's voice made Tommy's stomach hurt.

Under the spill of moonlight, Francesca ran across the estate, through shadows, past the gazebo, and the stables. She followed the winding creek, where cattails stood erect like obedient soldiers on its banks, past the wild purple loosestrife to the farthest corner of the property.

It was a warm night, filled with the sounds of cicadas, crickets, and the continuous trickle of water from the creek chugging over rocks. Owls hooted their night call. Small animals scurried and huddled when they saw Francesca running toward them as if escaping a fire.

Fifteen minutes later, Tommy found her by the creek's bank. Wrapped in a silk robe, fuzzy, pink slippers on her feet, Francesca's head rested on folded knees as the tears coursed down her face.

"You came." Francesca lunged herself on Tommy.

"Of course." Tommy brushed the rumpled hair out of her face. "What's wrong, Francesca? Are you hurt?"

"Hold me, Tommy. Just hold me."

Tommy folded her into his arms. "Cry whatever is bothering you out of your system, and then tell me what's triggered this," he said although he already had a good idea.

Sitting by the creek's bank, Tommy held Francesca. Her crying sound cutting through the silence of the night, he let her cry herself dry. Cried out, Tommy dried Francesca's cheeks with his hands. "What's bothering you?"

Francesca looked up through misted eyes to a velvet black sky sprinkled with stars as clear as glass. "Daddy got me out of bed to tell me I've been accepted to Stanford. Then, he handed me this." Francesca reached into her robe pocket for the plane ticket. "I'm supposed to leave this Sunday to get settled in before school starts in a couple of weeks."

Although Tommy knew this was coming, the words hit him like a quick, cold shock to his system. "Congratulations." Tommy pushed back the tears.

"Did you hear what I said, Tommy? I'm supposed to leave in three days. Leave you."

Tommy closed his eyes as the pain stabbed at him. "I heard you. Stanford is what you wanted." The ache in his heart at the sense of loss was unbearable. He'd felt the same void when his mother left him. It had yet to heal.

Francesca bolted to her feet. "Do you want me to go away?" she said, pressing fingers to her temple where the headache was drumming in a steady rhythm now.

Tommy rose, calmly walked to Francesca's side. "You know I don't, but it's Stanford. Your dream school," he said although he suspected it was to please her father, to satisfy her overwhelming need for his validation.

"It was until you came into my life. I don't want to leave you, Tommy. If I go, I'll be gone for six years. I can't stand being away from you that long." Francesca looked at him with eyes clouded with pain.

"Six years will go by really fast. You'll see. We'll talk on the phone every week, I'll write to you every day, and I'll visit you. You'll be home during school breaks." The words were said in vain because Tommy knew it wouldn't work out that way. The moment Francesca boarded the plane their lives would change—forever. "This is a great opportunity you can't pass up, Francesca."

"What good is a great opportunity if I have to be without you? I don't think I can stand being so far away from you."

Tommy brought his hand to rest on her damp cheek. "Of course you can. It's nerves talking right now. This is what you need to do for me. For us." He felt something crumble inside of him, and he pulled Francesca into the protective circle of his arms where he wished she could stay forever. "Look up there," he said, pointing to the sky. "Those are our stars and moon. Look up to them when you're missing me. We'll meet there because I'll be doing the same. Will you do that?"

Francesca nodded with silent tears slipping from between closed lashes. "I love you so much, Tommy."

"I love you, and will to infinity."

Francesca brought her lips to his, let then brush over his. There was a different kind of passion to her kiss. It was desperate, needy, and alive. She slid her tongue deep into his mouth, to taste, to tangle with his.

Francesca lifted young, vulnerable eyes to Tommy and slipped off her robe, but Tommy reached for it and slid it on. "Don't you want me?"

"More than you can imagine, but now is not the right time."

"It's what I want." She pressed a finger to his lips when he started to speak. "It's what I want," she repeated, and eyes never leaving his shrugged out of her robe.

Francesca watched Tommy's eyes fill with stunned appreciation as she slid the thin straps of her nightgown off her shoulders and let it fall to the ground. There was desire, need, and want in Tommy's eyes. No one had looked at her as Tommy did then.

Tommy breathed deeply, taking her in, appreciating the sheer beauty of the shapely curves, the skin as creamy and smooth as pearls. "You're so beautiful and so ... perfect."

A flush worked its way up to Francesca's cheeks. "I'm not perfect."

Tommy framed her face with his hands. His touch left a tingling feeling in her. "You are to me."

Francesca slipped her hands under his T-shirt. His trim body was muscled, hard as steel. The feel of him under her touch was as she imagined it would be. Inch by inch, she brought his T-shirt up until she slipped it off him.

"Make love with me, Tommy." I want to touch you, and I want you to touch me."

Francesca glided fingers over him. His skin was hot now, his scent relentlessly male. Conscious of the way his muscles tensed under her touch, she took her fingers over the broad shoulders, the iron-hard chest, over scars mapping his reckless youth.

Tommy could feel the heat moving up from his toes.

Francesca raked her fingers through his chest hair. She thought she felt his heart beat thick when she lay kisses on his chest. "I want you to love me tonight, Tommy," she said, her tongue sliding down his belly to the snap of his jeans with tormenting patience. "I want to feel your naked body pressed to mine. I want you to touch me, claim me," she whispered, tugging at his jeans.

"Francesca," he started to say, but she cut him off by pressing her mouth to his for a long, deep kiss.

Moonlight fell across her face when she tilted it up to his. "I want to feel you inside me. I want you to make tonight one I'll remember forever. Will you do that for me, Tommy? Will you love me tonight?" The sensation of her warm body pressed against his was electric.

Tommy ran his fingers over the curve of her cheek, looked into the eyes steeped in dreams. He couldn't deny her and himself tonight. This might be the last time he saw her, and he needed the taste of her in his system to take with him. Taking her hand, he brought her down to the ground with him, weedy grass cushioning them.

Tommy kissed her neck and shoulders softly at first, giving her the choice to step away, but she didn't. She couldn't. His breath against her skin felt like fire, and her ache for him only swelled into a drugging need. With a little moan, she begged for more.

Tommy combed her hair behind her ears. "Are you sure, Francesca?"

"I've never been surer of anything."

When his hands lowered to caress, her body trembled. She never anticipated the explosion of sensations that rushed at her when he set his tongue to taste and claimed that which she willingly gave to him. In one instant, his lips were on her breasts, circling her nipples with his tongue. Taking them into his mouth, he suckled until her body arched, and she sang his name like a prayer.

Feelings, sensations swarming her went beyond her wildest dreams. Tommy was tender, loving, and gentle. He was the great lover she knew he would be. Combing her hands through his hair, she wondered why she'd waited so long to let him love her like this.

Tommy's every touch, every kiss, set off every nerve in Francesca. Nothing prepared her for the sensations that shocked her body alive when Tommy slithered his tongue down her belly to the dark triangle between her legs. Slowly, seductively, his mouth lingered, clouding her brain, making her tingle with panicked excitement. When his mouth and tongue claimed her, an intense fire blazing and manic swept through her like an unstoppable wildfire. Every muscle in her body tensed, every nerve erupted with sensations she'd never felt before, never knew could feel so glorious, and she moaned his name into the night.

The shock hit her like a punch when the first peak rocked and dazed her. Her eyes stormy, her breath coming quickly, she latched onto his shoulders when the next orgasm ripped through her body with unrelenting force. Then he lifted her hips high, greedily took more, gave more until she arched against him. When the last wave struck her fast and intensely, she came, his name flowing from her lips into the dark of the night.

Straddling her, Tommy stared into her eyes. "I want to be inside you." He said softly. When she opened up to him, his eyes never leaving hers, he slipped inside her gently, tenderly. She was wet and hot, he was full of want and need, and he plunged himself deeper inside her. "Did I hurt you?" he asked when her breath caught.

Jolts of shocking pain sliced through her, but she gave him a silent headshake. Feeling him inside her made her feel complete, a woman loved. No one had made her feel so desired, so wanted, and so loved.

It felt so right and so perfect.

Aiming blue eyes her way, patiently, tenderly, lovingly, Tommy moved in and out of her sinking deeper into her with each stroke until they were fully bonded. Stroke for stroke, his blood hummed, every muscle tensed, as he neared that precipitous edge. Not wanting the moment to end, he held back.

Recording in his mind every wonderful sensation, the feel of her body under his Tommy made love with her. Sliding in and out of her, he told her how much he loved her. When he was ripe for release, instinctively, she tightened around him. Her fingers digging into his back, she rose and fell with him, mated with him in synchronized rhythm as if they'd done this so many times before. Swamped with love, he emptied himself into her.

IN A DAZED WONDER, HOT NAKED bodies, layered with a film of sweat from their lovemaking, Francesca and Tommy lay coiled in each other's arms. Faces to a starred sky, with their minds wrapped in thoughts of how everything now felt different, they listened to the night, the calm.

It was some time before Francesca turned to Tommy, and kissing him deeply said, "Thank you for making me feel so loved and for making it such a memorable experience. I'd always wondered what my first time would be like. I never imagined it would be so beautiful and wonderful."

Tommy cupped a hand under her chin, turned Francesca's face, so they were eye-to-eye. Francesca's eyes were teary and sad. Tommy wanted to tell her that for him, it had never been as it was tonight with her, but he couldn't get the words out. Instead, Tommy reached for her robe on the grass and covered her with it.

"I'll never forget tonight, Tommy."

He glided his lips over hers. "You're the best of me, Francesca. The best moments in my life have come since you've been in it. How you make me feel is what made our lovemaking so extraordinary and memorable, and I'll forever carry tonight with me."

Francesca let the tears come faster then. "Once I leave, our lives are going to change forever, aren't they?"

"Yes, they are." His heart wept for her. For him.

"I don't want it to change."

"I don't either, but..."

"Life is full of interruptions and complications," she finished for him.

"It is, but always remember whatever happens, wherever life takes us, I love you, and will to infinity," he said through his tears.

THE THREE DAYS LEADING TO FRANCESCA'S departure, she and Tommy met every night by the grove. Under the spill of moonlight, with the mellow sounds of the night and the gurgling waters of the creek, they made love until dawn when Francesca, with love in her heart, snuck back into her bedroom.

Eight

FROM A DISTANCE Tommy's eyes fixed on Francesca, he was deaf to the din of people and the constant announcements spewing from the airport's public address system. She wore the yellow sundress from their first date, and her glossy mink hair haloed her face as it had then. For the minutest moment, Tommy thought he could smell a subtle hint of her sweet perfume.

For a long time, Tommy watched Francesca, wishing he could touch her, talk to her, but her father's presence made it an impossibility.

When her flight was called, Tommy watched Francesca hug her father then, Mrs. O'Sullivan, before turning her eyes to scan the airport for him. Guilt and an unbearable pain squeezed Tommy's heart when he saw the hurt that filled her eyes when she didn't see him. For a brief five seconds, he thought of stepping out from behind the column, but her father's presence set him straight.

Tommy watched Francesca sling her tote over her shoulder, and take the carry-on from Mrs. O'Sullivan. He saw her take one last look around before she handed her ticket to the customs officer and crossed into the boarding area.

Francesca was on her way to California, and out of Tommy's life.

Tears running down Tommy's cheeks, he honed in on Francesca's sad eyes staring out the plane's window. For a moment, he felt their eyes meet and pressed a hand against the window glass. Tommy thought he saw Francesca doing the same against the plane window. If only for the briefest moment, Tommy thought they'd shared a connection minutes before the plane took off.

"I love you, Francesca, to infinity," he murmured, flipping through the memories they'd made over the past few months.

Would there be more, he wondered.

LOOKING OUT THE AIRPLANE WINDOW, FRANCESCA sensed Tommy watching her. She thought their eyes met. As the plane started down the runway, Francesca was sure she saw Tommy rest his hand against the second-story window to connect with the one she pressed against the plane's window.

THREE THOUSAND FEET IN THE AIR Francesca reached into her carry-on for a tissue to wipe the tears that swam into her eyes and found the envelope Mrs. O'Sullivan slipped in at the last minute. Recognizing Tommy's handwriting, eager fingers ripped the envelope open.

> *My Dearest Francesca,*
>
> *I'm not a writer, nor am I a poet, and at this moment, I wish I were both because I want only the perfect words to describe how I feel about you. Seeing, as I'm neither, I'm going to write what I feel in my heart.*
>
> *My mind can't sleep tonight. It's filled with you and the images of our lovemaking under a moonlit sky. I can hear the sound of the trickling water and nature's symphony all around us. The*

first time we joined as one, the world around me filled full of oxygen.

No one has made me feel as complete or as loved as you have. You saw past the reckless boy I was and loved me for the man I am, and who I am now is because of you. I'd shut down after my mom's death, and you showed me I could open my heart and be loved in return.

You taught me what true love means.

You, Francesca, are the best of me. You've claimed a place in my heart, and I will carry you with me forever.

As I write this letter, I'm looking out my bedroom window to the sky, at the stars and the moon that fills it because I already miss you and feel a huge void in my heart. In them, I see your face, and I feel you all around me.

I love you so much, Francesca. I love you more than there are blades of grass on this earth, more than there are grains of sand on the beaches of the world. I always will.

I will carry your heart in mine with me for as long as I'm on this earth. I will see you in every star for all eternity. I hope you do too.

With all my love, Tommy.

Crying silent tears, Francesca read Tommy's letter over and over the entire eight-hour flight.

TOMMY WROTE AND MAILED HIS FIRST letter to Francesca the day of her departure and every week afterward. Two months later, he still hadn't received a response, not a letter, not a call.

Clinging to hope, Tommy never stopped writing Francesca.

Nine

LILY MADISON GRANT, the daughter of Rex Grant, a Texan oil magnate turned conservative senator eying a run for the presidency in eight years, had an I.Q. that put most of the student body at Stanford to shame. Lily, however, was more interested in—as she called it—living the *Dolce Vita*. She was petite with a tiny upturned nose and large almond-shaped eyes. She had the type of curvy figure with a tiny waist that turned men's heads and got on every woman's nerves.

Lily and Francesca met the first week of school. Both looking lost, Lily introduced herself and told Francesca she at least find her way to a great milkshake and fries. After some coaxing, Lily led Francesca to The Malt Shop, where Francesca spent the rest of the afternoon watching Lily introduce them to every boy that walked in and by the end of the introduction had them sitting at their table.

The moment Francesca heard Lily's heels tap on tile, she wiped her face dry and tucked Tommy's letter under her pillow. In the five months Francesca had known Lily Madison Grant, she'd told her now best friend everything about herself, her life, and Tommy. Lily knew everything there was to know about Francesca, but for Tommy's letter. That was something that was hers.

"I knew I'd find you in here, hibernating as usual," Lily said in her Texan drawl, sashaying into Francesca's bedroom with her usual flounce.

"I thought you had cheerleading practice." Francesca heard the tears in her voice, and she cleared her throat to disguise them.

"Postponed until tomorrow." Lily looked past the dewy eyes Francesca tried to blink dry. The last time she'd made a big to-do about Francesca's teary eyes, she'd jeopardized their friendship, and she didn't dare risk it again. Lily had grown to love Francesca like the sister she didn't have. "So, I've come to rescue you from this dark hell hole." Lily rolled blinds up and opened windows to let the sunlight and air flow. "You need to get out of this place, Frankie. Come to The Malt Shop with me. Right about this time, it's full of those hunky football players with the rippling muscles and the oh, so tight behinds." Lily walked to the dresser, turned off the transistor radio that lately, in her opinion, only spewed nonsense of war.

"Is boys all you ever think about?"

Lily's brows slammed together. "Sugar, what else is there?"

Francesca turned the radio back on. "There is so much going on in the world, Lily. Dark war clouds are hanging over Europe. People are dying over there. Have you no interest in what Hitler is doing?"

"No, and neither would you if you weren't constantly filling your head with thoughts of Tommy and driving yourself into a depressed state, you become like a heat-seeking missile for misery."

"I'm not feeling depressed," Francesca said soberly, and when Lily gave her a raised brow added, "Okay, maybe a little, but I have a right to feel miserable. I haven't heard from Tommy in months. He promised to write and call."

"I know you're missing him, but from what you've told me of him, I suspect there's probably an excellent reason why he hasn't. For now, you have to snap out of it. It's not healthy. Worse, it's making me sad."

"And God forbid that happens."

"Exactly." Lily dabbed cherry-red lipstick on her lips, surveyed herself in the dresser mirror. "What do you think?"

"Looks great on you," Francesca said, to the dark-haired, blue-eyed beauty when she turned an extended pout her way.

"Red is me. I'm keeping this lipstick." Lily tossed the tube into her Hermès bag. "Now, enough of listening to horrible war nonsense. Throw on a pair of tight hugging jeans and a sexy top that exposes your assets. We're getting a chocolate milkshake and rounding me up a man."

"I need to study for a history exam." Francesca turned the radio back on as the newscaster quoted from Winston Churchill's speech that there was no chance of a speedy end to the war except through united action. What united action meant Francesca wasn't sure, but the words shot a shiver down her back.

If Lily heard the newscaster's report, she chose to ignore it because all she said was, "Both you and I know that's a load of cow doodle you're giving me because you'll ace the test. You always do. You have this intrinsic need to hole up in this bedroom because you feel a need to remain loyal to Tommy even though you haven't heard from him in months." Immediately regretting the hurt her words inflicted, Lily ran to Francesca's side. "I'm sorry, sugar, I didn't mean it. My mouth sometimes runs off without processing first. Forgive me, Frankie?"

A momentary silence hung in the air before Francesca said, "I can never stay angry with you. Besides, by now, I'm used to your mouth running off without thinking."

Exhaling a breath of relief, Lily wrapped Francesca in a hug. "I know you are. Still, I need to think more and talk less. Daddy says God gave me two ears and one mouth for a reason. I would have preferred two mouths and one ear." Lily gave Francesca a wink, and Francesca couldn't help but smile.

"You don't need to change for me. Your honesty is what I love about you."

"That being the case, I'll tell you you need to make friends."

"I have you."

"You do, but you need more sensible friends than me, and not necessarily of the male species," Lily added, anticipating Francesca's rebuff. "The fewer boys you attract, the more I have to entertain, and you know how much I love entertaining."

Francesca let out a snorted giggle. "No one can deny you an A-plus for initiative."

"And performance." Lily flashed Francesca, a wicked grin. "Now, all I'm saying is you need to get a bit of excitement in your life. But all you ever do is study, study, and study some more. I fear you're turning into a nun."

The sound of a riding lawnmower sounded off in the distance. In seconds the smell of freshly cut grass flooded the bedroom.

"I don't think a non-virgin can qualify." Francesca pointed out.

Lily waved a finger. "No. We're not going into the detailed account of the fantastic four days of memorable lovemaking you and gorgeous Tommy had by the creek. Now, how wrong would it be if you came down to The Malt Shop to keep an eye on me? You know how I have a tendency to get out of hand when surrounded by the male species, and how it usually ends up not favoring the governor's image." Lily fell back onto Francesca's bed. "God, I wish daddy would have chosen a line of work that didn't require me watching my every step. It's why I need you there. You're the conscience I lack."

"Whether I'm there or not, when your eyes latch onto a guy, you're like a tornado ready to strike. There's no stopping you when it happens. But you're right."

"Honey, when haven't I been? Although I'm not sure what I'm right about in this instance." Lily ran a sterling brush through dark curls.

"You're right about Tommy not having written to me and me having to get on with my life. He probably has." Pain swam into her eyes. He'd told her he loved her to infinity.

It had been five months since Francesca had moved to California, and just as long since she'd heard from Tommy. Francesca never thought after giving herself to him, after everything he'd said to her during those four days, during the months they were together, he'd walk out of her life without a second thought.

Francesca wondered if Tommy already had another woman on his arm. She couldn't bear the thought of her sitting with Tommy on the hood of his truck watching the stars, walking hand in hand down the boardwalk, or sharing a hamburger at Nick's. Francesca stopped short at the notion he was making love to her and saying the things he'd said to her.

She hated to admit that her father might have been right. Tommy was only after one thing—her money. With the thought gnawing on Francesca's nerves, she pushed off her bed, walked to her closet, pulled a pair of slim-fitting jeans and a tailored poplin shirt off their hangers.

"That's the spirit, sugar. Now, let's get those waves of yours brushed, and your pretty face made up." Excitement lifted Lily's voice and rummaging through Francesca's makeup drawer said, "Boys brace yourself for Lily and Frankie. Tonight they're painting the town red."

"IT'S GREAT TO HEAR YOUR VOICE, Mrs. O?" Francesca said, over the telephone line.

"It's nice to hear from you, Frankie. It's been ages since you've called home."

"I'm sorry, but school's keeping me busy." And I have no reason to call if Tommy wants nothing to do with me. "Anyway, I got your wedding invitation. I was over the moon when I saw it. You and Mr. Scott sure don't mess around."

"At our age, every minute counts. Besides, we're too old for all the courtship nonsense. We thought we'd jump into it feet first." It pleased Mrs. O'Sullivan to hear Francesca's laughter over the telephone line.

"Did you and Mrs. Scott get my wedding present?"

"Yes, we did, darling. Mr. Scott says he will keep your Baccarat vase filled with red roses."

"Your favorite."

"The man does like to spoil me." Mrs. O'Sullivan's smile echoed over the telephone.

"I'm so happy for you and Mr. Scott. You make a lovely couple, and you both deserve much happiness and love. I'm sorry I won't be able to make it back for the wedding, but there's so much going on in school, and Daddy thinks any time off will distract from my studies."

"More like it will keep you away from Tommy," Mrs. O'Sullivan murmured between clenched teeth.

"I'm sorry, Mrs. O, this connection isn't very good. What did you say?"

"I said your father knows best. You need not worry, darling. It's a simple affair at our church and a small reception. Not worth the trip. I'll send you loads of pictures."

"Yes, send me loads. Where are you going on your honeymoon? I hope it's somewhere romantic. Tell me everything."

"This is a long-distance call. It will cost a mint."

"I don't care. I miss talking to you, Mrs. O." Francesca hesitated for a moment. "I guess I should start calling you, Mrs. Scott."

"I won't be Mrs. Scott for another two weeks."

"All right, Mrs. O, tell me everything." Francesca settled in her bed, legs crossed in the air, and Mrs. O'Sullivan settled at the kitchen table with a cup of coffee.

Mrs. O'Sullivan caught Francesca up, ensuring to skirt Tommy's name and anything to do with him. Unless

Francesca asked about Tommy, Mrs. O'Sullivan wouldn't mention him.

Talked out, Mrs. O'Sullivan let the air hum long enough to give Francesca one last chance to ask about Tommy, although she doubted she would. Not after she'd found the stack of Tommy's letters in Peter's office desk, intercepted by his brother. Mrs. O'Sullivan could only imagine the hurt her girl was feeling thinking Tommy had abandoned her. Guilt smothered her at the thought she couldn't tell Francesca of her discovery, not after Peter forbade her to speak to her to his daughter about Tommy.

Mrs. O'Sullivan couldn't bring herself to tell Francesca her father's narrow mind couldn't see past the person Tommy used to be or that he was the reason she was thousands of miles from home. Worse, Mrs. O'Sullivan had to lie to Tommy when he asked about Francesca, but telling him, Peter considered him an undesirable, undeserving of his daughter wasn't an option. She refused to make her soon to be son feel unworthy.

Mrs. O'Sullivan damned Peter Thompson to hell. She wouldn't have invited him to her wedding, but it might have raised suspicion had she not.

"I love you, Mrs. O, and I'm so happy for you." Francesca ended the telephone conversation without so much as the mention of Tommy's name, and Mrs. O'Sullivan could only ask God for forgiveness.

Ten

TOMMY TUCKED THE paperwork into the folder when Mrs. Scott walked into the small kitchen of the red brick duplex on Cedar Street. She'd been living at the Scott home for one day, and everything already felt different. For the better, Tommy thought because every home needed a woman's touch.

"Honestly, how your father managed without a woman for so long is a mystery to me. This morning he couldn't find his razor blade although it was sitting right there on the bathroom sink." Mrs. Scott gathered the breakfast dishes, set them in soapy water.

"He needed a good woman like you," Tommy said because he wouldn't dare point out that after two men living on their own for so long, the addition of a woman into their midst set their world askew.

"You're not wrong there." Mrs. Scott stood by the sink, the sunlight streaming through the window haloed her black Fedora. "You'll wash these for me, won't you, Darling?"

"Of course. You get yourself sorted. I know dad's anxious to get to Niagara Falls to get this honeymoon of yours started." Tommy took the damp cloth from Mrs. Scott when she started wiping the table.

"Imagine an old biddy like me on a honeymoon. Will wonders never cease?" Mrs. Scott said, but Tommy's head was miles away. "I'm sorry she didn't make it in for the wedding, love. You know, the first year of university is tough even for a smart girl like Frankie." Mrs. Scott rested a hand on Tommy's shoulder and squeezed tight.

"I wasn't thinking of her," Tommy said, but when Mrs. Scott raised a brow, his shoulders went as limp as he felt inside. "I'm not going to be able to get away with anything with you around, am I?"

Mrs. Scott shook her head. She'd liked Tommy from the time she sat him down to have her motherly talk about Francesca. Now, he was her son, and she loved him as her own. "I know you expected Frankie to make the trip if not for the wedding, at least to see you, and I'm sorry she didn't, darling. But you must know her actions had nothing to do with you."

"I know." Tommy tried to disguise his hurt, but Mrs. Scott could see the injured expression in his eyes, the pain that filled them.

"I'm sorry you're hurting so much, darling. You deserve better, but you mustn't hate or blame Francesca. I want you to believe me when I tell you none of this is her doing."

"I don't blame Francesca for anything, and I certainly don't hate her."

Francesca had been gone for six months, but it felt like a lifetime to Tommy, and he feared forgetting the taste of her kisses, her scent. In time he'd forget her face, the sound of her laughter just as it had with his mother. If it weren't for the picture of his mother on his night table, Tommy wouldn't remember her face anymore.

After calling up to tell her husband his wallet was on the nightstand, Mrs. Scott sat next to Tommy. "I saw Mr. Thompson talking to you at the wedding reception."

"It was nothing." Tommy dismissed the comment with a wave of his hand.

Mrs. Scott watched Tommy agonizing like a child whose lollipop was taken from him. "You're like a son to me now, and you won't mind if I treat you like one, will you?" When Tommy shook his head, Mrs. Scott said, "All right then, sit up straight, stop brooding, and tell me what Mr. Thompson said to you." Mrs. Scott's blazing eyes told Tommy he'd better do as told.

"He told me to stop writing to Francesca. Said she needs to concentrate on her studies. He said she has a new life now, and if I cared for her, I'd let her live it."

There was so much pain in the solemn blue eyes staring at Mrs. Scott she couldn't help but let out a string of Gaelic curses. Calmer now, Mrs. Scott fixed her eyes on Tommy. "I saw him hand you a package."

"It was the letters I've written to Francesca, unseen, unopened." The sense of loss, the ache in Tommy's heart was unbearable.

The sorrow in Tommy's voice turned Mrs. Scott's eyes to a fiery blaze, and she set off on an oath driven rant in intelligible English this time. Oathed out, Mrs. Scott breathed in for calm. "I'm so sorry, love."

"He's right. I need to let Francesca get on with her life, and I need to get on with mine." The despair and defeat clear in this tone.

Mrs. Scott drew Tommy into her ample bosom to hold and comfort as a mother would. "Wait for me in the car," she mouthed, waving Mr. Scott away when he walked into the kitchen. Knowing better than to question her or the scene playing out before him, he scurried along. "Do you want me to talk to Frankie, lad?"

"No. Mr. Thompson is never going to allow us to come together, and it will just make things more difficult for Francesca—for me."

Mrs. Scott thought she heard something desperate in Tommy's voice, and she couldn't escape the nagging sense of dread in her gut. "You're not going to do anything rash, are you, lad?

"Of course not. You better get going." Tommy urged Mrs. Scott to the front door when the car horn sounded off.

"He is an impatient one, isn't he? I'll have to do something about that." Tommy smiled, thinking if anyone could change his father, it was her. "I'm worried about you, Tommy. Your father and I can just as well cancel our honeymoon and stay here with you."

"I'm a twenty-two-year-old man. I certainly don't need my new mommy around to take care of me." Tommy's words melted Mrs. Scott's heart, and she folded him into a tight embrace. "You get off. I've heard the falls in February is a winter marvel. Just make sure you don't come back telling me I'm going to be a big brother in nine months."

Mrs. Scott let out a boisterous cackle. "You cheeky bugger."

"I'm glad you and dad are together. I'm glad you're in his life. You're going to be good for him. Promise me you'll take care of him, of each other."

"Of course, I will. And as your mommy, I'm taking care of you too."

Tommy pecked Mrs. Scott on the cheek. "I love you."

"I love you too, lad," she said with the nagging sense of dread becoming stronger.

ONE WEEK LATER, ON THEIR RETURN from Niagara Falls, Mrs. Scott found Tommy's letter propped on the fireplace mantel. The moment she read it, she screamed out for her husband.

Eleven

TOMMY WAS GLAD when a few days after enlisting, he received his order to ship out. He was sorry he didn't get the chance to say goodbye to his father or mother, but running was what Tommy needed to do. Leave behind the misery that was his life was what Tommy had to do. Slinging his duffel bag over his shoulder, Tommy set off for England to fight alongside the thousands of men of the First Canadian Infantry Division.

To say Tommy's decision to enlist to fight in the escalating war in Europe was a rational or patriotic one would be a lie. Tommy's decision to enlist was an emotional one, which came to him when Peter Thompson handed him the stack of unopened letters.

The moment Peter set those letters in Tommy's hands, it drove a reality he'd refused to accept home. Peter was going to do everything in his power to ensure he'd never be a part of Francesca's life. The bottomless well of hope, which had kept Tommy believing there was still a chance for him and Francesca, hit bottom. The following day, an inconsolable Tommy picked up the forms from the recruitment office.

War, Tommy decided, was the perfect distraction for his broken heart and the unbearable ache of loss. If he died along the way, so be it.

"WHAT DOES FRANKIE DO OUT ON the terrace at sundown every day?" William asked Lily as both stood at the kitchen window, watching her.

"She says she needs to look up at the stars."

William sipped coffee contemplatively. "Why?"

"She says she's connecting."

William drank the last of his coffee, and walking to the refrigerator reached into the freezer for the tub of chocolate ice cream. "Would you like a scoop?"

Lily nodded. "Can you make a bowl for Frankie, Professor? I'll take it out to her."

"Sure. Grab the scooper and three spoons from the drawer behind you." William reached into the cupboard for bowls. "Do you know what it is she reads every night while she's connecting?"

"She tells me everything, except for what's in that letter, and I haven't pressed her. Some things are your own. You know. I think this is one of those things for her. I know Frankie often cries after reading it, and there's nothing I can do for her. It breaks my heart, Professor Thompson. Tears it in two."

"Me too." William felt a heaviness in his chest.

William wondered if Peter cared how much his daughter was hurting. Several times, William tried to discuss Francesca's depressed state with his brother only to be dismissed and told it was teenage angst, and she'd get over it soon enough.

Peter had always been driven, self-centered, cold-hearted, an uncaring brother, but growing up, William idolized his older brother and overlooked his character flaws because who was perfect. As they got older and Willian got wiser, they drifted apart. It was why there were thousands of miles between them. Family sometimes worked best when kept arm's length. But now, seeing the pain and hurt in the niece he'd come to love as his own, William couldn't tolerate Peter's callousness toward Francesca. Francesca was hurting, and William suspected it was for Tommy Scott, the man Peter determined to keep her from seeing.

"As her best friend, you must know more than I do." William scooped ice cream into bowls. "Aside from you, does Frankie have any friends, a boyfriend?

"She has no interest in making friends or meeting people. I've tried to get her to socialize, but she'd rather lock herself in her bedroom and study. Not that there's anything wrong with that," Lily added when her reply caused William to lift a brow.

William walked back to the window to peel concerned eyes on his niece. He regretted now agreeing to intercept Tommy's letters for Peter. He wished he'd never kept them from Francesca, but William believed Peter when he'd told him Tommy was an ex-convict, bad news, and keeping Francesca shielded from him was what had to be done.

William wished he'd gone with his gut and cast doubt on his brother's portrayal of Tommy. A man who writes weekly and continues to do so without receiving a response is a man in love. He's looking to build something that mattered with the woman he loved. He's not a low-life criminal with disregard for law and humanity as Peter made him out to be, William, conclude.

Anger darkened William's eyes, and there and then, he decided to do what he should have done months ago.

AS THE DAYS WORE ON, TOMMY'S squad spent their day's training for the day the orders to spearhead the Allied attack came. The training was arduous, the days long and tiring for the men. Nights were the worst. It was when the loneliness and homesickness set in. Not for Tommy. He kept busy. Focused on anything other than Francesca not only helped Tommy escape the pain and heartache but turned him into the consummate soldier.

Tommy volunteered for any patrol mission going. Trying to avoid sleep—sleeping resulted in dreams of Francesca—Tommy took on night patrol duty for weeks on end. Often, Tommy had to restrain himself from being too quick with the trigger when thoughts of Peter Thompson entered his mind.

Fighting on the frontline was what Tommy signed up for, the distraction he needed, and when the orders to engage in combat were delayed for months, his disappointment was huge. Until the orders came, Tommy spent his time training and guarding England against a possible German invasion.

While the men in his squad spent their downtime fraternizing at the mess hall or the pub, Tommy spent it reading the books Francesca wanted him to or staring up at the stars, hoping she was doing the same. Keeping to himself drove the men to distance themselves from Recluse-Tommy, and that was fine with him.

Putting distance between him and the men who on their downtime only talked of home, family, wives, and girlfriends to fill the boredom was what he wanted. Tommy didn't want to talk about home. He had nothing to say, and the only photograph he carried with him was of a woman he loved and lost.

Tommy's sadness, pain, and despair rolled into indifference, the type that makes a man overlook his wellbeing. Whether he was injured or met with a bullet was of no concern to Tommy. His disregard for his welfare drove him to take risks that gave rise to outperform every man on his squad, and soon enough, the promotions started rolling in. Not that moving up the ranks was his objective. Tommy was there to forget and put the past behind.

Letters from home—mainly from Mrs. Scott since his father wasn't much of a writer—came often. They were mostly about the goings-on at the garden center. With the shortage of men back home, Mrs. Scott was now working alongside her husband to keep the garden center running. Tommy felt a heaviness in his chest at the thought he'd let them down. He should have been running the business while they enjoyed a well-deserved retirement.

Mrs. Scott often joked in her letters Tommy hadn't yet become a big brother, but that he shouldn't give up hope. Her love for his father came through in all her letters. Tommy was happy to know his father was loved and well cared for. He deserved to be happy.

AFTER GOING THROUGH FRANCESCA'S PERSONAL BELONGINGS while she was at school and finding Tommy's letter under her pillow, William dialed Mrs. Scott's telephone number. Guilt, the overwhelming weight of it smothered him. The words in that letter spoke of a man in love, not of a criminal out to take advantage of a naïve, young girl as Peter led him to believe.

When William Thompson called Mrs. Scott to offer to fly Tommy to California to surprise Francesca and was told he'd enlisted to fight overseas, he lapsed into momentary silence. Men with broken hearts did foolish things, but William couldn't help but shoulder some of the responsibility for Tommy's reckless decision to enlist. Had he gone with his gut feeling and passed the letters to Francesca instead of doing what Peter asked, Tommy wouldn't be in Europe, William concluded.

William looked out to the terrace where Francesca stared up at the canopy of stars sprayed against a black-blue sky. He had to correct this. William couldn't stand to see Francesca hurting anymore. Francesca was a wonderful, intelligent, caring woman who deserved happiness, to be making memories at this young age, not shedding tears. How Peter could do this to his only daughter and to what purpose, because if William knew Peter, there was a bigger scheme in play, only proved his brother's callousness.

"He's been gone three years now." Mrs. Scott dried soapy hands on the apron at her waist.

"I'm sorry to hear, Mrs. Scott. Is he ... well?"

"He's fine. Luckily, he hasn't seen combat—yet. He nearly got shipped off to participate in the Dieppe raid, but his commander kept him back to train the men left behind.

Tommy's somewhere in England right now. Has been for the better part of his deployment, but you and I know it's only a matter of time before he gets his orders to go into active theater. God help him."

William heard the anxiety in her voice. The regret and remorse were like two vicious, heavy blows to his gut. "I don't suppose you know where in England he's stationed."

"He can't tell us, but I have a mailing address if that's what you're after."

"It is. Do you suppose Tommy would oppose me filling Frankie in on his whereabouts?"

"He would, but not me. The boy needs to hear from Frankie. He needs to know she's thinking of him. It may save his life, Professor."

William smothered the quick pang of guilt. "Yes. You may be right about that, Mrs. Scott."

"Professor, you know your brother isn't going to be as agreeable to Frankie..."

"You leave my brother to me, Mrs. Scott," William finished, letting raw temper carry him out. "I'm sorry, it's just that Frankie has been miserable since she got here. I may be a Professor of law at a high ranked school, but I'm a man, and it's taking me this long to figure out what she's suffering from is a broken heart."

"Unfortunately, men react differently to heartache. Tommy's broken heart, I believe, is what made him enlist. Frankie and Tommy, Professor Thompson, are meant to be together. The love they share for one another is rare and special."

"Agreed," William said, reaching for pen and paper to jot Tommy's address.

WILLIAM INDICATED THE SOFA AND FRANCESCA sat down. "I want to talk to you."

Francesca set Bear, the lively Yorkshire terrier William gave her on her last birthday to cheer her up, on her lap. "What about, Uncle Will? Is anything wrong?"

"Nothing's wrong, darling." William poured himself a brandy before joining Francesca on the sofa. "I spoke with Mrs. Scott last night."

"You did? Why? Is she all right? Is Mr. Scott?"

"Both are fine." William ran a hand over Bear's head and got himself a grunt of pleasure. "You know I love you like a daughter."

"I know that, Uncle Will." Bear settled his head on Francesca's lap and, in seconds, fell asleep. "He's had a tiring day."

"Yes, chewing my shoe all morning will do that." When Francesca smiled, it warmed William's heart. He rarely saw her smile. "I never had children of my own because, well, as an educator, I inherit hundreds every year, and to me, that's enough. So I'm not sure how to deal with…"

"Just spit it out, Uncle Will." The worry line between Francesca's eyebrows grew deeper.

"All right. You tell me if I'm crossing a line or wording anything wrongly." Odd, there could be so much emotion swirling in him, William thought, and he swilled most of his brandy, hoping to infuse the courage he needed. "I want to talk to you about Tommy Scott." With a jolt, Francesca sat up straight, and when she started to speak, William held a hand up to hold her off. "I thought you'd want to know he's overseas, Frankie. He's gone to Europe with the First Canadian Infantry Division."

Realization dawned slowly. When it did, Francesca stiffened. "Infantry? He's in the military?"

"He enlisted shortly after you arrived here." William swilled more brandy.

"He's gone to fight in the war? Is he all right, Uncle Will?" Emotion choked her voice.

"He's fine, darling. He's somewhere in England right now. Has been for the better part of his deployment, but as I understand it, his squad is waiting on orders to go into active theater." The truth and nothing but was what Francesca deserved.

"Oh, God. Does that mean he's going into battle?"

"I'm afraid so, darling." William's throat dry as sand, he walked to the bar for a refill.

"Tommy's going to fight, with bullets and bombs exploding all around him." Francesca's raised voice stunned with shock, she startled Bear, and he lifted his head, swayed it from side to side studying an agitated Francesca.

"Yes, darling. I'm sorry." William picked up his glass, drank deeply.

"Are you sure?" Francesca asked, refusing to accept what she was being told.

"It's just a matter of time." William gave her hand a squeeze hoping to dim the fear in Francesca's eyes.

Nervous energy searing, Francesca rose to pace the room. She'd heard the reported atrocities taking place in Europe on the radio reports, seen it on the newsreels at the theater. Never in a million years did she think Tommy was in the middle of it. Tommy—the man she knew—couldn't hurt a fly, let alone kill men. Francesca stiffened at the thought.

"Why, why would he do that, Uncle Will? Why would he risk his life that way?"

William swilled more brandy. "Sit down, darling." Francesca's anxiety all too real, when she sat down Bear laid his head in her lap, aiming adoring eyes at her. "Because that's the difference between men and women. You sit out on the terrace looking up at the stars hoping to see him in them while crying your tears of pain. A broken man unleashes his pain by ramming their fist into a wall or, in this case, going to war."

"It's my fault. For leaving him, isn't it?"

William was glad when Francesca dismissed the star comment, which he'd inadvertently let slip out. "No, it wasn't your fault." It was Peter's and his for going along with him.

"Oh, Tommy." Francesca fell into William's arms. She felt so small for the anger she'd carried for Tommy for deserting her, for blaming him for her pain, her heartache. "I don't want him to die, Uncle Will."

William could hear the dread in Francesca's voice. His eyes were dry, but his heart wept for her. "He won't."

"Don't make promises you can't keep, Uncle Will." Francesca pushed away from him, but William pulled her back into the chain of his arms.

"I'm sorry to upset you, but I thought you'd want to know. I thought maybe you'd like to write him," William said, brushing her hair from her face as a confused Bear looked on.

"I would. There's so much I need to say to him." Tears ripped through the words.

THE ORDER CAME AT THE END of June. Tommy and his men were to participate in Operation Husky, an Allied invasion of the south-east shores of Sicily. The aim, to take the island of Sicily from the axis power was to be led by an amphibious attack, along with airborne and naval support, followed by a six-week land campaign, which fell to the First Canadian Infantry.

Unlike the rest of the men in his squadron, there was no fear, no apprehension of going into war in Tommy. Fighting was what he'd signed up for, and with nothing in his life to look forward to, Tommy couldn't wait.

On Tommy's walk through the camp, out to his place of solitude where he spent his downtime, he walked past men sharing cigarettes discussing what was to come. For some, it was the first time in active theatre, and the fear of war touching them felt too real. The tension in the air was palpable. Many of the men wrote letters—what they perceived as their last—to loved ones or drafted their wills.

There wouldn't be much sleep to be had tonight, Tommy thought.

None of the tension, the nerve-wracking what-was-to-come thoughts crossed Tommy's mind. This was what he'd signed up for, and focusing on the what-ifs was a futile exercise for Tommy. War was an unpredictable business, at best.

Tommy sat on the grass-covered ground and leaned against the beech tree. Firing up a cigarette, he slid one arm behind his head and set eyes to the sky. The night was ripe with heat. To the north, Messerschmitt fly-bys lit the sky with fire. Closer to camp, a melodic nightingale sang out in chorus with blackbirds. Above, the moon was sliced in half, its glow sharp in a dark sky glowing with stars. Looking up to them, Tommy thought he could see Francesca's face and his mind filled with thoughts of her. She was rooted in him, and as hard as he tried to push her out of his mind, he couldn't. After some time, Tommy resigned to the fact he'd carry Francesca forever in his heart and mind.

The memory of the first night they made love flooded him, and a smile creased his lips. Francesca had never been with a man before him. But the passion that flowed from her was one he'd never felt until her. The sensations Tommy had shared with her were extraordinary; the feeling of her warm body pressed to him fiery. He thought he could taste her just then, smell the subtle hint of the soap on her skin, the musky scent of her shampoo. Tommy heard Francesca's breathy voice moaning his name as he drove her to fly. He felt the fierce pull of desire for her flood his body.

Tommy hadn't been with a woman after Francesca. Not that he hadn't had plenty of opportunities to indulge. War and the possibility of impending death made women much more willing to share their bed and bodies. But none of them were Francesca, and he couldn't bring himself to slide into bed with them.

"I figured I'd find you here." Pimpled face Mike fell to the grass beside Tommy. "What do you do here, sarge?"

"I watch the stars," Tommy said to the only person in the camp he considered a friend.

Mike, a seventeen-year-old who'd enlisted for the romance of war, had a shock of blonde hair. His eyes were as innocent as they were blue. Mike kept mostly to himself, didn't ask many questions, and didn't pass judgment. It was why Tommy liked him and took him under his wing to watch over and protect.

Mike tilted his face up to the sky, tried to see what Tommy saw. "They look like dots of light to me."

Tommy breathed in smoke, making the tip of the cigarette glow red in the darkness. "There's so much more there, Mike. There are dreams, memories, and secrets. Those stars see everything." Tommy expelled a thin white cloud of smoke, watched it swirl upward.

Mike took a closer look. "Yeah, I still get nothing," he said, taking the cigarette Tommy offered and drawing in smoke. "You know you're the only man on the squad that isn't freaking out about tonight's announcement."

"Why bother freaking out over something you have no control over."

Mike sighed out, smoke. "You're a strange fuck, Tommy. It's as if you don't give a shit about yourself, of your life. We're about to go into combat, and you're as cool as ice."

"That's me, the iceman." Tommy took the cigarette back from Mike before he smoked it down to the filter. "Did you come out here to give me a philosophical talk?"

"Oh shit. I almost forgot. I got a letter for you from back home. I couldn't find you earlier, so I held it for you. It smells nice, like a dame." Mike rose to his five-nine and reached into his pants pocket.

"It's probably from my mom." Tommy stubbed the cigarette out, reached for the letter, but Mike pulled it back.

"Nu-huh. Your mom's envelopes have never smelled this good, and wouldn't it be disturbing if they did? It smells of Chanel." Mike's comment caused Tommy to lift a brow. "What? The summers I worked at a department store, the Chanel girl used to spray that stuff everywhere. Must be a classy dame. Chanel's pricey." Mike took one last whiff before handing Tommy the envelope. "I gotta get some shut-eye, or I won't make it through training tomorrow. See you later."

"See ya." Tommy breathed in the envelope's scent. The kid was right, definitely Chanel. He knew only one woman who wore it religiously.

Under the faint spill of moonlight, Tommy read the face of the envelope and felt something catch in his throat. The delicate flowing script was Francesca's.

Twelve

TOMMY STARED AT the envelope for a long while.

It had been over three long, heartbreaking years since he'd heard from Francesca. Over three years since she'd boarded the plane that whisked her out of his life. Three years since he'd spoken with her.

All this time, Tommy thought Francesca didn't reply to his letters because she'd moved on with her life. A life meant to be shared with men of wealth and intellect, not with men like him. When days turned into weeks, and weeks into months, and Tommy still hadn't received a response from Francesca to any of his letters, he'd felt broken, alone, miserable. Tommy felt as if their time together meant nothing to her.

Tommy breathed a sigh of relief when Peter set the stack of unopened letters in his hands. It was proof Francesca hadn't replied because she'd abandoned him, but because she hadn't seen any of his letters. When Tommy imagined Francesca had almost certainly felt as abandoned and hurt as he had, his first instinct was to ram his fist into Peter Thompson's lawyerly face.

Peter was fortunate they were at his parent's wedding reception at the time, and Tommy banked his anger for their benefit. Otherwise, Tommy may have ended up doing his second stint behind bars—for manslaughter. Instead, Tommy settled for the more restrained approach and let the air out of all the tires on Peter's Ferrari. Tommy didn't get the satisfaction he would have if he'd broken Peter's jaw or a few of his ribs, but it felt good nonetheless.

Staring at the envelope, Tommy wondered why Francesca would write to him after all these years. Her reasons for doing so, all bad, roiled in his head. Was Francesca writing to tell Tommy she'd found another? Was Francesca writing to say to him she was getting married? Was it a Dear John letter?

For a long moment, Tommy debated whether to open the envelope. He couldn't handle more disappointment, not from Francesca. Tommy struggled until he couldn't hold back any longer. Letting out a long breath, Tommy tore the envelope open.

> *Dear Tommy,*
>
> *I write this letter to you from my terrace where I spend most nights looking up to the sky while I read the only letter I have from you.*
>
> *Since the beginning of the war, I've listened to news of the escalating conflict in Europe never in my wildest dreams did I imagine you were in the midst of it. When Uncle Will told me tonight you'd enlisted, I felt sick to my stomach, for so many reasons, but mainly because of the anger I've carried all these months in me for you for thinking you'd deserted me.*
>
> *Until tonight, I thought you'd abandoned me. I thought our time together meant nothing to you. Until tonight, I thought all the beautiful things you said to me were fluff, and I'd hate you.*
>
> *I'd hate you so much, Tommy.*
>
> *But I also love you so much and to tame my hateful feelings I'd read your beautiful letter. It's wrinkled and brittle from handling now. Anyway, as much as*

*reading your letter helps dull the pain, it
makes my head reel in confusion. I didn't
know what to think, and all I do is hurt
again.*

Tommy's hand bunched into a tight fist when
Francesca's words left him sick. That she'd felt this way,
all this time, made anger war with fury. Goddamn Peter
Thompson, Tommy thought, pushing to his feet and
ramming his fist into the tree's trunk. He leveled a second
punch, just because. Wrapping the bandanna around his
bleeding knuckles, Tommy picked up the letter and
continued reading.

*I'm sorry, Tommy. I'm so sorry for
thinking of you the way I have these past
few years. I should have trusted you more,
but I was hurting so much.*

*I try not to think about you being
over there, but I can't escape the images
rushing at me. Why, Tommy, why would
you put yourself in the path of such
danger? I don't want you to end up hurt
or worse. I want you to come back to me.
Please come back to me, Tommy.*

Francesca aroused feelings in Tommy that had been
long since buried. Suddenly a wonderful peace washed over
him, and life had meaning. "I want to go back to you too,
Francesca."

*I want you to know Tommy there's
never been anyone but you. Even after all
the hurt and the anger I've felt, you're the
only man that fills my thoughts. I often
think of the times we watched the stars or
walked the boardwalk. I think back to the
first night we made love and how*

beautiful and wonderful it was. I want to do all those things with you again, Tommy. I want to feel your body pressed to mine. I want to feel your lips on mine. I want to feel your breath on my face.

You claimed my heart, Tommy Scott, and I want you to reclaim it. You told me I was the best of you, but you, Tommy, are the best of me.

Please come back to me, safe and sound.

With all my love—

Indifference melted into inspiration. Tommy hadn't felt this full of life, not in years. The passion he'd lost long ago fueling him again, he looked up to the sky. "I promise I'll come back to you, Francesca."

"Sarg. Hey, Tommy." Mike's cries shocked Tommy out of his reverie. "We're pushing out tonight."

"What are you talking about? We're not leaving for a couple of days." Tommy called back.

"Guess they changed their mind. We need to pack up. We leave for Sicily tonight."

Thirteen

WAR WAS HELL.

That was how it now felt for Tommy.

Bullets whizzed by from every direction; rocket-propelled grenades came out of nowhere to destroy, mutilate, and kill. Death and destruction were all around. This, Tommy thought, was hell on earth.

Tommy would never be bored with simple and silence. He'd wallow in it the first chance he got.

"Spread men. Run for Cover," Tommy shouted over the sound of gunfire and exploding rockets. Black smoke billowed into the sky, over the shattered mortar. The screams of dread choking men running for their lives, pleas and prayers never prayed from the nearly dead men tangled with the sound of destruction. "Mike, get to cover," Tommy screamed, but Mike was frozen on the spot. Amid the battle and barrage of bullets coming at them from everywhere, the abject terror rooted in his eyes, Mike could only stare at the mangled body he'd stumbled over.

When the Panzer rounded the building and aimed the gun in their direction, pure adrenaline had Tommy picking Mike up like a rag doll. "We gotta get out of here. Now." Tommy threw Mike over his shoulder and running over rubble, past burning cars, avoiding craters, got him to safety. At a safe distance, Tommy set Mike down on his feet and slapped the shock out of his system. "You okay, kid?"

"Yeah. Yeah, I'm fine," Mike said as if waking from a trance. "I'm sorry, sarge."

"Stay close to me. Keep your rifle aimed at all times, and you have to remain vigilant, Mike. Always. Those German bastards are coming at us from everywhere. Understood?" When Mike nodded, Tommy slapped him on the back. "You'll be fine, kid. Let's go."

With the onset of dusk, under white flashes of detonating artillery, the sky began to change colors. Until darkness fell, Tommy and Mike stayed in the shadows as much as possible. Darting from doorway to doorway, they scanned for the enemy, pointed rifles, and snipers on rooftops. Danger was everywhere lurking in the darkness.

"There's a sniper up in the church bell tower." Tommy tilted his chin up to indicate the location when bullets whizzed by. "I need to make it across the street and up there to take care of him. You're going to have to cover me. Can you do that for me, kid? Do exactly as I taught you in training, and you'll be fine." Tommy wrapped his hand behind Mike's neck. "You can do this."

Mike's eyes darted to the bell tower and back to Tommy. "I can do this, Tommy. You can count on me," he said, taking a deep breath and aiming his rifle toward the tower.

The moment Tommy sprinted across the cobbled street like a seasoned runner, Mike fired a series of shots toward the tower for distraction. It took Tommy seconds to make it across the street, up the winding stairs to the bell tower. By the time he got there, blood was pumping from the bullet hole and pooling around the German's head.

"Jesus, the kid, has excellent aim," Tommy said, giving Mike the clear signal.

If Tommy weren't so busy trying to keep Mike and himself alive, the mangled body parts of shot soldiers, the dead bodies all around him, the blood flowing and pooling like rain on the streets would have slid into his psyche then. Killing to survive was the only thought in Tommy's mind.

The days that followed, they marched over hilly terrain for miles, through dusty roads, under an insufferable one hundred degrees. It was physically and mentally exhausting, yet the First Canadian Division, along with Allied forces seized town after town, driving the enemy out.

The unexpected Sicilian attack resulted in an unqualified success with few Allied casualties, but the war didn't end there. The fighting went on for days. Under the cloak of darkness, the skies lighting up under enemy and friendly fire, the First Canadian Division, along with Allied forces advanced in the shadows, over rocky ground, through muddy trenches.

Huddled in a grove of olive trees under a clear sky set alight by bomber planes dropping their loads in the distance, Tommy looked over to a sleeping Mike. Since his freeze-up, Mike hadn't left Tommy's side. "I'll take care of you, kid." Tommy dug into his shirt pocket for the half-smoked cigarette, lit it, and settled in to read Francesca's letter. He read it when he could, although it had been some time since he'd had the chance to do so.

Everything changed since Francesca's letter. She'd given Tommy a reason to live. His only goal now was survival and rushing home to make a life with her. It was strange the unexpected twists a man's life took by the expression of love, Tommy thought.

Damn Peter Thompson, Tommy decided. Whether Peter approved or not, after the war, Tommy planned to marry Francesca. He planned to buy her a little house. It would be a considerable step down from the sprawling estate she was accustomed to, but he was confident she'd be okay with that. Tommy hoped she wanted children because he wanted loads of them with her. As soon as he got the chance, he'd write to tell her.

With the smell of gunpowder wafting in the wind and the skies lighting bright, swamped with the taste, the heat of their last kiss, Tommy sunk into sleep with Francesca on his mind.

IN THE MORNING, OVER TERRAIN THAT dipped and lifted, the First Canadian Division headed east toward Mount Aetna. It was a typical sunny Sicilian day. The air was dry, and the temperature was nearing an unbearable one hundred. Mount Aetna's peak covered in a white cape of snow, rose majestically into the clouds. Lugging his gear and weapon, a thick film of sweat on Tommy's face, he thought when they came out of this, he'd go back to visit Sicily. Once the devastation of war faded away, Tommy imagined an island with quaint towns, cobbled streets, and white sand beaches. A beautiful, peaceful place.

The moment the men, Mike, and Tommy reached the base of Mount Aetna, they proceeded up the rocky hill into the unknown. Without warning, the German's came at them from every angle. Ambushed by the barrage of artillery fire, hundreds of bullets flew past Tommy, Mike, and the men, pinning them in a circle of death.

"Spread out. Take cover." Tommy shouted over the chaos.

"Take cover in there, Mike," Tommy called out, gesturing toward the doorway of a vacant home. Mike did as Tommy said—he always did.

As the gunfire persisted, Tommy watched the men scatter, taking cover in and behind buildings, cars, trucks, anything with a solid wall to protect themselves from enemy tanks rolling into the town. Firing tanks, enemy and Allied, set off a multitude of explosions. Fires raged around them, the smoke billowing dark and thick was blinding. Tommy watched in horror as men from both sides ran out of exploding buildings in flames, swatting themselves to douse burning uniforms.

Assessing their surroundings, Tommy determined they had to get out of the building where they took cover. The half-blown doorway they stood under wasn't sufficient cover from the flying bullets, Tommy decided.

"We gotta make it across to the monastery, Mike. It's one of the few solid buildings still standing. We'll take cover there. You with me?"

"I am, sarge. I got your back," Mike said, hoping Tommy didn't hear the fear in his voice.

"You go first. I'll cover you," Tommy said to Mike scanning their surroundings.

Tommy randomly fired his rifle as Mike ran, taking cover when he could, sprinting past the blizzard of bullets until he reached the monastery. Tommy followed next. Ducking and dodging the onslaught of bullets, grenades, and rockets, he screamed instructions at Mike to shoot to cover him. But nothing. Mike froze amid the attack—again.

Tommy watched Barlow and Connor go down when a bullet got them in the leg and shoulder.

When the bullets started coming faster, Tommy called out, "Mike, Mike take cover," as he dived behind the wall of rubble.

To Tommy's left, debris shot up hundreds of feet in the air when the rocket-propelled grenade struck the building. Part of it tumbled like a deck of cards. Tommy's eyes peeled on Mike, he watched his body propelled into the air before it slammed against the monastery wall. Mike's body slumped like a deflated balloon to the ground.

"Mike, Mike." Tommy sprinted to his feet. He had to get to Mike. He'd promised he'd take care of the kid he considered his little brother. "Hold on, Mike."

In the confusion, the explosions, the bullets, the billowing smoke, Tommy didn't see the massive chunk of concrete descending from the sky onto his head.

THERE WAS ONE OF THOSE HESITANT beats during the telephone conversation that told Mrs. Scott, Francesca, was processing the shocking news, and she let the silence hang for a moment. "I'm sorry, Frankie."

Francesca slid down the wall onto the floor. "When, where did it happen?" The tears that swam into Francesca's eyes blurred her vision.

"A few days ago. I don't know where. We received the telegram last night. I'm sorry I didn't call you until this morning, love, but his father and me well, we were in shock. We still are."

Francesca breathed for calm. "Yes. Yes, of course. I'm sorry, Mrs. S. How's Mr. S?"

"He's devastated. He's still in shock. Tommy was his only child. He was everything to him," Mrs. Scott said, as steady as her shaken nerves allowed.

"Please let him know how sorry I am and how much I love Tommy. He'd want to know that Tommy is very much loved." Pain, bright and sharp, stabbed at Francesca's heart as the wave of memory unspooled in her mind.

Tommy's smiling face swam into her mind. In her daze, Francesca waved her fingers in the air as if she was sweeping them through his wild, swirl of dark hair. She saw the blue eyes staring down at her as he made love to her. She imagined the familiar curve of his mouth against hers, the silky slide of his lips and tongue. Francesca imagined Tommy tucking a strand of hair behind her ear as he'd done so often.

Francesca heard his voice telling her he loved her. The realization she'd never hear those words from Tommy again was crushing.

"Frankie, are you there, love?" Mrs. Scott's voice came over the telephone.

"I'm here," Francesca said, after a long contemplative silence. "Mrs. S, we need to keep our faith. Missing in action doesn't mean Tommy's dead. It means he's missing that he's still out there. He's out there, Mrs. S." She firmed her lips in determination, mopped her cheeks dry. "I know it. I can feel it."

"Oh, love." Mrs. Scott refused to tell Francesca the blast from the explosions had maimed many of the bodies beyond recognition.

"They didn't find a body because Tommy's not gone. He's still alive somewhere out there," Frankie said with conviction.

"Darling…"

"He's alive, Mrs. S. I can feel it in my heart, in my bones. Tommy's out there. He may be physically injured, knocked out, but he's not dead. I refuse to believe it."

Mrs. Scott's heart squeezed. "Honey…"

Francesca slid her hand into her jeans pocket to connect with Tommy's letter. "He's alive, Mrs. S."

Mrs. Scott knew better than to argue with Francesca when her voice firmed as it had, and her mind set as it did. Mrs. Scott only hoped Francesca's blinder of denial was temporary, and in time she'd accept the truth. Denying Tommy's death was bound to end up hurting twice as much when reality set in.

When Francesca hung up with Mrs. Scott, she walked out to the terrace. The rain scented California air on her tear-stained cheeks felt cool. Sitting down on the stone steps, she let the tears flow. Were she and Tommy never meant to be together? It felt as if the world was conspiring against them.

"You can't be dead, Tommy. You can't be. I asked you to come back to me. Please, Tommy, please come back to me." Francesca tilted eyes to a cloud-drenched sky that had swallowed every star in sight.

Fourteen

FRANCESCA SET HER suitcase down and cast her gaze around the opulent foyer. Streams of gold from the skylight illuminated the expansive entrance. Wood floors were polished to a sheen. Yellow daisies from the garden speared out of the Waterford vase on the Cocobolo rosewood table at the center of the foyer. It had been six years since Francesca was home, and although everything looked the same, it felt different.

Francesca set Bear down to let him roam his new home. After a short probing walk, Bear leaned into her and sighed. She knew precisely how Bear felt. It all felt new and strange to me her. On hearing the voices flowing from the kitchen, Francesca gestured Bear to follow her down the hallway lined with portraits of her mother, father, and the Thompsons long gone where she found two women fussing over a coconut cake.

The older woman was trim with sharp, dark eyes set in a ruddy face. She wore thick-soled loafers, a starched, baby-blue inform with a white collar, and a lace apron hung around her waist. Her hair, as black as night—due to the regular application of Henna—was tied up into a tight bun that gave her an instant facelift.

Next to her, in a black maid's uniform, stood a younger woman. She was pretty with delicate features. Thin eyebrows, a small puckered mouth, a tiny upturned nose, and the greenest eyes Francesca had ever seen were set in an oval face. Her hair, also tied into a bun, was shades lighter than the older woman's.

"Miss Thompson, we weren't expecting you for another hour." The younger curtsied while the older woman eyed an exploring, sniffing Bear, with disdain. "I'm Missy, the new maid, and this is my mother, Jean Richards, your cook."

"Nice to meet you both, and I'm sorry I didn't let you know about my early arrival. The flight made good time. Something to do with favorable winds. I'm Frankie, not Miss Thompson, and please don't curtsy."

"But Mrs. Thompson…"

Francesca held a hand up to silence Missy. "I don't care what my dad's wife said to you. I'm not the queen of England, and she certainly isn't either."

"All right, Frankie." Missy liked what Francesca was made of. "And who is this?"

Francesca bent down to pick up Bear. "This is Bear. Say hello to the ladies, baby." At the command, Bear offered a smile and his right paw. "Go ahead, shake it."

"Isn't that darling," Missy said, taking Bear's paw.

"Not in my kitchen, it isn't. There's food all around and that…"

"Beautiful little dog is part of the family, Mum." Missy scratched Bear behind the ear. "Mum's very particular about her kitchen."

"I am. I'm sorry about my abruptness, Miss Thompson. You will be Miss Thompson to me," she pressed the point when Francesca opened her mouth, "and I will be Mrs. Richards to you."

"She won't let up, so best to agree," Missy murmured, then turned to her mother. "Mum cut Frankie a piece of cake. I'll get her a cup of coffee. That'll hit the spot after her long trip. How about you Bear, are you hungry? I picked up some of that Puppy Chow your mommy told me you liked." Bear's ears perked up. "I guess that means yes."

"That is not eating in my kitchen," Mrs. Richards piped up when Missy filled Bear's bowls with food and water.

"Would you like to eat on the terrace, Frankie? It's a beautiful summer day. I'll set Bear's bowls out there too. Have a seat, and I'll be out there in a minute."

Missy set cake and the steaming cup of coffee before Francesca. "I know this is your home, Frankie, but for your sanity, well, mainly mine, would you mind doing what Mum says? See, you seem like the diplomatic, polite sort, but I'm not. I tend to get violent when frustrated, and I know you don't want me to end up as your first client."

Francesca snorted a laugh. "Don't do anything just yet. I still need to pass the bar exam later this month," she called after Missy as she walked into the kitchen and came back out with Bear's food.

"You'll ace your exam. Any girl who walks out with a Ph.D. from Stanford will have no problem passing the bar." Missy set bowls of food and water down. "This is for you, Bear."

"Thanks for your confidence." Francesca watched Missy's lips curve when Bear sidled up to chow down, his tail happily wagging. Anyone who treated Bear as well as Missy did was all right by her. She and Missy were going to be good friends.

"It's a fact. Poor baby, he was hungry."

"He's always hungry. For a small dog, he has a bear size appetite."

"Ah, hence the name." Missy eyes shot upwards when a pair of blue jays winged by in the sun-drenched, blue sky.

"By the way, I'd hide your shoes if I were you. And it's not a Ph.D. I have."

"My shoes aren't worth much. You're welcomed to them." Missy ruffled Bear's fur. "It'll give me a good excuse to replace them without having mom harping about me spending money needlessly. And whether a Ph.D. or some other degree it's more than I could ever do. It takes brains to do what you've done, Frankie. Anyway, I better get back to it," she said when she saw her mother eyeing her. "Can I get you or Bear anything else?"

"No, thank you. When is Mrs. Thompson going to be home?" Francesca asked with reluctance.

"She's out," spending your father's hard-earned money. "Won't be back for a while. She said she'd be staying at the downtown condo to give you some time to settle in." With that, Missy headed back into the house.

"Hmm, how benevolent."

Nothing was the same. Her father had remarried, and Tommy was gone. Mrs. Richards had replaced Mrs. Scott since her return to Ireland with Mr. Scott to start anew after Tommy's loss caused him to spiral into a deep depression.

"I need to take him far away from here. There are too many memories causing him pain. Everywhere he turns, he sees Tommy. I'm afraid if I don't take him away, he's going to die of a broken heart." Mrs. Scott had said to Francesca, and six months later, they'd sold their home, the garden center, and set off to start a new life abroad.

The Scott's leaving was a shock, but not as much as Peter's marriage to Tiffani. Tiffani—with an I as she insisted on pointing out—was thirty years younger than Peter and only six years older than Francesca. That Tiffani had the I.Q. of a sloth didn't play into the equation when Peter proposed. That Tiffani had a spill of platinum blonde hair, a double D cup size, a tiny waist, and up until they married had been a cheerleader for the national football team did.

Francesca disliked Tiffani the moment they'd met. Not so much because her father had never told her about Tiffani or his intention to marry her. Not so much because Peter introduced Tiffani as her stepmom over their twenty-four-hour layover in Stanford on their way to their month-long honeymoon in Hawaii, but because Francesca saw through Tiffani's perky façade.

Women like Tiffani controlled the tide of a man's life, and Francesca saw just that in the way Peter was twisting himself into a pretzel for her. Barbie's interest was in Peter's bank account, not him, and her tight, curvy body blinded him to Tiffani's real motive, but not Francesca.

Nothing was the same.

Mrs. Scott was gone, her father had remarried, and Tommy was lost to her. Francesca felt a horrible, heavy sadness press down on her chest.

"You're out there, Tommy. I know you are, and I'm going to find you." Francesca vowed although it was going on two years since the arrival of the telegram from the war office.

FRANCESCA DARTED EYES UP FROM THE newspaper to Peter. Framed in the doorway of her office, he seemed to fill it with his imposing presence. In a gray pin-striped suit, wisps of gray woven through his hair at the temple, he looked handsome and distinguished.

"The war is over."

"Front page news." Francesca set the newspaper down.

The sadness resonating in her eyes told Peter she was thinking of Tommy. Three years gone, and Tommy was still stopping Francesca from moving on with her life. Peter hadn't seen Francesca with a man or date anyone. She attended the company functions, stiffly, but dutifully. Francesca refused to participate in the country club functions or spend time with her friends. Her days were filled with work, home, and Bear.

Peter wished Katherine was around. She'd know how to help Francesca move on with her life. He missed his wife. Peter missed talking to her. He missed her laugh and lying next to her in bed. Tiffani was a sexual woman and fulfilled his needs in the bedroom beyond his wildest expectations, but she had the intellect of dead bark. Katherine was his intellectual equal, and sometimes a thoughtful exchange with a woman was more gratifying than a quick a roll in bed.

"I want to talk to you, Frankie." Peter closed the door behind him. End of war news making the rounds in the office had the staff abuzz with excitable chatter and laughter. "Do you keep any alcohol in this office?"

Francesca shook her head. "Just water. Can I get you a glass?"

"No." Peter sunk his six-foot frame into the wide-backed guest chair across Francesca. "I want you to take first chair on the John Adam case, Frankie."

"The physician suspected of physically abusing his wife and ultimately cracking her skull open."

"That's the one. He called me a few days ago, asking if I would take his case. Yesterday, I spent most of the morning at the Brockville prison speaking with him. Here are the notes."

Francesca locked a stunned gaze on her father's face. "It's a murder case, Daddy. I just started practicing. I can't take on such a big case yet. Besides, I don't know that I want to defend a wife-beater."

"You're a lawyer, Frankie. You won't always have the luxury of choosing who you represent. Moreover, I believe him to be innocent. And not only do I think you can defend him, but I believe you can win the case. It's the perfect case for you to make your name."

"Are you saying that as my father or my boss?"

"Both. As your father, I'm looking after your best interest. As your boss, I want you to succeed." Peter stretched out his long legs, crossed his feet at the ankles. "This is a great opportunity for you. It's the perfect case to make your name. He's a broken man who needs your help, Frankie."

Mulling the idea in her head, Francesca tapped the pen in her hand in a see-saw motion on her desk. "But I'd be going up against James Templeton. He's one of the best criminal prosecutors in the business."

"That's where you're wrong. I'm the best lawyer. Pfft, he only has ten years of litigation under his belt."

"That's ten more than I have." Francesca rose, turning her back to Peter as he walked to the window.

It was a bright September day, filled with sunshine, renewed hope, and celebration. Horns beeped, strangers shook hands and hugged at the news the men were coming home. Possibly physically injured, maybe mentally damaged, but they were coming back nonetheless. Tommy wasn't.

"You have to jump into the shark-infested water some time, Frankie," Peter said.

"James hasn't lost one case, Daddy."

"Until now. You're a Thompson, Frankie; you can do this. Meet with John and feel him out. You'll have me to consult when needed and all the office resources at your disposal. How about it, Frankie?" Peter eyed his daughter, gauging, for her response.

She took a deep, clearing breath. "All right, if you think I can do this." Francesca saw her father brighten as she hoped he would. She was a grown woman, and validation from her father was still what she needed most.

"Of course you can do this. You're a Thompson." The prideful expression that welled up in Peter was one Francesca thought never sat comfortably on his face.

"I am," Francesca said, doing her best to shield her apprehension.

Francesca was right to doubt herself. Peter knew his daughter wouldn't win the case. She was too inexperienced, but she'd put up a good fight, which is what Peter wanted. There was nothing like a woman challenging a man's intellect to stir his juices and work up his interest, and with Francesca going up against James Templeton, she'd do just that.

Trap and prey set, he'd let Francesca play out her part. When the time was right, he'd move in to rescue the case.

Fifteen

DAYS PASSED QUICKLY, and before Francesca knew, the case of the Crown versus John Adam was underway.

The courtroom was packed with angry women hoping to see the man depicted as a wife abuser by James Templeton and the media get his just desserts. From everything they'd read and seen on television, Dr. John Adam, a privileged man with an imposing stature who beat his petite, frail wife, regularly, was guilty until proven innocent. The woman defending him was a disgrace.

On her way up the steps into the courthouse, Francesca was booed, shamed, and called names that did little for her already fragile confidence.

The Honorable Mark Spencer, a septuagenarian with a shock of gray hair, beady, blue eyes, and the road map of his life carved deeply into his face, banged the gavel with a forceful hand to silence the room to no avail. He detested the type of cases that attracted so many women to his courtroom. They were boisterous, loud, opinionated, and they were going to be the death of him. He came to work in search of the quiet his wife—a boisterous woman herself—didn't afford him at home.

As the Honorable Mark Spencer was about to bang his gavel for the tenth time, a hushed silence fell in the courtroom when James Templeton rose to his six-foot height. In a gray, three-piece Armani suit, his dark hair stylishly combed back, and his fashionable stubble perfectly trimmed, he looked as if he fell out of the glossy pages of a lawyerly magazine. His rich, brandy-brown eyes gleamed with a confidence that made every woman sigh.

"Your Lordship, ladies, and gentlemen of the jury, my name is James Templeton." Applause erupted in the courtroom.

His Lordship let out a long breath of frustration. This was how it was going to be, he thought banging his gavel. "Silence or everyone one of you will be asked to leave."

Silence descending in the courtroom, James sent the gallery a quick smile. "I'm the crown prosecutor, and I will prove Dr. Adam is guilty of murdering his wife Elizabeth Adam, a soft-spoken, frail woman who deserved better than to be whacked on the head to her death."

Francesca bolted to her feet. Her hair was tied back in a low flat twisted bun. Her cheeks were lightly dusted rosy, and her lips were glossed in soft pink. The professional, conservative, blue suit she wore didn't convey the confidence she intended. "Your Lordship, I resent the use of the word whacked to describe Elizabeth Adam's, ummm … injury."

"Miss Thompson, you can't interrupt Mr. Templeton during his opening statement." The Honorable Mark Spencer pointed out with sarcasm in his voice that rang clear.

A slow flush worked its way up Francesca's throat to her cheeks. "I'm sorry." She sank to her seat.

"Thank you, Your Lordship. As I was saying before I was interrupted. I will prove Dr. John Adam is guilty beyond a reasonable doubt of this heinous crime, which he claims to be an accident." James flashed the jury and spectators an all-perfect-teeth smile that arrowed into every woman's fantasy and heightened Francesca's nerves.

When James sat down, Francesca hesitantly rose. The hissing and boos from the gallery filled the silence James left.

"I will not have this type of disorder in my court. If this keeps up, I will have the gallery cleared." His Lordship grinned when the courtroom went quiet. "Please proceed, Miss Thompson."

Francesca took a moment to compose frazzled nerves. "Thank you. My ... ah, name is ... Francesca Thompson." She remembered then to acknowledge the most influential people in the room and proceeded to correct her oversight. "Ummm ... Your Lordship, ladies, and gentlemen of the jury, I'm the defense counsel for Dr. John Adam, a respected physician who has served his community for the past thirty years," she said, taking her seat. When Francesca saw the lines around James' eyes deepening in a smile that said: I got this in the bag, sweetie, she stood. "I'm sorry. I have more to say."

"We're listening with bated breath," His Lordship's comment netted snickers from the gallery.

"We will show to Your Lordship and the ladies and gentlemen of the jury that Dr. John Adam is an innocent man and that what Mr. James Templeton is claiming to be murder was nothing but self-defense." Francesca flicked a smug grin at James and thought she got a wink in return.

The weeks that followed didn't get easier for Francesca. James' confidence and skillful lawyering skills deflated her, and she stumbled over her words. One of her key witnesses failed to appear, and her investigator couldn't locate him. The day before John Adam was expected to take the stand, he called Peter Thompson to demand he step in for his daughter.

"I will be Francesca's second chair tomorrow. At any time during her questioning, you want me to stand in for her, just give me the signal. But I can't stress enough, John, how much better the optics are with a woman defending you. And John, her suggestion that you focus on your close bond with your wife during your cross-examination is an excellent one. There are six women in that jury," Peter said, hoping to sway Dr. Adam's mind.

Peter saw the look in James' eyes as he followed Francesca across the courtroom. It was the look of a man fascinated by the woman challenging his ego. Peter considered Francesca's stumbling over herself every time she cross-examined a blessing. In his opinion, men loved women who challenged them but didn't quite reach that level of bruising their ego.

Peter's plan was working better than anticipated.

Soon enough, he'd have a son-in-law and successor for his multi-million dollar empire. Peter would have liked Francesca to take over the firm, but that wasn't in the cards. It was difficult enough for a woman to be taken seriously in the legal world, let alone at the helm of a multi-million dollar company. James Templeton III had the name, the connections, and the old family money that garnered respect.

"I call Dr. John Adam to the stand," Francesca said.

Boos and hisses from the women in the gallery followed Dr. Adam to the witness stand, but his movements remained sharp, resolute. They weren't those of a guilty man. Unbuttoning the gray jacket Francesca picked out to add an air of dignified respectability, Dr. Adam sat and crossed one leg over the other. Blue eyes set in a clean-shaven, handsome face, haloed by a sweep of silver hair, turned to gaze at the jury long enough to establish contact before turning to Francesca.

"Dr. Adam, are you testifying today against my advice you do not take the stand?" Francesca asked.

"Yes."

"Why are you testifying?"

"I want the truth to be told." Dr. Adam's eyes connected with the six women in the jury box.

"Then let's do that, Dr. Adam. Did you kill your wife?"

There was no hesitation from Dr. Adam. "Yes, I did."

The comments from the gallery followed.

"I knew it."

"Murderer."

"Lock him up. Now."

"You cowardly bastard."

Oaths Francesca hadn't heard a woman utter before were crisply shouted. His Lordship banged the gavel, but it was drowned by the raucous outraged voices from the gallery.

"I'm warning all of you. One more outburst and the bailiff will clear the gallery. Am I clear?" His Lordship's warning silenced the room. "Proceed, Miss Thompson."

"Thank you, Your Lordship." Francesca turned to Dr. Adam. "Did you mean to kill your wife?"

"I did not. I love ... loved my wife. Lizzy and I were married for thirty-five years. Lizzy was the mother of my five children. We have ... had a good life together." Genuine sadness ran across his face.

"In the thirty-five years, you were married, were you ever unfaithful to your wife?"

"Never. I did not need to turn to anyone other than Lizzy. She fulfilled my every need, intellectually, emotionally, physically. She was a perfect wife and a great mother. Ask any of my five children."

Francesca scanned the faces of the jury gauging for their reaction. It looked encouraging, and her confidence surged. "Then, how did you end up in a situation where she ended up dead?"

"Lizzy," he hesitated for a moment to gather himself, "suffered from Alzheimer's, and she wasn't dealing well with it."

Francesca let a stretch of silence hang for the jury to digest the crucial piece of information coming to light. "Did anyone other than you know your wife was diagnosed with Alzheimer's, Dr. Adam?"

"No." Dr. Adam's gaze reflected on some memory. "Not even our children knew. Lizzy didn't want anyone to know. She was having problems dealing with it."

"Can you elaborate on what you mean by 'she was having problems dealing with it,' Dr. Adam?"

"She wouldn't accept the diagnosis, the fact she was afflicted with the disease, and therefore she refused to take her medication or keep her doctor's appointments."

"You're a doctor, a medical professional, couldn't you help her deal with or manage her decease?" Francesca's voice flowed with more confidence with each question.

"I could only do so much. Alzheimer's is a complicated disease, and my expertise was limited. I'm not a neurologist, which is … was, I'm sorry I can't get used to the past tense." Dr. Adam's voice broke, and the gallery heaved a sigh that sounded like sympathy.

"Would you like a break, Dr. Adam?" His Lordship's face radiated empathy.

Dr. Adam breathed in air. "I'm fine. As I was saying, my wife needed the medical care of a neurologist of specialists. I could only do so much." Dr. Adam turned to the jury. "I'm not God. There was only so much I could do. Only so much I could do," he repeated, bringing trembling hands to cover his face.

"What happened that day, Dr. Adam? The day of your wife's death."

"When I walked in through the front door of our home, she didn't recognize me. I believe her refusal to take her medication, to seek the medical treatment she needed made her unravel on the spot. She became paranoid, and she came at me with a knife. I tried to hold her off, but she was persistent and surprisingly strong. We wrestled for some time, and when she came at me again with a chef's knife, I pushed her off me. I, oh, Jesus. God, forgive me. I was too forceful. I know that now, but it all happened so fast." He stopped to take a deep breath, and you could see him replaying the horrible moment in his mind.

"She fell back and hit her head against the kitchen table. She fell to the ground, and her head bounced off the tiles. I can still see it in my mind. It plays out over and over in excruciatingly slow motion. I killed her. I killed my wife. I'm so sorry, Lizzy."

"Do you need some time, Dr. Adam," Francesca said softly.

"I'm sorry, no."

When Dr. Adam seemed calmer, Francesca said, "Was that why you initially confessed to killing her?"

"Yes. Can't you see? I killed my wife. Me. Me." Dr. Adam struck his chest with a flat hand over and over. "I pushed her and caused her to hit her head. My first instinct was to stop the bleeding, and I did. I tried my best to stop it. There was blood everywhere, pools of it spreading on the tiled floor. When I'd done what I could, I called for the ambulance." The tears glimmered in his eyes, and he covered his face with the hands that had healed so many.

"I know how difficult this is for you, but I have one last question. Dr. Adam. Did you mean to kill your wife?"

"No," he said without hesitation. "I desperately miss her. I miss talking to her. I miss not having her next to me in bed at night. I hate coming home to an empty house. There are nights when I sit in our closet for hours, breathing in her scent. Just breathing her scent." Someone sighed, and the sound spiked in the hushed room. "When you share your love, your life with someone for more than half of your life, losing them is the hardest thing." Dr. Adam choked on his words as the tears now streamed down his face. Many of the women in the jury and gallery broke down with him.

Francesca felt the sting of tears choke her own throat. Dr. Adam's loving words resurrected thoughts of Tommy, and she bit back her tears. Her life with Tommy would have been as remarkable as Dr. Adam and Lizzy's. Francesca made a mental note to place her monthly call to the Veterans Affairs office.

"Thank you, Dr. Adam. The defense rests." It couldn't have gone better, Francesca thought. "Your witness."

When James Templeton got to his feet, all eyes in the room followed him to the witness stand. "Do you need a moment, Dr. Adam?" he said with a feigned sympathy that didn't play out as well as he'd hoped.

"No, I'm fine." Dr. Adam took the tissue the judge handed him.

James asked, "How tall are you, Dr. Adam?"

"Five-eleven."

"Hmm. How tall was your wife?"

"Five feet."

"Five feet," James repeated, rubbing a hand over his chin for effect. "So are you telling us that a petite, five-foot woman overtook a fit, five-eleven man?"

"Mr. Templeton, have you ever had to confront a person with an ill mind?"

"I'm the one asking the questions, Dr. Adam."

His heart thumping like a herd of marching elephants, Dr. Adam persevered. "They could be rather tenacious, and you'd be surprised at the strength they possess. That, combined with their confused mind, makes dealing with a person with an ill mind a challenging one. It sounds like something beyond rational belief, but a human being with an irrational mind manifests into superhuman strength."

James bypassed the comment. "Your wife was a hefty five feet." His voice was laced with a sarcasm that garnered him unexpected boos and hisses from the gallery.

Francesca shot to her feet. Her eyes sharp and hard on James, she said, "Objection. Your Lordship, I don't hear a question."

Before his Lordship could tell the jury to disregard the comment, Dr. Adam jumped in with his response. "Mr. Templeton, I love my wife. I would have never killed her, let alone beat her as you claim I did. I'm a doctor sworn to the Hippocratic Oath. If you don't know what that is, I'll enlighten you."

"You tell him, Dr. Adam," shouted one woman.

"Stop, bullying him, you cold-hearted suit," barked another, and the women in the gallery cheered in support.

"Order, order," his Lordship shouted until silence fell in the courtroom. "Proceed, Mr. Templeton."

For the next thirty minutes, James posed questions. With each question, he sensed the room turning on him, and he elected to cut his cross-examination short. "No further questions," James said to Francesca's delight.

He gave up, Francesca thought with a smile creasing one corner of her mouth.

PETER WALKED INTO FRANCESCA'S OFFICE. "HOW are you holding up, Frankie?" Seeing the nervous look on her face, Peter put a hand on her shoulder, squeezed conveying a sense of solidarity. "It's going to be fine. It's now in the jury's hands."

"It's my representation that will steer them to their decision." Francesca reached for the glass of water to lubricate a persistently dry throat. "Jesus, what if they find him guilty. John could end up in jail for decades. Not to mention the fact I'll have to see that smug look on James Templeton's face."

Peter laughed at that. "You're on your way to becoming a great lawyer, Frankie. Winning is fifty percent the satisfaction you get from exonerating your client. The remaining fifty comes from slapping that smug look off the opposing counsel's face."

"You're not wrong about that. How I'd love to slap that smugness of James' face." Francesca reached for her shrilling telephone. After a short one-sided conversation, she hung up. "They have a verdict."

Peter didn't conceal his shock. "They've been deliberating for less than a day."

Francesca's lips curved, slow, easy. "I guess they don't need any more time to determine John's innocence." She reached for her briefcase. "Well, are you coming?"

"I wouldn't miss your first judgment for the world."

Sixteen

ALL EYES IN the courtroom were on his Lordship as he read the verdict then bounced over to the foreman when he said, "Has the jury reached a verdict?"

The foreman stood. "We have your honor." The unreadable expression on his face intensified the tension in the room.

"What say you, Mr. Foreman?"

"On the charge of murder in the first degree we find Dr. Adam," there was a moment's hesitation that felt as if it stretched into an eternity.

Dr. Adam closed his eyes and bowed his head as if slipping into deep prayer. Francesca closed a hand firmly over Dr. Adam's folded hands to soothe as much as to calm herself. The silence in the courtroom was smothering, and his Lordship relished in it because once the verdict was read, he expected all hell was going to break loose.

"Not guilty," announced the foreman.

Unsure he'd heard right, Dr. Adam rolled eyes nearly translucent with shock toward Francesca. "You heard right, John."

It took him a moment to process. When it finally sank in, Dr. Adam broke into silent tears—of sadness. The taste of victory was a bittersweet pill. Francesca thought she heard him say, "I'm sorry, Lizzy. I'm so sorry. How am I going to live without you?"

Francesca's hands still wrapped around his, squeezed tight. "You'll never forget her. She'll always be in your heart and thoughts."

Sitting next to Dr. Adam's, Peter's eyes glazed with shock. "Jesus! She got a not guilty verdict against James Templeton III," he muttered under his breath.

There were cheers, applause, cameras clicked, and reporters posed questions. Many shouted words of support, some hugged. The judge gave up pounding his gavel and throwing his hands up in the air in surrender, sunk deeper into the marshmallow-soft chair to watch the spectacle unfolding in his courtroom.

Francesca looked over at James Templeton. Her lips curved with amusement as he gathered his paperwork and thrust it into his briefcase. Fighting his rising anger, he grunted, "Congratulations," as he walked past her.

Francesca had won her first case, and it was against the renowned James Templeton III.

Today was one she'd remember forever.

SITTING ACROSS FRANCESCA, PETER WAITED HIS turn to speak with her. The days following the Adam verdict, Francesca's telephone hadn't stopped ringing. Reporters, the guilty, the accused, girlfriends, wives, family members were queuing to talk to her to beg for her to take on their case. There was nothing like a desperate caller begging you to represent them to get your confidence level dialed to eleven.

Peter heard it now. For the first time since Tommy Scott slipped out of Francesca's life, he heard a sense of purpose in Francesca's voice, saw it in her eyes. There was newfound enthusiasm in Francesca, a sense of direction. Peter hadn't seen her this confident and alive in a long while. Francesca Thompson was ready to take on the world, and no one could have been more pleased than Peter.

Things may not have worked out with James Templeton, as Peter hoped. A temporary deviation from his plan, he decided focusing on the positive. If he knew his daughter, she'd sink knee-deep into her work and hopefully put Tommy behind her. Once he thought it was safe to proceed, he'd pick up where he left off and put his plan to get Francesca and James together back into motion.

Francesca covered the telephone with her hand long enough to say, "Give me a few more minutes, Daddy."

Giving Francesca a take-your-time nod, Peter rose to stretch his legs. The office looked like a florist shop. There were congratulatory bouquets of roses; their scent painted the air. A crystal vase brimmed with birds of paradise— Francesca's favorite. Curiosity had Peter reaching for the card.

> *Congratulations on your win.*
> *Would love to buy you a drink.*
> *James Templeton III*

"I don't want you saying another word over the telephone, Mrs. Gruber. I'll drive up to the prison Thursday. We'll talk more then." Francesca returned the handset to its cradle. "Sorry for making you wait, Daddy. Since my win, it's been crazy."

"I can see that. You're certainly in demand. Soon you'll be asking me for a raise and a bigger office." Peter's comment made Francesca snort a girlish giggle. "Did you know there are five flower arrangements here from James Templeton? Costly flower arrangements and each accompanying note is an invitation for drinks."

"Hmm?" Francesca flipped through her appointment book.

"Frankie, pay attention." Peter pinched her chin to lift her face to meet his.

"What are those?" Francesca asked when Peter waved the cards in her face.

"Invitations from James Templeton to join him for drinks. Don't you think you owe him a courtesy call?"

"He's also left several messages inviting me to dinner. And no, I'm not interested. I don't like him, Daddy. He's smug, self-centered, and rumor has it he's a womanizer."

Francesca picked up the stack of message slips, flipped through them.

"Rumours and innuendo. You know there's plenty of that at the club. We're talking about James Templeton III, Frankie. You know him, his family." Peter watched Francesca separating the messages into call and do-not-call piles. He saw her set one of James' messages in the do-not-call pile. "Do you know how many women would kill for an invitation from James?"

"I know who he is. I know his family, and I know women trip over themselves to spend even a second with the man. I'm not one of them." Francesca made notes on the margin of the documents she retrieved from her IN basket, set them down in the OUT basket. "I don't like him. Never have."

"It's drinks, not a proposal of marriage. Honey, promise me you'll think about it."

At the affectionate term, Francesca sunk back in her seat and looked up at her father. He hadn't called her honey since forever. "You really want me to accept his invitation."

"Give us a minute, Jennifer." Peter waited until Francesca's petite, blonde, assistant with the exceptional hearing closed the door behind her. "It's just drinks, dinner, not a lifetime commitment. You both have so much in common."

"We do?"

Peter watched Francesca uncap and cap the Mont Blanc. Even as a child, she'd had nervous fingers, always had to fidget with something or other. "You're both lawyers. You both grew up together in the same circles."

"We didn't grow up together, Daddy. He's ten years older than me."

"Why don't you start with a simple drink? Do it for me, honey."

The sheer pleasure of hearing her father speaking to her with such tenderness made her relent. "Okay, Daddy, I'll call him, but I'm not promising anything."

"It's all I ask, baby." His plan was back on. Sometimes things worked themselves out.

FRANCESCA MET JAMES AT WINSTON'S. THE air, ripe with the scent of sautéed garlic and seared meat mingled with old money and privilege. Ceilings were high, walls were covered in dark mahogany, and floors in a thick pile green carpet. Chandeliers from the ceiling dripped with crystal teardrops that twinkled in the light spilling from them. Servers wore black and white livery.

James stood the moment he saw Francesca. He looked dignified, handsome, and perfect in a navy, silk suit. His dark hair was perfectly styled. His eyes were a perfect rich brandy-brown. He was perfect.

Francesca hated perfect.

"Hi." James leaned forward, pecked her on the cheek in a familiar way. The tauntingly sweet scent of her perfume—Chanel, he deduced—reached out to him.

Black, silk whispered against her curves. A waterfall of diamond dangled from either side of her face, neck, and wrist. The luxurious, chestnut hair spilled around the beautiful face with lips painted cherry-red. James liked what he saw, as did every man in the room.

"You look stunning." James scraped the chair out for her. "I took the liberty of ordering a bottle of Kristal." He snapped his fingers at the waiter and had him pour Francesca a flute. "I hope you like it."

"I do. Thank you."

"Serve the dinner, please," James instructed the waiter, then shifted eyes back to Francesca. "I hope you don't mind. I asked the chef to prepare us his specialty."

"That sounds fine."

They dined on Cobb salad, asparagus risotto, Kobe steak, and garlic roasted potatoes. Dessert was a decadent chocolate soufflé, which James had the chef make especially for them. The meal was Michelin star worthy, but Francesca would have been happier with a greasy burger, onion rings, and Tommy sitting in James' place.

"Here's to your win." James touched crystal to crystal.

Francesca took a long sip of her champagne as she studied James' face. "You do surprise me."

"I'm the mysterious sort."

Hazel eyes steady on brandy-brown eyes, Francesca smiled. "I should thank you for the flowers."

"So, you did get them." James took another gulp of bubbly.

"I'm sorry, I didn't call you sooner. How did you know birds of paradise is my favorite flower?"

"A good lawyer does his research."

Francesca left her fingers on the stem to run up and down. "Frankly, I was surprised when you called to invite me out for drinks after..."

"You beat my ass. I won't lie. I resented the loss— deeply, but after I calmed down, I came to my senses. Bottom line, you argued the case masterfully and better than I did."

"I did, didn't I?" Francesca let out a soft, feminine laugh, which to James' surprise, slid into him. "Please, both you and I know I was tripping over my words most days."

"Then, you tripped well because you got to the judge and jurors to see things your way." When James met her eyes, Francesca could see the look of a man wanting an itch scratched, and she stiffened for a moment. "You're very beautiful, Frankie."

She hadn't meant to jerk back, but she found herself in retreat. "It's getting late. I should get going."

James wanted to reach out for her hand, but the timing wasn't right. Francesca was the type of woman who fell into things in her own time. "It's only ten. I thought we'd head out to The Blue Note. I know you like jazz." When Francesca raise a questioning brow, James said, "I always do my homework when entertaining a beautiful rival I need to ingratiate myself to. Especially one who kicked my ass in the courtroom. What do you say?"

Francesca didn't know what to say. She didn't have much experience with men, and certainly not a player like James. Francesca wondered what Lily would do. Tommy had been the only man in Francesca's life, but he wasn't there.

The Veterans Affairs office had no news for her again. It had been eight long years since she'd seen Tommy, and as long since she'd allowed a man into her life, her heart, and bed. Francesca couldn't deny the fact James Templeton had piqued her curiosity, but she wasn't ready to move on—not yet.

"What do you say we pop into The Blue Note? If, after we get there, you don't want to stay, I'll take you home." James helped her out of her chair.

"My car is here."

"I'll drive you back to pick it up. I'm not anything if not accommodating." James brought his hand up to toy with a curl that flirted in her face.

"Umm, sure, all right."

THE MUSIC WAS STIMULATING AND THE company enjoyable, and before Francesca knew it, it was two in the morning when she and James left The Blue Note. Reluctantly, James drove Francesca back to her car. He would have preferred to take Francesca back to his place, and up to his bedroom, but she wasn't the type of woman to be rushed. He was a patient man.

The following day, James sent Francesca a dozen birds of paradise. The note read: Into each life, some rain must fall, and you are my rain. James. The Ella Fitzgerald song reference put a smile on Francesca's face. As much as she hated to admit, James Templeton was getting to her.

Seventeen

"I HEAR YOU took the Gruber case." Peter headed straight for the bar cart he'd had put in Francesca's office. "Ambitious of you to take on the woman who alleges to have been battered for most of her married life by her husband and ultimately conveniently kills him. You know that's going to be difficult to prove." He tossed back Johnny Walker.

Francesca set the telephone down. "I'm a Thompson, and Mrs. Gruber is innocent. I've read the medical records, seen the photographs of the many injuries she sustained during their marriage. That bastard deserved what he got."

"You're indeed a Thompson, and your cynicism is..."

"Enlightening?" she finished. "It's new to me. The cynicism, I mean. I guess it's an occupational hazard."

Peter nodded. "Cynicism tends to sneak into your thought process after a while." He waved the glass in her direction in offer. Francesca shook her head. "Let me know if you want me to take second chair."

"I was thinking of Robert Tunney as second."

"Hmm, you want to do this without your old man." Peter walked to the window, gazed at a blue, July sky drenched in sunshine.

"Something like that. No offense."

"None taken."

Peter admired Francesca's tenacity. For a moment, he considered appointing her as his successor. She was a Thompson and would undeniably make an excellent CEO, but she'd never be taken seriously by her male counterparts.

She was too pretty, too female. Peter was looking for a respected, influential man to take control of his company. What he needed was James Templeton III.

At sixty-five, Peter was ready to pack it in and move to an exotic locale to spend the rest of his days lounging by the pool and watching his young wife parade around those skimpy bikinis he liked. Peter's plan needed to come to pass sooner than later.

If Katherine had given him a son, he wouldn't be at an impasse, but he had no one but himself to blame. If they'd started a family when they'd first married as Katherine wanted instead of putting his ambitions ahead of his family, they would have had more children, and he'd have had the male heir to take over his empire. By the time Francesca came along, Katherine was forty years old. Too old to bear him the boy he wanted. Turning to James was Peter's last option, but he needed a successor, and James ticked all the boxes. He'd be the perfect husband to Francesca, the ideal son-in-law, and perfect CEO. It was the perfect plan.

"So, how was dinner with James?" Peter considered not raising the topic, but curiosity had the better of him.

"It was okay."

"Just okay?" Peter perched himself on her guest chair, focused his gaze on his daughter. Her intelligent hazel eyes, the chestnut tumble of waves, the delicate face it was as if Katherine sat before him.

"Maybe better than okay. He was attentive and considerate. Not at all like the man I remembered or the arrogant one I saw in court."

"So, you'll be seeing him again?"

"Maybe," Francesca said, surprising Peter. "I'm thinking about it." She felt the twinge of guilt and betrayal for Tommy and found herself crossing to the bar to fill a glass with the brandy she didn't want. "Why are you so interested in getting James and me together, Daddy?"

Peter's eyes met his daughter's with the straight-on gaze he set on his rivals in court. "I want you to be happy,

Frankie. I want you to find the same happiness your mother and I shared. It's been eight years since…"

"Tommy," Francesca curtly finished when Peter couldn't bring himself to say his name. "His name is Tommy Scott."

Peter noted Francesca's use of the present tense. Six feet under and Tommy Scott still had a firm hold on his daughter.

"You still can't bring yourself to say his name. Why do you hate him so much, Daddy? Tommy is kind, caring, and he loves me. And I love him. He's the only man I will ever love." Francesca's heart suddenly ached for him.

"I don't hate him. I just knew him better than you."

"You don't know him at all, and still, you judge."

Peter rose to close her office door. "I know him very well, Frankie. The man you claim to be kind and caring seriously injured a man who had to be rushed to the hospital. He would have ended up behind bars for years was it not for me taking on the case as a favor to his father. The boy was constantly getting into trouble. If you don't believe me, have Jennifer draw his file from the storage room. It'll be easy to find. It's the thickest one down there."

If Francesca was shocked by the revelation, she didn't show it. "I don't need to read his file. That's in the past."

"How would it look if my daughter got together with the criminal I got off?" Peter refilled his glass, drained half of it.

"That's not the man Tommy is anymore."

"Once a criminal, always a criminal." Realizing his poor choice of words would fuel Francesca's anger, Peter rushed to correct himself. "No father ever thinks any man is good enough for his little girl, and in my eyes, Tommy Scott, wasn't good enough for you, Frankie."

"And James Templeton is? Why? Because he has the right lineage, the right name, the right friends, the fancy manners, the right amount of wealth, and fancy education."

"Yes, Frankie. Why is it so wrong to want my little girl to have the best in life? It's why I've worked my fingers to the bone. To give you the best."

"Daddy, we both know you've worked your fingers to the bone to satisfy your ego." Anger had Francesca absently taking in most of the brandy in one swallow. She winced at its pungent taste and the sting at her throat. "Besides, I'm not a little girl anymore, Dad. I'm a woman who can make her own decisions."

"I know you're a woman. It's just hard for me to accept you're not my little girl anymore." A wistful expression came over Peter's face. "All I want is for you to be happy, honey. Don't you think you deserve to be happy? It's been almost eight years since you've allowed anyone into your life, someone into your heart. Don't you think Tommy would want you to be happy?"

A storm of emotions blew through Francesca. Her heart wouldn't allow her to let anyone take Tommy's place. She'd tried, maybe not hard enough, but she'd tried to let others in. But Francesca had compared them to Tommy, and no one ever measures up to him. There were times when Francesca wondered how she could be so in love with a ghost because that was what Tommy was becoming as her hope of ever seeing him alive evaporated.

"You argued your case well, Mr. Prosecutor," Francesca said. "If it means so much to you, I'll call James. I'll go out with him again and see where it takes us."

"And I promise I won't bring the topic up again." Peter rose, crossed to the door. "Whether James Templeton or someone else, Frankie, ultimately, it's your choice. It's your life. I just want you to be happy. Okay?"

Always the statesman, she thought giving her father a silent nod.

IN THE WEEKS THAT FOLLOWED, FOR her father's sake, Francesca accepted James invitations to the opera, the theater, the symphony, and the many dinners. A couple of Fridays, after a draining day in court, needing to unwind, they closed The Blue Note. At the end of the night, James drove Francesca home, walked her to the front door, and like a perfect gentleman, pecked her on the cheek before driving away. The following morning a bouquet with a thoughtful message always found its way to her desk.

Slowly but surely, James was slipping into Francesca's life.

Peter couldn't have been more proud when Francesca, draped in a red silk gown and James in a tuxedo, walked into the Lawyers Association Gala arm in arm. After dinner, when the music began to flow, Peter's lips ripe with a smile watched Francesca and James flawlessly circle the dance floor. His work was done.

James slid into the driver's seat of his Jaguar, loosened his bow tie. "Are you tired, Frankie?"

"What do you have in mind?"

"Going back to my place for a nightcap?" James dared to say what he'd wanted to for weeks.

"All right," she said, surprising him and herself and wondering where tonight was heading.

Once home, James led Francesca into the living room. Shrugging out of his jacket, he draped it over the back of his leather sofa. "Please make yourself at home while I make my famous martinis?" he said, crossing the expanse of his living room to the bar. "I make the best dry martinis this side of town."

"You do, do you?" Francesca darted eyes around the room. "You have a lovely home."

High ceilings, dark wood floors, two luxuriously long, ivory leather sofas were the highlight of the room. Colorful abstracts decorated tan walls. A crystal chandelier collared with a medallion spilled light as did the two Tiffani lamps on the Ashley console table flanking the sofa. Russet curtains were drawn open to expose the colorful garden lit by the beams of floodlights.

"I've always thought it needed a woman's touch." James poured dry vermouth, set the lid on the cocktail shaker.

"It's perfect as is." Francesca watched James shake the martini before pouring into glasses. He'd looked handsome in his tuxedo, but now with jacket and bowtie shed, the top buttons of his shirt loosened, he looked doubly so, and she couldn't help but stare.

"Are you all right, Frankie?"

"Yes, I was just ... admiring the Bertram Brooker piece behind you." Francesca sunk herself into the buttery soft sofa.

James handed her the martini glass. His rich brown eyes never left her as she crossed long, shapely leg that widened the slit of her gown to expose a creamy, white thigh. Whether intentional or not, he appreciated it nonetheless. "You know your artists."

"Some," Francesca said as James dropped the needle on Ernie Birchill's album, and Dream A Little Dream of Me flowed. "This is a good martini."

James dimmed the lights before sitting beside her. "I'm glad you like it."

The silence that followed was the type that stirs up emotions. It made Francesca feel vulnerable, and she began to regret being there. Francesca knew full well where tonight was headed when she'd accepted James' invitation to his home, but until now, she hadn't regretted her decision. What was she thinking? She couldn't slide into James' bed and betray Tommy.

Francesca rose, walked to the patio doors to put distance between them. "Your garden is lovely."

"You're lovely, Frankie, and you look stunning tonight. You were the most beautiful woman at the ball." James breathed the words reverently as she felt his arms go around her when he met her at the door. "I want to make love with you, Frankie. I want to touch you, and kiss you, and taste you," he said, kissing Francesca's bare shoulders then, spinning her around, so they were face to face when he offered her his hand.

Francesca's weary gaze rested on his face for a long moment. She wanted to be touched, held, and be loved. She wanted to feel a man's touch on her, feel his naked body pressed to hers. Francesca wanted to bond with a man in the way love brings two people together, to share in the tender moments, but she couldn't bring herself to do so with anyone other than Tommy.

But Tommy wasn't there, hadn't been for eight years. With that thought lingering in her mind, she reached for James' hand and let him lead her up the winding staircase to his bedroom.

It was a manly room, Francesca thought when James threw the door open. Walls were washed in brown. A solid four-poster bed was covered in creamy, silk sheets. A thick, Persian rug in reds and blues lay in front of the marble fireplace, which tonight wouldn't be lit. It was September, and the night was too warm for a fire.

While Francesca freshened up, James set the mood in the room. He lit candles and dimmed lights. He slid the window up to let the warm night air flow, and with it came the rich scent of sweet alyssum and lemon verbena from his garden along with the sounds of the night. Crossing to the record player, he dropped the Duke Ellington record.

In the darkened room dancing in shadows under the flicker of candlelight, the soulful strains of *In a Sentimental Mood* filling the silence, James walked up to Francesca when she stepped out of the bathroom.

"Are you sure about this, Frankie? I don't want you regretting tonight or me in the morning." James ran his hands through the hair that shimmered under the glow of candlelight.

James' touch and Duke's breathy voice had her pulse jumping, and she nodded. "You've been so patient with me and wonderful these past weeks. I want this, James. I want to be with you."

She looked nervous, James mused. He liked that. Nothing like a woman's flustered insides to inflate a man's ego. "God, you're beautiful." James laid butterfly kisses on her forehead, nose, and cheeks. Tenderly he trailed a lazy line of kisses down her neck and shoulders while breathing her in. "And you smell great. You always do. It's been driving me crazy all these weeks."

James lifted his mouth to press it against the kissable lips he'd been dreaming of kissing. His mouth on hers was quick, experienced, and full of energy. While their lips brushed, his hands busied themselves sliding the zipper down on her dress and slipping it off her body. James' gaze skimmed over the red, lace bra and panties beneath the silk.

Watching Francesca's face, his hands skimmed over her body. He liked it when her body quivered under his touch. He loved the feel of her warm, silky skin, and his hand roamed.

Under his touch, her body churned like an overheated engine and tossing caution and logic to the wind, her fingers tore at his shirt, unsnapped his pants. His body was toned with a long smooth line of muscle. His arms were muscular, and his shoulders broad. Unlike Tommy, there were no scars anywhere on his body. It was a perfect body. Francesca hated perfect, but she wanted this right now, and when he led her to his bed, she willingly let him.

Limber muscles rippled when James got on top of her. "I want to make love with you all night, Frankie. I want to feel you under my touch." Eye to eye and mouth to mouth, she could feel the heat of his breath on her face "You're shaking. Do I make you nervous?"

Francesca forced herself to concentrate on forming a coherent sentence. "I'm not, ah, very experienced."

"That's very sexy." James didn't think women like her existed anymore. Francesca was twenty-six and inexperienced. But then, women all professed to be pure simply because society dictated they portray themselves as white doves. When it came down to it, James had yet to meet a woman that wasn't a tigress in bed.

"Really? I figured you're used to experienced women."

"I am, but I don't want them. I want you." James traced the edge of red lace that covered her breasts with his lips before unhooking her bra and letting his mouth feast on her breasts. He lingered there until she bucked under the waves of pleasure he shot through her.

Her shuddering body thrilled him, aroused him, and needing to claim more of her for himself, he slipped his fingers under her panties, into the heat. She was wet, and he let his fingers slide until her body shuddered.

"You like that?" he murmured.

"Mmm-hmm." Her breathy voice was like music to him.

There was a satisfied smile on his face. "Stay with me, Frankie. Let me enjoy you for a while," he whispered, letting his fingers sink deeper into her.

And she did, and when he felt her self-control slipping, he drove her first orgasm to burst with long flowing waves of unexpected delight.

"Do that again for me," he murmured. "Let me hear you when you come this time."

When Francesca came that time, she let out a loud orgasmic moan that made James feel like a king. "Do it one more time for me, Frankie. This time cry my name out. I want to hear my name on your lips," he said, tearing her panties off and claiming her with his mouth.

When the wave of heat struck her with the intensity of a geyser erupting after its long slumber, James' name shuddered through her lips.

Hearing his name moaned as the orgasm tore through her body, his need to be insider her became urgent, and rolling on top of her, he spread her legs and plunged deep into her.

Francesca watched James sliding in and out of her, the pleasure deepening in his face with each quick thrust. His groaning sounds growing louder, she closed her eyes and let her thoughts drift back to the creek and Tommy as he made love to her for the first time in her life.

Eighteen

BEFORE FRANCESCA KNEW it, September turned into October, and December came fast. She was spending more time with James. Colleagues, friends, and Peter referred to them as a couple—the perfect couple. As did James, but in Francesca's mind, their relationship was a physical one, not emotional. By Francesca's standards, it wasn't based on love or the deep-seated emotions that came to pass between two people meant to be together. That love and emotion were reserved in Francesca's heart for Tommy. It always would be.

Peter was thrilled by the turn of events, and he'd already set the wheels in motion. James would be offered a seat at Thompson and Associates board of directors table. Peter wouldn't table the offer until the vows were said, but that was a matter of time. Days ago, James had asked Peter for his blessing to ask Francesca for her hand in marriage.

JAMES JOINED FRANCESCA AT THE FRENCH doors and handed her the flute of Kristal. "You look deep in thought. Are you resenting me for having turned down your father's invitation to spend New Year's Eve on the beaches of Ibiza with him and Tiffani?"

Francesca shook her head. "I think you know I'm not a fan of Tiffani's. Besides, this was perfect. Dinner was wonderful, the company is great, and the view is spectacular. Look at how pretty everything looks covered in snow," Francesca said, gazing out the patio doors to where a white moon cast a soft, silver glow over the city. Thick, large flakes of snow drifted, weighed down tree branches and blanketed rooftops and everything under layers of white. It was a scenic winter wonderland that lent a romantic feel to the night.

"It is a beautiful sight," James skimmed fingers over her arms. She looked stunning in the short, teal Fendi dress he'd picked up for her. It tightly hugged the curves he'd become intimate with over the past few months. "Will you stay the night, Frankie?"

"If you'd like me to."

"I would." James clamped a hand on her arm when she started to swill her champagne. "Not yet. It's thirty seconds to midnight."

"All right."

"Come sit with me." James took Francesca's hand, led her to the fireplace. Helping her down onto the Persian rug, before the crackle of flame and wood, they waited for the stroke of midnight. At the sound of the chiming clock announcing the incoming year, James touched his glass to hers. "Happy New Years, Frankie," he said, brushing his lips to hers then, reaching into his jacket pocket, got down on one knee.

"I love the time we spend together, Frankie. I love being with you, and I want to wake up next to you every morning. I want to come home to you at night. Will you do me the honor of doing all those things for me? Will you marry me, Frankie?"

Although Francesca had seen it coming and worked through in her head what she'd say when the moment came, she froze. Nausea rose so fast, so sharp it stole Francesca's breath. For a long moment, the snap of burning wood was the only sound in the deafening silence of the room as she stared at the diamond ring.

Feeling the thump of panic, Francesca bolted to her feet and put distance between them. That ring symbolized so many things Francesca wasn't ready to deal with: change, a new future, a fresh start, stability in her life. It brought finality to Tommy and her. The thought made Francesca's chest constrict, but she needed to stop aimlessly drifting through life, waiting for Tommy's ghost to appear.

Determined it was time to move on, to push aside, once and for all, the notion of Tommy returning to her, Francesca looked into James' eyes and saw James' eyes narrow and his jaw clench.

"You're supposed to say yes, I'd love to, James, without a second thought."

She'd hurt him, embarrassed him, and that wasn't her intention. "I'm sorry. I didn't mean to upset you. It's just that marriage is a serious matter, and I... Do you think we've known each other long enough to make an informed decision? I mean, we've been together for less than six months."

Everything about James hardened. "There's no timetable to falling in love. It just happens. I fell in love with you the moment you walked into the courtroom, but it's now clear to me you don't feel the same way I do. If you did, you wouldn't be questioning my proposal—us. I've misread you all along."

Francesca watched James walk away from her toward the patio doors.

"To think that all the times I made love to you was nothing but a roll in the sheets for you. You led me to believe you were sexually unsophisticated. You're anything but. Isn't that the truth? I've been spending my nights with a professional." James' anger cut through Francesca like razor blades, but she blamed no one but herself for inflicting the type of pain that hatched such hurtful words.

Francesca never meant to hurt James. He'd been patient, caring, and understanding. He hadn't once pressed her for intimacy, waited until she came around. James had been the perfect gentleman all these months, and now she'd hurt him for doing nothing more than love her.

Tommy's shadow walked beside Francesca, but James was here, flesh and blood with his heart asking to love her.

"I'm sorry, James. I didn't mean to hurt you. It's just, well, that you surprised me." Francesca's words stumbled over one another.

James slammed his glass of Johnny Walker on the bar, spilling half of it and startling her. "Goddamnit, Frankie. Proposals are meant to be spontaneous. They normally trigger a positive, emotional response. Not a regrettable one, which is what I hear in your voice, see on your face."

The injured expression on James' face was clear, and it tied her stomach in knots. "I didn't mean to upset you, James."

"I'm not upset. I'm disappointed, Frankie. I've tried to do everything right by you." There was a sharp note of irritation. "Your father told me you might react this way, but I dismissed him."

"My father? What's he got to do with anything?"

"I spoke to him a couple of weeks ago to ask his permission for your hand in marriage. I'm wondering now why I bothered. You try to do everything right, and this is what you get." James hurled the whiskey glass into the fireplace.

Francesca wrapped arms around herself when crystal hit brick and shattered into pieces.

"He told me you're hung up on someone from your past. Someone who's been dead for years, but who you won't let go," James said, walking to Francesca, and fisting his hands in her hair pulled her face inches from his. "Were you thinking of him when we were in bed, Frankie? When I was inside you?"

Putting on her lawyerly poker face, Francesca braced herself to lie. "No, of course not. I wouldn't do that. I ... I love you too much to think of anyone other than you when we make love."

"If you loved me, you would have accepted my proposal without hesitation."

"It's hard for me to open my heart to anyone, to let people in. People leave you. It's been that way for me since

I lost my mother," and Tommy. "Please let go of me, James."

"Yes, I'm sorry." James gentled his hold of Francesca's hair. "Did I hurt you?"

"I'm fine." Francesca started to raise a hand to massage her scalp but resisted the urge for fear of triggering a reaction from James.

"Why didn't you tell me this before?"

"It's not something that comes easily for me to say. It brings back too many memories."

"I'm sorry I reacted as I did. It's just that I love you so much, Frankie, and your father telling me about a past lover and you turning my proposal down. Well, it all played badly in my head."

Her father was going to get an earful for stoking James with his misguided notions. "I understand."

"Do you, Frankie? Do you really? You know I'd never hurt you." James tenderly tucked a strand of hair behind her ear. "Are you in love with this, Tommy, still? If you are, I'd understand. He was your first love. I know how that feels."

A frown creased Francesca's brow. "You do?"

"Of course. I, too, had a first love. Her name was Jasmine White. She was my high school sweetheart, and we spent every minute together. On our way from the prom, we were hit head-on by a drunk driver." James breathed deeply. "She was killed on impact. I, unfortunately, survived the accident. I've had to live my entire life with the guilt of surviving that night."

Francesca's face softened when she saw the pain in James' eyes. Walking over to him, she lay a hand on his cheek. "I didn't know. I'm so sorry, James."

"It was a long time ago, but it still hurts. I think it always will." James took her face in his hands. "She's an important part of my past. I'd hoped you never expect me to forget Jasmine."

Sensing his pain, feeling it herself, Francesca's hands came up to meet his, and he felt a sense of unity with her. "I'd never dream of it."

"And I'd never dream of making you forget your past."

Francesca felt the room fill with oxygen, and a wave of love washed over her for James. "I would be proud to be your wife, James."

"You're sure, Frankie?"

Francesca's eyes tracked over to his. "I am."

At her words, James fished into his pants pocket for the ring. "It was my great-grandmothers. I hope you like it." Dimples flashed as he slid the shimmering diamond, encircled in rubies on Francesca's finger.

"It's beautiful, James." Francesca held her left hand up to admire.

"You've made me the happiest man alive, Frankie." The tears rolling down James' cheeks, he lowered his mouth to kiss her deeply and sweetly. At the end of the kiss, Francesca reached for his hand and led him to the bedroom.

Nineteen

IT WAS A perfect day for a wedding. A bold June sun poured out of a dreamy blue sky over trees crowned with the greenness of summer. A warm breeze carried the scents of the blooming gardens. Blue jays and starlings flitted through the air in song.

The gazebo where Francesca and James were to exchange their vows burst with white roses. Chairs were wrapped in ivory taffeta. The cobbled path leading to the gazebo was covered in rose petals and flanked with lanterns that would bloom with light the moment Francesca made her way to James. Inside the tent, which would accommodate five hundred guests—handpicked by James and Peter—dozens of wait staff set up to James' specifications.

It was starting to look as James envisioned his wedding day.

Peter stepped onto the terrace, handed James the bottle of beer. "Everything looks great, James. I hope you're pleased."

James tapped his bottleneck to Peter's. "I am, and I know Frankie will love it the moment she sees it. She's still upstairs getting ready. Has been for the past hour."

"It's not like her to be so girly. You've been good for her, son." Peter drained part of his beer.

James followed Peter to the wicker chairs, sat when he did. "Thank you, sir."

"Peter. We're family now and should be on a first-name basis."

"All right, Peter. Thank you for letting us have the wedding on the estate. It's a stunning property. It's why I chose to get married in June. I thought an outdoor wedding would be perfect amid your stunning gardens."

Peter waved a hand. "There's no need for thanks. Consider the Thompson estate your home now. You and Frankie can move in tomorrow if you like." Peter drained his beer as he watched ice sculptures being set up at the multiple bars. James certainly spared no expense.

"Thank you. I'll give that some thought, but Frankie insists on working at the firm after we marry, and my downtown home is minutes from your office and mine. Maybe I can talk Frankie into spending weekends here." Squinting against the sun, James scanned the property and made mental notes of the changes to be made to accommodate his taste.

"Well, you won't have to do much to talk Frankie into spending time here. She loves this place." Peter heard the beating of drums, the twang of guitars, and the sound of brass when the band launched into rehearsal. "After your honeymoon, I want you and me to sit down for a talk."

"About what?" James made a mental note to tell the wedding planners to switch the ice sculptures set up on the north and south bars. He'd been precise in his instructions, but good help was hard to find.

"Business. It's no secret I've thought you'd be a great addition to the Thompson and Associates team. Why you chose to go into public practice is still a mystery to me. With your talent, you could have made so much more money in private practice." Peter watched the beads of sweat trickle down the side of his beer bottle down to the armrest forming a circle around its base.

"I felt it was time for a Templeton to give back to the world in more ways than philanthropy. Handing money over to charity is a simplistic way of relieving your guilt for enjoying the comfortable lifestyle the generations of Templeton's have made possible. I felt a moral obligation to give back, and offering my legal services pro bono is my way."

"Very noble, but you're an excellent attorney who should aspire to more than public defense."

James stretched out his legs, crossed his feet at the ankles, and let the sun pour over his face. "What do you have in mind, Peter?"

"Here, you both are." Both men turned to meet Tiffani's overly painted face appreciating the sensual swing of her gait. Her flowing hair was golden under the afternoon sun, and the rubies at her ears and neck twinkled under its light.

"You look stunning, baby," Peter said, salivating over the ripe breasts spilling over the edge of the cream, silk dress she'd purposely chosen to outshine the bride.

"Thank you, darling." Tiffani gave him her right cheek, and he planted a kiss.

"I want you to get upstairs right now to make yourself pretty for me. I laid out your tuxedo on the bed. No. No more talking," Tiffani said to Peter when he started to speak. "Scoot now. Guests are due to arrive in under an hour,"

"All right, I'm going." Peter gave her butt a suggestive squeeze. "Talk James into doing the same," he said over his shoulder.

"He's right. You need to get yourself upstairs too. Francesca looks beautiful, and the groom needs to as well. You don't want her upstaging you, do you?" Tiffani linked her arm through James' and walked him into the house.

ALL EYES TURNED TO FRANCESCA. FLASHES from cameras came from every angle. In the white, lace gown and cathedral veil James handpicked for her, Francesca looked like a fairy Princess.

With a giant smile on his face, looking tall and handsome in a white-tail tuxedo, James watched Francesca make her way to him. His heart beat thick as each step brought Francesca closer to becoming Mrs. James Templeton III.

Vows exchanged, James passionately kissed his wife. "I love you so much, Mrs. Templeton, and I can't wait to start our new life."

"Me too, James," Francesca said, letting him lead her to the translucent dance floor James had installed atop the blue waters of the pool for their first dance as husband and wife.

Camera flashes winked as Francesca and James circled the dance floor to the sound of *The Anniversary Song*. As they spun, cheek to cheek, arms chained around one another, James kissed his wife and vowed his love to her. Francesca reiterated the sentiment, although deep down she wished she was saying the words to Tommy. Closing her eyes, Francesca conjured his image. She saw the flowing dark hair, the smiling blue eyes full of love for her.

"May I cut in?" Peter took Francesca's hand when James stepped back and turned Tiffani over to his son-in-law.

"You look beautiful, honey. Your mother would think so too, and she'd be as proud as I am of you today." Peter fell into long, smooth steps with his daughter as the band segued into *Moonlight Serenade*.

Francesca felt her lungs choke up. "Thank you for saying so, Daddy."

"I know she'd like James." Peter saw right through the contrived smile, shadowed in sadness. "I know I haven't been the perfect father, and I'm sorry about that, but your mother's death was difficult on me."

"Don't, Daddy."

"I need to say this, Frankie. I know you'll forever blame me for keeping you and Tommy Scott apart, but I was doing what I thought was best for you. You know it's not easy to be both mother and father." Peter glided his daughter past James and Tiffani, who was stepping off the dance floor heading for the bar. "I know you don't love

James, but he loves you and will take care of you. Will you at least give him a chance to do so?"

"Don't worry, Daddy. He's my husband now, and I'll play the role of the loyal, devoted wife. You can go ahead and make him the offer to join your board of directors." Francesca's glossed lips curved into a cynical smile when the shock flew into Peter's eyes. "You think Thompson and Associate's is immune to the rumor mill?" Francesca waved a hand in Peter's face to silence him. "Please don't say anything else that will insult my intelligence."

"Honey."

"The honeys and sweethearts won't work anymore, Dad. If you'll excuse me, I need a stiff drink." Francesca gathered her dress in her arm. "Mom would have loved Tommy," she said before walking off the dance floor.

AT THE SOUND OF THE MAN and woman's laughter coming from the hallway bathroom, Missy ducked behind the pillar. Her brows lifted when she watched Tiffani peek her head out to make the coast was clear.

Stepping out, Tiffani leaned in for one last kiss. "That was fun, darling. It always is with you. You're very talented." She skimmed a finger down his cheek. "I better get back to my husband."

Missy watched Tiffani adjust the mussed hair, and smooth the front of her dress before she made her way down the stairs. She'd always known the woman was a cheap skank.

Remaining in the shadows, Missy waited for the man to step out. When he finally came out of the bathroom, wide-eyed, Missy watched him finger-comb his disheveled hair and adjust his belt buckle before heading downstairs to rejoin the party.

Twenty

FRANCESCA COVERED HER naked body with a white T-shirt. Barefoot, her hair tumbling in waves over her shoulders, she stepped out of the bedroom onto the terrace of their honeymoon villa. The air that rushed at her was hot, laced with the scents springing from the lush tropical gardens hemming the property, of all that was Bora Bora, and she breathed it in.

James outdid himself when he booked the secluded villa, Francesca thought scanning the panorama. The pool gleamed against the reflection of the sun. Beyond it, the turquoise lagoon deepened into a sapphire-blue as it stretched to the horizon to meld with sky. Strokes of greens and deep browns from the chain of mountains created a postcard-perfect scene.

"Good morning, Mrs. Templeton?" James chained his arms around Francesca and rested a stubbled cheek against hers.

"I'm sorry if I woke you." Francesca's scent wrapped around him like the Polynesian heat.

"You didn't. I turned to you in bed, hoping to make love to my wife, and you weren't there," James said, kissing her neck and shoulders. "But then I did keep you up most of the night. I can't seem to get enough of you, Mrs. Templeton." James nibbled on her ear. "You look great in my T-shirt, by the way."

"I hope you don't mind. I grabbed the first thing I came across."

"Of course, I don't mind. What's mine is yours now, Mrs. Templeton. Even my T-shirts." James walked her to a wicker chair lined with soft cushions and gestured Francesca to sit on his lap.

His hair sexily tousled, his chest bare, and his jeans carelessly fastened, he looked handsome and desirable. Wealthy, a respected prosecutor, and a great lover, James certainly ticked all the boxes. Why couldn't she stop thinking of Tommy?

Francesca had thought of Tommy every time she and James made love last night. She'd imagined Tommy's mouth and tongue feasting on her body each time James had. Francesca had wished it was Tommy kissing her, inside her instead of James. Her feelings of betrayal for Tommy when James made love to her was as overwhelming as the remorse she felt for not being the loyal wife James deserved. She was Mrs. James Templeton now, Francesca told herself, and she had to stop fixating on Tommy before James sensed something.

"Are you all right, Frankie?" James asked when Francesca's gaze focused on some faraway point. "You've seemed distant since we got here."

Francesca aimed the eyes she knew would give away her guilt from James to the lagoon where sunlight sparkled diamonds over glass-smooth water. "I'm fine. I ... I just wished my mom had been at our wedding," she said, aiming to distract the probing eyes.

James chained his arms around her. "I'm sorry. I should have guessed."

"No. It's me who's sorry for sounding so sad on our honeymoon. Let's not talk about it." Francesca brushed her lips over James to end the conversation, which would drive her to pile lie after lie, and that tower was getting mighty tall. "I can't get over how beautiful this place is."

"Do you like it?"

"How could I not? It looks like I imagined paradise would." Francesca watched a flock of birds set off from one tree to another in synchronized flight.

"Well, it's all ours. The house, the lush gardens, the white sand beach that stretches for miles. It's all ours."

Francesca's eyes opened wide. "What are you talking about?"

"It's my parent's wedding gift."

"They never said anything."

"Because they wanted me to surprise you."

"Well, you have. They have." Francesca's smile curved wider. "We're definitely coming here often."

"If you like. I want to make my wife happy." James caught sight of her erect nipples straining against the T-shirt, and he slipped his hand under cotton to fondle. The sensation of her hot skin under his touch was like fire. He felt himself go hard. He had to take her there now.

Seeing the stunned arousal in his eyes, feeling it against her leg, Francesca pressed her hands to his chest. "James, the staff will see us out here."

"I don't give a shit what they see." James temper bubbled at an alarming speed, unnerving Francesca. "They can turn around and leave if they don't like what they see. You're my wife, and I want you here. Now." He suckled on her nipple, liked it when she winced in pain when he bit down hard on it. "God, you taste great."

"Let's go back to bed." Francesca was half off James' lap when he gripped her wrist and pulled her back down.

"Didn't you hear what I said?" James' eyes were so intense they burned through her. "I want you here now. I'm sick and tired of rolling around in a comfortable bed. I need more excitement than that, and as my wife, you should want to please me."

"I do want to please you, but not here where everyone can see us."

"Stop being such a prude and focusing more on pleasing me."

"I want to please you, but not out here." Francesca started to push to her feet.

"You don't walk away from me," James snapped like a German Shepard before the unexpected backhanded slap that left Francesca dazed came.

Francesca's breath caught at the suddenness of the strike. Pain, hideous pain reared up. When she started to turn away, James' hands gripped her waist and spun her to face him. The anger Francesca saw in his eyes was huge, and she feared he was going to hit more forcefully this time.

This wasn't the James Francesca knew, and all she could think to do was mumble an apology. "I'm sorry I've upset you."

"Don't give me that teary-eyed, innocent look. All I said was that I want to fuck you right here and now. Is it so wrong of me to want to fuck my wife? Jesus Christ, Frankie, I just gave you a goddamn villa. You'd think you'd want to bend over backward to please me."

"I do want to please you." Francesca struggled with the tears that wanted to come but refused to shed.

"I'm glad to hear it. Bend over. I want to take you from behind."

"I've never…" Francesca's strength was no match for James' when he wrapped his hands around her waist to force her into position.

"Today, you will because it's what I want."

Francesca couldn't hold the tears back anymore. "You're hurting me, James. Please stop," she cried out, bucking against the pain.

James enjoyed the sound of her trembling voice. "Stop wriggling." His hands ruthless and rough, dug nails into her hips to hold her still. "I need to be inside you right now."

Francesca swallowed hard when he plunged himself into her with a savagery she hadn't known James to possess. Speechless, disorientated Francesca remained silent the entire time James drove himself in and out of her without regard for how much he was hurting her.

"I think this suits me just fine. It's better I don't look at your face when I'm fucking you. You don't think I can't sense you're miles away every time I have. Like it's a chore for you. Are you thinking of *him* every time I'm inside you? Do you wish it was him?" The anger Francesca heard in James' voice went deep. "Get back inside. Can't you see we're busy?" James snapped at the young maid when she appeared on the terrace with the breakfast tray he'd ordered.

Francesca couldn't have felt more humiliated than she did when the maids' eyes widened in shock then waned into what she construed as pity for her.

"Get back to the kitchen. Now," James shouted.

Fearing for what James might do to the eighteen-year-old maid, Francesca, said, "It's fine. Go back inside, Samaria." Only then did the gawking, dark-haired Polynesian maid walk away. "You're hurting me, James," Francesca cried out, her voice and her dignity breaking.

"Maybe now, you'll remember that it's me who's fucking you and not that criminal you're so in love with."

"I ... I don't know what you're talking about?"

"I didn't ask you to talk." James slapped Francesca's left cheek hard enough to leave his handprint stamped red. "I can't compete with a goddam memory you won't let go of."

James waited for the cries, the complaints to come, but Francesca sucked up the throbbing pain reverberating through her from the strike, and all he heard was her deep breath of distress. Aroused by her discomfort, James' body bucked. With a hideous groan of triumph, he released himself inside her.

"That was the best orgasm I've had with you in the time we've been together. I need to wash you off me now," James said, pulling out of her and walking back to their bedroom.

Frankie lowered the T-shirt to cover herself, her shame and collapsing into the lounge chair, coiled herself into a fetal position. With the sound of chirping birds and the scent of paradise, Francesca cried her humiliation out of her system.

HATE, ANGER, FEAR, CONFUSION, MASHING INTO a storm of emotion, Francesca spent the night in her darkened bedroom, alone, crying. James, her newlywed husband, the man who'd sent her flowers weekly, who'd been nothing but attentive, loving, and kind, had done the unspeakable to her. He'd degraded, shamed, broken, and stolen her trust.

At dawn, when the world was still asleep, Francesca aimlessly walked the miles of beach next to the endless blue curving on the horizon, trying to come to terms with what had happened. Twenty-four hours later, and she still couldn't wrap her head around the horrendous violence her husband, the man she'd come to trust, inflicted on her.

Francesca blamed no one but herself for James' reaction. James had never lost his temper before. She was his wife now and should have tucked her thoughts of Tommy away the moment James slid the ring on her finger. She should have stopped fantasizing about Tommy when James made love to her. Francesca's eyelids shuttered close. She vowed to become a better wife. She'd put all thoughts of Tommy away.

Francesca took several cautious steps back when James walked into the bedroom.

"I slept in the guest room last night. I thought I'd give you space—from me."

Francesca said nothing.

"Did I do that?" James asked when he caught sight of the yellowing bruise she'd tried to hide under a layer of makeup.

Francesca said nothing.

"I'm sorry, Frankie. I'm so sorry for hurting you."

Francesca promised herself she wouldn't give James the satisfaction of crying. The bruises would heal in a few days, the deep scars he'd inflicted would take much longer.

"Please, look at me, Frankie. I need you to look at me so I can properly apologize to you." James waited for a beat to give Francesca the time to consider. When she turned, she shot him a look meant to wither a man. "I'm so sorry for what I did to you yesterday. You know that's not me."

Francesca heard the remorse in his voice, but she stood her ground. "It may not be who you are, but it's what you did."

"I know, and I ask for your forgiveness. It's just that... It drove me crazy when I saw the distant look in your eyes every time I made love to you when we were dating, but when I saw the same look after exchanging vows after we became husband and wife, I couldn't bear it anymore. In my mind, I can't help but think you wish I were him."

"I don't, James." Francesca lied with conviction and reaffirmed to herself she had no one to blame but herself for James' actions. "I was exhausted. Our wedding day was a long one, and we'd barely slept that night. Then the trip was even longer. By the time we got in, I was so tired, and when you turned to me the moment we got in, I didn't want to disappoint you. Like I didn't want to disappoint you on our wedding night. I just need some sleep. That's all it is."

James got a good look at Francesca, saw the swollen eyes, the fear in them, the pale face, and guilt balled in his stomach. "Why didn't you say so, Frankie? I'm sorry. I didn't realize I've been so physically demanding. It's just that I love being with you, and the thought of making love to my wife thrilled me. Promise me you'll be more forthcoming in the future. If this marriage is going to work, you have to tell me what's on your mind. Promise me you'll talk to me and tell me how you feel." James flashed a sincerity and a sweetness that reached deep into Francesca's tangled thoughts and frayed emotions to heal.

Calmer eyes swept over James. "I promise."

James offered his hand and waited for Francesca to take it. When Francesca eventually did, James walked her to the bed. "You get the rest you need," he said, pulling back the covers.

"But I thought you wanted to go into town today."

"We can do that another day. Right now, I want you to get some rest." James started to help her out of her T-shirt. When she let him, he proceeded to unhook her jeans and helped her into her nightie.

"Are you sure you don't mind, James?"

"Of course not. I only want what's best for you, Frankie. I always will." There was soft sympathy in his tone. "Don't worry about me. I'll have the kitchen staff whip me up some lunch. And for the rest of the day, I'll relax by the pool."

"If you're sure."

"I don't want to hear another word. You rest up for as long as you need." He covered her, and touching his lips to hers said, "I love you, Frankie."

"I know."

FRANCESCA WATCHED YOUNG SAMARIA STEP OUT of the guest room. Her luxuriously dark, shiny hair spilled around the pretty, heart-shaped face. "Good morning, Samaria," Francesca said, somewhat uneasy. She couldn't take back what innocent eyes had seen yesterday, nor could she explain the complexity of the situation.

Samaria jerked back several steps when the unexpected voice came at her. "*Madame*, bonjour."

Noting Samaria's agitation, Francesca gave her a sunny smile she hoped would telegraph all was fine. "I didn't mean to startle you. You're in early."

"*Oui*. Madame." Samaria's tone betrayed her discomfort.

How, Francesca wondered, was she to explain what she'd seen yesterday? "Everything is fine. Do you understand, Samaria?"

"*Oui,* I think so."

Francesca drew in a breath of relief. "Good. Do you know where Mr. Templeton is?"

Samaria pointed a finger to the closed bedroom door. "I, ah, take *Monsieur* Templeton towels. He says he take a shower," she said in an unusually loud voice.

"I needed to rest, and he slept in the guest room so he wouldn't disturb me," Francesca explained, stepping around Samaria, and just as she reached for the doorknob, James threw the door open. He wore nothing but a white towel wrapped low on his hips. His hair was tousled from sleep, and his eyes had a euphoric look to them.

"I heard your voice." James leaned in to peck Francesca on the cheek. "You look rested."

"I am." After their talk last night, Francesca slipped into a satisfying dreamless sleep and woke up refreshed.

"I was about to step into the shower. Come in and wait for me. We can go down to breakfast together." James stepped aside to let Francesca in.

"By the way, Samaria, you look pretty with your hair flowing loose. Don't you think she looks great, James?" Francesca urged James to agree hoping the compliment would paint him in a better light in Samaria's eyes.

"Yes, she certainly does," James said, and the moment Francesca walked into his bedroom whispered, "You looked great from behind too," giving Samaria's butt a suggestive squeeze.

The smile on Samaria's lips bloomed wide. "You are very kind for saying so, *Monsieur*," she said, reaching down to stroke his crotch and feeling him go hard. "Hmmm, nice. Too bad, I must go, but you call me anytime. And next time, five hundred dollars more gets you S&M, which I suspect you like." Samaria slipped her hand under James' towel, wrapped her hand around his steel-hard erection. "*Madame*, Monsieur, please let me know if you need anything," Samaria said, loud enough for her voice to carry into the bedroom.

"I will." James watched Samaria sway the tight butt that had given him such pleasure all night.

Twenty-One

SINCE HIS HEARTFELT apology, James was the perfect husband, and Francesca told herself no one needed to know about "the incident," and she told no one. It was a one-off, Francesca reasoned that had to be glossed over since she'd instigated it with her refusal to let go of Tommy. A marriage between two people and the ghost of a past lover did not make for a successful marriage. Regardless of how Francesca felt for James, he was her husband now, and he'd have to be the only man in her life. She had to put Tommy and their memories out of her mind. She had to focus on James if her marriage was to survive. And the moment they returned from their honeymoon, Francesca sank into her work. There were depositions to take, meetings to attend, and a stack of calls to return. Francesca had Jennifer book back to back appointments with potential clients. Between work and home, Francesca barely had time to breathe. As she hoped, keeping her mind busy kept thoughts of Tommy at bay.

Francesca stopped making the monthly call to Veterans Affairs. She stopped writing government officials for help tracking Tommy down. Francesca shredded all logs of her calls and conversations with Veterans Affairs and the "We regret" letters she'd received over the past five years.

"From your husband, for your three month anniversary." Jennifer breathed the scent of the red roses before setting them in the vase. "And these are your messages." Jennifer set those on Francesca's desk. "You're a lucky one to have such a romantic, thoughtful man. Not to mention gorgeous and successful."

Francesca set the law book she was scouring through on her desk. "I am lucky, aren't I?"

"I need to find myself a James. Someone who sends me flowers just because. Someone who plans our nights, and willingly goes clothes shopping with me as your James does to help pick out the perfect outfit. I'm so tired of doing all those things for myself, by myself. I need a James Templeton III. God, even his name sounds sexy. Does he have a brother?"

"Sorry, he's an only child."

"A friend?" Jennifer poured water into the vase, rearranged the roses.

"I can ask, but have you met Bart Risk? The young, handsome grad we just brought on."

Jennifer reached deep into her memory. "Is he the one with the green eyes and dark, shaggy hair?"

"That's the one. He's handsome, and rumor has it available. Better yet, I've seen the way he looks at you. There's definite interest there."

"Really? I never noticed it."

"You never noticed him walking past your desk more than he should or eyeing you the entire time he does." Jennifer shook her head. "That's your problem. You're too focused on your work. Not that I'm discouraging it, but you need to pay closer attention if you're ever going to..."

"Reel one in." Jennifer finished.

"Sure, that works." Francesca rose, walked to the bar cart, and poured herself a glass of water.

"Hmm, Bart Risk. He is cute." On further consideration, Jennifer said, "I think I will pursue the Bart Risk avenue."

Francesca surveyed the petite blonde, with the long, lashed eyes that were as blue as the sky and the shapely body she hid under the ultra-conservative suits. "May I make a few suggestions?"

"You know you can." Jennifer took one of the guest chairs when Francesca gestured her to sit.

"Your thick, honey-golden hair should be flowing around your face, not tied into a granny-bun. And you have a body that shouldn't be hidden under layers of gabardine."

"A granny-bun?" Jennifer glanced up at Francesca as she brought a hand to her head. "But this is a professional office."

"Sorry about the granny-bun comment. And it is an office, but it's not a convent. You can show a few curves and wear your hair loose. I'm going to make an appointment with my hairdresser, and you're what, a size six?" Francesca guessed, and Jennifer nodded. "I'm going to bring you a handful of my outfits. If you don't feel comfortable wearing them, you don't have to."

"Of course, I wouldn't feel uncomfortable. You're very stylish, but I mean, they're probably expensive, and I can't..."

"You can and you will, and I don't want to hear another word." Francesca raised a finger when Jennifer opened her mouth. "One last thing. When things work out between you and Bart, could you not make it too obvious? You know how my father frowns on office romance."

Jennifer gave Francesca a brisk nod. "They're the spawn of the devil." She thought of poor Shyla and Bob from the mailroom who personnel walked out the door when they were found canoodling in the supply closet at the Christmas party. "I'll keep it on the QT, and, Frankie, thanks."

"It's my pleasure and the least I can do for everything you've done for me." Aside from Lily, whom Francesca spoke to on their weekly telephone call, and Missy whom she kept in touch with, Jennifer was the closest thing she had to a friend.

Jennifer walked her stunned self to the door, paused with her hand on the knob. "I can't wait for you to take over this company. Not that your dad isn't a brilliant man, but it's time for a woman to take the helm."

Francesca gave her a twinkling grin. "Can't argue with you there."

"Oh, I almost forgot. You should return Noah Mulligan's call. It's the top message. I think you'll be interested in what he has to say." Jennifer pointed out before returning to her desk.

FRANCESCA HAD LEARNED never to underestimate her legal assistant's intuition, and Noah Mulligan's case was no exception. Her conversation with the man released from jail four months ago on a hefty fifty thousand dollar bail, who'd fired two prominent attorneys, and ultimately called her, piqued her interest. Noah Mulligan's case was a defense lawyer's dream. It had everything careers were built on—if she won. Regardless of the histrionics between Noah Mulligan and his former attorneys, Francesca's gut feeling told her she could win it for him. She told Noah Mulligan as much when she agreed to take him on as a client.

As Francesca made her way to the meeting table, she focused her gaze out the unblinded window. Bright sunlight spilled over the city. In the distance, Francesca saw a gaggle of Canada geese crossing a clear blue sky in V formation. Pouring herself a cup of coffee, Francesca settled in at her round meeting table and reached for the top folder. Opening the folder, Francesca read Jennifer's report on Noah Mulligan's police statement.

Noah Mulligan was thirty-five, and Elsie—the wife he was accused of choking to death—was twenty-seven at the time of death. Married for five years, they had no children.

Elsie Mulligan, born Tremblay, was the heiress to the Tremblay media empire. As the only daughter of Baron and Marguerite Tremblay on their death, Elsie stood to inherit the whole enchilada—Jennifer's wording—worth in the vicinity of fifty million dollars. Until then, Elsie had a very generous trust fund worth in the range of eight million dollars, which daddy gave her when she turned twenty-one.

That piece of information was new to Francesca, and her brow raised in interest. For a brief moment, sipping coffee, Francesca mulled that over. The case was becoming more interesting by the minute. Francesca made a couple of notes on the margin of the report before reading on.

On June fifteenth, the Mulligan's maid went up to Elsie's bedroom. She and Noah Mulligan slept in separate rooms. (I don't know what it is about rich people and separate rooms.) Jennifer wrote in brackets. Francesca made a note for Jennifer in red ink: As much I appreciate the editorial comments others reading, the report may not be as acquiescent.

Frida, the maid, Francesca read on, went up at around noon, which was when Elsie started her day. With lunch in hand, Frida opened Elsie's bedroom door to find her splayed on her bed. Frida called out Elsie's name several times, but she didn't respond, which was unusual for her. Frida claimed Elsie was a demanding woman who needed attention from the moment she woke until she passed out at night.

When Elsie didn't answer Frida's call, she crossed to the bed. Frida stated that Elsie's silk knight gown was riding high up her body, and her panties were on the floor. Once Frida got close enough, she described Elsie as looking pale to the point of translucent and her eyes wide open like an owl's. Sensing she was staring in the eyes of death, Frida dropped the food tray and ran out of the room, screaming for Noah.

That matched to Noah's deposition, Francesca concluded flipping to the next page.

Noah Mulligan ran upstairs, and when Frida told him what she'd seen, he told her to stay in the hallway and went into the room. Jennifer made a notation questioning why Noah didn't tell Frida at that point to call for the police. Jennifer didn't know what Francesca did, which was that Noah claimed Elsie had a cocaine dependency they and the household staff kept hidden from everyone—even her parents. If Elsie was passed out on a high was something Noah would have wanted to keep concealed, Francesca reasoned, and aside from Frida, Noah, and Francesca, no one knew.

Reaching for the red ink pen, Francesca made a notation in the margin: The medical examiner found coke in Elsie's system, but not enough to knock her out. They did find petechiae and finger marks the size of a man's hands-on Elsie's neck, she added.

Francesca reached into the folder, pulled out the enlarged photographs of Elsie's neck, and spread them on the table. What she saw was consistent with strangulation, but the police report stated there was no sign of a struggle. There were no broken fingernails or skin under them, proving there was a struggle. An odd outcome, Francesca thought since anyone being strangled, even for someone as petite as Elsie, the typical human reaction would be to fight back. And a woman would scratch and kick, but they found no skin under her nails, no injuries on her feet.

"Either Elsie knew her assailant, or it was rough sex gone wrong," Francesca thought out loud.

"Wow, how damaged do you have to be when you need to be strangled to get sexual satisfaction?" The quick flash of surprise in Jennifer's eyes mirrored in her voice.

Francesca couldn't help but smile at the stunned look on Jennifer's face. "There are people who are into S&M or erotic asphyxiation where you intentionally restrict oxygen flow to the brain for the sole purposes of increasing sexual stimulation. I've been reading up on the reason for being choked during sex." Francesca clarified when Jennifer's brows winged high. "Is that for me?"

"I figured you'd be hungry." Jennifer set the salad and ice tea on the table. She donned a pale blue high waist sheath dress—one of the many dresses Francesca gifted her—and her hair now trimmed into a short bob was highlighted blonder. Lance was an artist when it came to hair. Her eyes were lightly shaded in bronze makeup, and her lips glossed pink. Jennifer looked beautiful and confident.

"I'm starving," Francesca said, taking a forkful of salad. "Grab your salad and join me."

"So, you don't think it was suicide, as Noah Mulligan claims?" Jennifer said, walking back into the office with her Cobb salad and taking the chair across Francesca.

Shaking her head, Francesca reached for the roll, slathered it with butter.

"She choked in a moment of passion? Is that going to be your defense?

Francesca crossed one slender leg over another. "It's one option I'm considering. From my research, it's not as uncommon as you think."

"I'm all for adventure in the bedroom, but Christ, this does take it to another level. God, there are depraved people out there, aren't there? I'm guessing that if she was into that type of sexual deviance, it wasn't her or her assailant's first rodeo. People into that stuff aren't novices. I mean who says to themselves, 'hey let me try choking you so you can have a better orgasm.'"

"That is something to consider." Francesca never thought of it in those terms, and her mind flashed back to James and "the incident." Could it have been a one-off? James hadn't asked her to do anything as unorthodox in the bedroom again or been rough with her. Still, Francesca couldn't help but wonder if he'd tamed things because of her. "What is it, Jennifer?" Francesca asked when she watched Jennifer contemplatively running her fork through her salad.

Working out just how to approach it, Jennifer remained silent for a moment. "If I tell you, you have to promise me to protect my friend, Frankie."

"You know I will do what I can. What is it?"

"She can't lose her job. As much of an asshole as the medical examiner is, she needs to keep her job. She makes good money working for Dr. Sampson's office."

Francesca rested a hand on Jennifer's. "I promise you I will protect her."

"Cindy, that's my friend's name, is Dr. Sampson's secretary and a friend from secretarial school. We do lunch once every few weeks. During our lunch this week, I mentioned we'd taken on the Mulligan case. It was when she told me." Jennifer's head cocked. "You have to promise, Frankie."

"Jennifer, please."

"She told me Elsie was raped."

Francesca's brows pressed together in what looked like reflective puzzlement and dropping her fork with a thud, reached for the medical examiner's report. "There's no mention of rape—anywhere," she said, after flipping through it.

"I know. She told me they had her delete it from the final report. She couldn't make sense as to why they'd ask her to remove such a critical piece of information, but who was she to question anyone. She told me the request had to have come from high up the food chain. You can't make a change like that, willy-nilly."

"Yes, that's correct." Excitement flashed into Francesca's eyes. "Has Cindy told anyone other than you?"

"No, she wouldn't jeopardize her job."

"You sure she won't tell anyone." Francesca looked at Jennifer for confirmation.

Jennifer shook her head. "She loves money too much, and I'm her only gossip-buddy. She trusts me to keep it locked in the vault."

"Let's hope so. Excellent work, Jennifer. Note this on paper." Francesca turned over pen and paper. "Have Lamont see if he can come up with the rape information. Specify under no circumstances is he to question the ME or his staff during his investigation. Also, it's my understanding Noah Mulligan wasn't a wealthy man when they married. See if Lamont can dig into his spending habits, gambling, women, that sort of thing." Francesca rose to pace the office. She thought better on her feet.

"I don't expect him to find anything, but I don't want any surprises in court. Have them check on how he stands to benefit financially from Elsie's death. You know wills, bank accounts. Have them check as to whether there's a prenup, legal documents drafted that were never signed off on. If my hunch is right, Mr. Baron Tremblay has to be concerned right now."

"I'll get it done right away." Jennifer finished making the notations. "You know, Frankie, this is going to be a high profile case. It's going to become part of the daily news cycle for weeks. It's going to be one monumental circus."

"I know. It's why I have to make sure no stone is left unturned, and I have nothing but the facts."

THE RAIN CONTINUED INTO THE WET, gloomy, windswept morning its pattering sound, the boom of thunder, always translated into romance for Francesca. Today that wasn't the case. Today the bleak weather sounded as dreary as she felt deep inside. Staring at her reflection in the mirror, Francesca ran fingers over the swollen, darkening bruise on her right cheek, and she decided not to go into the office. Francesca could conceal the bruises on her arms where James had gripped tight and the back when he'd tossed her against the door. She could put away those on her ego and heart, but the one on her face where he'd punched her was too deep and dark to be camouflaged behind makeup.

Francesca questioned herself, her judgment. How could she be so stupid? She had to fill her boots, put her ego ahead of everything that she'd overlooked doing thorough research on the Noah Mulligan case. Like James had said in the moment of rage she'd now rather forget: Did she think she was a better attorney than him? She wasn't. If she were, she'd have anticipated James was the prosecuting attorney.

Francesca slid a close glance at her reflection in the bathroom mirror. How could she go up against James? Against her husband? It was her fault she was in the situation she was in. It was her fault James reacted as he had.

Gingerly dabbing concealer on her face, the worst thought of all came to Francesca. Jesus! What if she won? The image of that deranged look in James' eyes flashed in Francesca's mind, and cold, hard panic snaked through her. The fear sprang hot in Francesca at what James might do to her if she beat him in court.

Francesca had no option but to lose the case.

But how could she, in good conscience, send an innocent man to jail, Francesca reasoned? Based on the information she had, Noah Mulligan was an innocent man. Francesca debated whether to break protocol and disclose her solicitor-client communiqué to James. She could be disbarred, but so be it. Francesca could make a plea bargain and settle out of court. That was an option to consider, but one Francesca concluded James would dismiss. James would find a plea bargain a sign of weakness, of being handed the case.

The terror and dread choked her. James was going to kill her.

Francesca ran her hands over her face, through the mussed hair James had pulled until she thought it would separate from its root. Feeling small, defeated, Francesca turned away from the reflection in the mirror.

"How did I get here?" Francesca asked the question out loud as her eyes began to swim.

No answer.

Francesca's body as limp as her resolve, she picked up Bear, tip-toed out of the bedroom and down the stairs. Seeing James' briefcase missing from the foyer made the ice-edged panic in her wane and picking up her keys and purse, she ran out of the house.

She was going home.

Twenty-Two

FATIGUE WEIGHING DOWN on Francesca, she wrapped herself in a thick throw and with Bear in tow, walked onto the terrace. The familiar, comforting scents of her youth came at her through the crisp fall day. Francesca breathed them in, let them soothe her. This was precisely where she needed to be.

Taking a seat at the patio table, she and cast eyes to the grove. Trees were crowned in the golds and russets, scarlets and bronzes, of fall their leaves fluttering in a crisp wind laced with the scent of the incoming winter. The cool breeze caressing her face, Francesca closed her eyes and let the memories she'd pushed to the back of her mind come.

Love ran over Francesca's battered face when the memories came to her as vividly as if it happened seconds ago. Francesca reached deeper for memories of Tommy's smile, the feel of his arms around her, his mouth on hers. A smile came to Francesca's face when she thought of their first date, sitting on the hood of Tommy's old, dusty truck watching the stars. It was the best night of her life. It was the night she'd fallen in love with Tommy.

Tommy would never hurt her. Never.

"Missy told me you were out here." Peter startled Francesca out of her thoughts. "I didn't think you and James were stopping by until tomorrow."

"I'm here alone. James's at work." Francesca took the offered wine glass. "I'm playing hooky from work today. I needed some me-time. I thought you and Tiffani were in the Bahamas." She steered the conversation away from her.

"We came back early. Tiffani got severe sunburn—everywhere." Peter's playful grin made Francesca smile when she did, she winced. "Are you all right, Frankie?"

Raising fingers to caress her heavily powdered cheek, she said, "I'm fine. I just felt a chill for a moment."

Peter slid a glance over his daughter. "I heard you took on the Mulligan case."

Francesca bent down to pick up Bear, set him on her lap. "Yes, I did."

"Were you aware that James was the prosecuting counselor when you did?"

"Yes." Francesca hugged Bear tightly.

Peter took a long sip of his drink as he studied his daughter's face. "Does James know you're the defending counsel?"

Francesca thought of the bruises on her cheek, arms, and back. She felt the tight-fisted punch he'd driven to her ribs. She envisaged James' dark, piercing gaze, which had shot her heart to her throat and made her fear for her life. Absently, she rubbed a hand there, left it to rest as if guarding herself against James' choking grasp.

"Yes, we talked it out, and he's good with it." Francesca drank wine to wash the nasty taste of lie from her mouth. "I'm sorry. I know this puts a wrench in your plans. Now you'll have to wait until we finish working the case to offer him a seat on the board of directors."

"Don't worry about that. This will be the case of the century. Husband and wife, Templeton versus Templeton who come to oppose each other in court while living under the same roof. Do you know the publicity this will garner our firm? I hope you never forget that you're a Thompson, and you kick Templeton ass." James raised his glass to Francesca, drank deep.

Her father, always spinning everything to his benefit, Francesca thought. "I'll do what I can," Francesca said because how could she tell him that for her safety, she was mulling the idea of throwing the case.

THE MOMENT PETER SET OFF TO his downtown apartment, Francesca got into her car and went for a drive. She needed to clear her muddled head. She needed to put last night's attack out of her mind. For an hour, Francesca drove.

Tires crunching over rural roads, the splattering rain had turned slick, and muddy Francesca drove past cozy homes painted in pastel colors with white shutters and wraparound porches. Francesca rolled by apple orchards heavy with fruit, fields layered in cabbage and pumpkins, dotted with golden hay bales. Cows grazed over green grass mist over with dew, and horses lazed.

When the road twisted ahead, Francesca caught sight of the St. Elizabeth's cross rising heavenward. Feeling the unexpected tug, she veered toward it. She couldn't remember the last time she'd been to church. Father Albert wasn't going to be pleased by that, Francesca thought, and he wasn't one to hold back on sharing his feelings. Although he'd lecture her about neglecting her spiritual obligation to herself and her God, he'd welcome her with open arms, and right now, she needed was someone to talk to. Father Albert would give her a listening ear and the comfort she needed.

Walking into St. Elizabeth's, the scent of burning candles and incense came at Francesca. Colorful stained windows, which on a sunny day, were a beacon of light and brought the church to life looked just as she remembered. The stream of music from the organ filled the peaceful silence and the smell the fresh flowers hung in the air. Crossing herself, Francesca proceeded to walk down the aisle to the back, past the narrow hallway to the vestry where she hoped to find Father Albert.

The door to his office was wide opened as she expected it to be. Father Albert insisted on it because, according to him, his church and heart were always open to everyone. Francesca gave a light wrap on the door before walking in.

The room was empty, the sign on the desk read: SIT YOURSELF DOWN. BE BACK IN FIVE.

Francesca sat down and waited.

At the sound of the approaching footsteps, Francesca rose, swirled toward the door. Her eyes fixed on the man arched at the doorway in the long-sleeved, black robe with the clerical collar. For a long while, speechless, dazed, and shocked Francesca stare.

His lips curved into a friendly smile. "May I help you?"

Hearing the voice, Francesca felt herself sway, and her vision went gray and hazy. For a long moment, Francesca found herself unable to speak. "You're not Father Albert," she said when she found her voice.

"No, I'm his replacement, Father…"

The sound of his voice drove Francesca's pulse to gallop so fast she could barely breathe. Her knees didn't buckle they evaporated, and she fell to the floor.

Twenty-Three

FRANCESCA'S HAND TIGHTENING on the glass of water he'd poured for her she drank.

"Are you all right?" At her silent nod, he walked past her and rounded his desk to take a seat.

"You may have a bump surface where you hit your head."

Her breath steadier, her nerves calmer now Francesca said, "I'm fine."

"I don't think I've seen you in church before. Are you new to the area?"

Francesca furrowed brows in confusion. Although the lines on his face leaned more towards dashing than aging, he was older, more mature. A vertical scar marred his chin, and the one above his eye sliced through his eyebrow. His dark, thick flyaway hair was now short and neatly combed back. His steel-blue eyes were wiser, and he was thinner, but it was Tommy. Her Tommy.

The gnawing shock, relief, and excitement fluttering in Francesca's stomach like a swinging pendulum, she said, "Tommy, it's me. Francesca."

"I'm Father Matthew, not Father Tommy. I've met most of Father Albert's parishioners in the past two months, but I don't recall meeting you." He settled back into his chair. "You seem upset. Are you all right, Francesca?"

Francesca's stunned eyes traveled over Tommy's face. "You've been in town for two months, just a couple of miles from my home, and you never thought to look me up?" Her voice broke.

The hurt swirling inside her came too fast and too hard, punched her like a fist to the stomach. It felt like crushing despair. Why wouldn't Tommy look her up? She'd mourned his loss all these years, and he didn't want to see her. Why, why wouldn't he? He'd told her he loved her. Francesca sat back, closed her eyes.

"I'm sorry, Francesca, bur Father Albert never left instructions to look you up."

Francesca opened her eyes, glanced up at Tommy with disbelief. "You have to be told to look me up?"

Father Matthew brushed over the obvious spiking anger in her voice. "Well, I'm new in the area, so, for now, I could only go by Father Albert's instructions."

Disappointment robbing Francesca of speech, she pushed to her feet and paced the office before stopping at the window. Dew clung to the panes in beads. The garden was infused with fall colors from chrysanthemums in glorious bloom. A lush carpet of sweet alyssum in shades of white and pink covered the ground. Lemon-yellow goldenrod and purple flowers and silvery-green foliage from Russian sage popped with color. No doubt, Tommy had a hand in its design.

Francesca turned, her gaze cutting straight to Father Matthew. "You don't know who I am, do you?"

Father Matthew's eyes calm and level on her, he said, "Of course I do. You're Francesca."

The smile on her lips bloomed. "Yes, that's right. I'm Francesca."

Father Matthew curiously stared at Francesca. "Yes, you are. You just told me so."

Cold washed over Francesca, and she wrapped arms around herself when she put it together. "You have no idea who I am."

"Difficult to know someone I've just met."

Francesca's thin shoulders hunched when the realization that Tommy had no memory of her hit her. Why? How? They'd spent a summer together. How did you forget someone you've told you loved? How could Tommy forget her? Francesca asked herself over and over.

A head injury or post-traumatic stress, Francesca concluded. That's what was affecting Tommy. Over the years she'd searched for Tommy, she'd read about soldiers sustaining traumatic injuries and losing their memory. That was why she couldn't find him, why no one could, Francesca reasoned. Tommy Scott was lost. He was now Father Matthew.

"If you're up to it, we can get to know each other. As a new priest to the area, I like to get to know my parishioners." Father Matthew felt the instant pull that overcomes a man at the sound of a crying woman. "Are you all right, Francesca?"

"I'm sorry, Tom ... Father Matthew. It's been a long couple of days." Francesca's eyes swam when she lifted them to his face.

Father Matthew would have asked about the gash that became visible when the tears that sprang from Francesca's eyes washed the makeup away stood out stark against her pale skin, but thought best not to. Father Matthew surmised there were other bruises on her body, but Francesca's state of mind was too fragile for questions. He'd have to gain her trust before delving into something he sensed led down a dark rabbit hole.

"I'm sorry you've had such a rough time, Francesca. Would you like to talk about it?" Father Matthew handed her a tissue. "You know life is full of interruptions and complications, but that's what I'm here for," he said when she hesitated.

Recognizing the words, Francesca lifted the tear-stained face to Father Matthew with newfound hope in her eyes. "Do you know who said that?"

Father Matthew shook his head. "But it's very profound and so apt, don't you think?"

Francesca started to tell him they were his mother's word, but when she looked deep into the blue eyes, they weren't Tommy's. They belonged to a stranger she didn't know. Francesca felt the wind knocked out of her for the second time in twenty-four hours. Feeling defeated, tired, and alone, Francesca tipped back her head and closed her eyes.

"I think I need to go now." The words slid soundlessly from Francesca's mouth as she ran out of the office.

FRANCESCA PULLED THE BLANKET OVER HER head when Missy walked into her bedroom. Since her return from St. Elizabeth's last night, in bed, with Bear by her side, was where she'd been brooding, and wallowing in self-pity

Although Tommy hadn't recognized her, although he was lost, a stranger to her, he'd stirred feelings in Francesca that made her realize how much in love she still was with him. Francesca thought of James and guilt, the overwhelming weight of it, smothered her. How would she feel if James was focused on another woman? Or if his heart belonged to another while they shared a bed? Maybe, just maybe the feeling of rejection she inflicted manifested itself into the violence James visited on her, Francesca rationalized.

What was she to do now that Tommy—or the man she knew as Tommy—was back in her life? Francesca asked herself. Tommy didn't know who she was or how much they'd meant to one another. Tommy wasn't the man she knew. He was a priest now.

Life was full of interruptions and complications, and regardless of the challenges, Francesca wasn't about to let Tommy slip out of her life, not again. She'd waited too long for him, and she wasn't going to let him go.

"No use hiding under the covers. I've already seen the gash on your cheek, Frankie." Crossing to the burgundy curtains, Missy threw them open to let the morning sunshine in. "I won't press you on it because I sense you're not ready to talk about it, but I can guess how it got there."

Missy lifted a hand, palm out, to stop Francesca from talking when she opened her mouth. "Don't insult my intelligence by denying it. That was what you were about to do, isn't it?"

Sighing, Francesca appeared from under the covers, sat up in bed. "It's nothing."

Missy felt the quick jolt of anger, then pity, and sadness. Her anger quickly surged again when she came closer and got a better glimpse of the purpling gash on Francesca's cheek. "That sonofabitch did that, didn't he?" When Francesca raised a humiliated hand to her cheek to conceal the cut. Missy's eyes flicked to the purpling man's hand imprint on Francesca's upper arm. Guessing there was a match beneath her left arm sleeve, Missy set off into a swearing tirade that sent Bear hiding beneath the bed cover.

"He did that too, didn't he? What else did he do?" At Francesca's silent stare, Missy set off into a more colorful swearing rant complete with hands curled into fists that wanted to inflict as much pain as she imagined Francesca had endured. "I could kill that cowardly, sonofabitch. That bastard, that…"

"Was there a reason why you came up?" Pressing fingers to her aching temples, Francesca jumped in.

"I'm not just your maid, Frankie. I'm your friend. You know you can talk to me." Missy walked back a couple of Tylenol and a glass of water from the bathroom, watched Francesca toss pills and water back. "I promise I won't go off on you. I've gotten it out of my system now—mostly." Missy rested a hand on Francesca's. "No one deserves this. And you deserve better, Frankie."

"I brought this on myself. I should never have married James. I don't love him as much as…"

"Tommy." Missy finished.

Francesca shook her head. "I was going to say as much as he deserves to be loved, and he senses it, Missy. This is my fault."

"No, it's not, Frankie. No one had the right to lay a hand on you."

Francesca dabbed at her eyes with the tissue Missy handed her. "You don't know everything."

Missy sat at the edge of the bed. "Then tell me."

"I'm not ready to, but only because it's best, I don't involve you."

"You don't need to worry about me, but whether me or someone else, you need to talk to someone, Frankie. You need to talk about it. More importantly, you need to understand this is not your fault."

Francesca hugged Missy. "Thank you for saying so and being such a good friend." Gratitude gushed from her voice.

"You're welcome. You can come out now, baby. Auntie Missy won't be swearing at the top of her lungs anymore." Missy flipped the bedsheet off Bear. Ears up, head slightly cocked, Bear watched Missy, and after a few seconds of consideration, bounded toward her open arms. "There's nothing like the love of a gutless dog," she said, kissing him.

The tender moment shared between Missy and Bear made Francesca smile for the first time in days. "Why did you come up, Missy?"

"Oh yeah, I forgot. Father Matthew from St. Elizabeth's is here to see you."

Francesca's heart pounded into her ribs. "He's here?"

"Downstairs. He wouldn't say what it's about."

Francesca paused for a beat. "He's here?"

"Yes, in the living room. Waiting."

Tommy came looking for me. He remembered where to find me, Francesca thought to herself, and scrambling out of bed, she sprinted to the closet.

"I didn't know you knew him. If you ask me, he's too pretty to be wasted as a priest. Anyway, make yourself decent. I'll bring in tea and a plate of scones when you're ready. And I'll get you a treat," Missy said to Bear, getting herself a lick of appreciation.

"Do you think you can round up lemonade and oatmeal cookies instead?"

"I can." Missy's brows shot up when Francesca rifled through her closet for the perfect outfit. "Jeans and a T-shirt would suit the priest just fine."

Francesca ignored Missy.

"What are you up to, Frankie?"

"Who says I'm up to anything?" Francesca loosened her hair out of the ponytail and letting it spill finger brushed it.

"That silk, low buttoned shirt and those slim-fitting Jeans you've slipped into tells me you're up to something. You know he's a priest. A celibate priest."

Francesca slanted a look over her shoulder. "Don't let that imagination of yours run off into some deep, dark hole."

"Right, my imagination," Missy murmured, staring at the face that had turned from miserable to glowing.

"Please let him know I'll be down shortly. I just need a few minutes to make myself presentable." Francesca called out from the bathroom.

"And, don't forget to dab lots of foundation on that gash to cover up those bruises." And whatever other bruises there are.

"Right." Shrugging out of her nightgown, Francesca dressed, dabbed loads of foundation on her cheek, and ran gloss on her lips. And taking one last look at her reflection in the mirror, headed downstairs.

Father Matthew rose to his feet. "Good afternoon, Francesca. I hope I'm not intruding."

Tommy's smile sprinkled light throughout the room, bringing it to life, Francesca thought, and she couldn't help but stare. In that instant, she saw him like the Tommy she knew. Francesca wanted to reach for his hand, feel his arms around her.

"Of course not. Please, have a seat."

He was pleased to see her more upbeat. "And who's this little fellow?" Father Matthew delighted Bear with head scratches when Francesca set him on the sofa between them.

"This is Bear. Say hello to Father Matthew."

Father Matthew's dimples flickered when Bear offered his paw. "You're one smart dog."

"Lemonade and oatmeal cookies," Missy announced, walking into the living room unannounced.

"My favorites." Father Matthew reached for a cookie, found it warm and toasty. Just out of the oven, he thought. Nothing beats home cooking. He missed *Signora* Capitano's cooking. "How did you know, Missy?"

"I didn't. It was Frankie's idea. How do you suppose she'd know?" Missy's eyebrows shot up suspiciously toward Francesca as she hefted the lemonade jug and poured two glasses.

"I'll take it from here, Missy." Francesca subtly lifted her chin toward the door.

"Mmm-hmm," Missy hummed, making her exit.

Francesca turned to Father Matthew when the door closed behind Missy. "It's nice of you to look me up."

"I needed to see you." The lemonade was tart, swimming with pulp. Also, homemade Father Matthew thought-feeling that prodding sense of familiarity since he'd arrived at St. Elizabeth's.

"You did?" Francesca's beaming smile left Father Matthew, staring at her.

The large hazel eyes, the chestnut hair that fountained over the beautiful face, the broad smile beneath the rosy cheekbones stirred something in Father Matthew. A spark of recognition came over him, and he dug deep into his memory. Nothing came to him.

"When you ran off yesterday, you left this in my office." Father Matthew turned Francesca's purse over. "I'm sorry, but I had to go through your wallet to get your address." He didn't tell her about feeling the nagging sense of familiarity when he had.

An unbearable sadness weighed down on Francesca's heart. "You're here to return my purse and for no other reason?"

Father Matthew's matter-of-fact nod felt like a twisted knife in Francesca's heart. "I figured you'd need it. I've been told losing a purse is like losing a limb for most women."

Tommy had slipped away from her again. To have him so near and yet so far.

"Yes, thank you for bringing it by." Francesca Picked up her discarded glass of lemonade, took a quick sip to wet the mouth that had gone bone dry.

"Well, I should get going."

"Don't," Francesca blurted out when Father Matthew started to push off the sofa. "I mean, stay for lunch. A thank you. I, ah, I can have Missy round up something light. A sandwich and salad."

When Father Matthew mulled his response for too long, her eyes deepened with a plea of need he couldn't rebuff. "I'd like that. We can get to know each other better," Father Matthew said, garnering a smile that lit the room.

TO KEEP THEM FROM PRYING EYES, and listening ears, Francesca had Missy serve lunch in the dining room. Over Monte Cristo sandwiches and Caesar salad while Francesca injected names such as Mrs. O'Sullivan, and Scott's Garden Center into the conversation. Francesca mentioned Nick's Burgers, the boardwalk, and Musselman Lake, but nothing triggered the reaction Francesca hoped for in Father Matthew.

"They sound like interesting places." Father Matthew scanned the room bright with sunshine spilling through the large bay window.

Sunflowers speared from the Waterford vase on the buffet table. Mahogany furniture and wood floors shone to a perfect polish. French doors opened to the slate terrace, which stretched the length of the house. It was a room meant for family gatherings. It was a room that set off that nagging sense of familiarity that had hit him since arriving at St. Elizabeth's.

"My mother loved this room. She wanted to fill it with children, but as fate would have it, I ended up being her only child. You don't smoke?" Francesca asked, pouring coffee.

"It's a nasty habit," he said, and she smiled at that. "And I'm sure your mother still enjoys the room, the home. It's a stunning place." Tommy had often told her it was too big, too cold.

"Mom passed away when I was a young girl."

"I'm sorry, Francesca."

Yours did too, Francesca wanted to remind him. "There's a creek that winds through the grove and runs through the property," she said when Father Matthew walked to the window and cast eyes to the grove. She remained hopeful when she thought he looked reflective.

"It's a beautiful property."

A compliment, Francesca thought, feeling limp. All she got was a compliment. Determined not to give up, she said, "If you like, I can take you to some of the places I've mentioned. You know, since you're new to the area."

"I'd like that."

Francesca's eyes kindled. "Good. I'm free this weekend and at your disposal," she offered knowing James or her father wouldn't set foot on the estate.

"I'll check my calendar, and I'll call you."

For the rest of the day, Francesca anxiously waited by the telephone.

Twenty-Four

FRANCESCA'S GRIN SPREAD when she saw Tommy. His blue eyes were curved into the familiar smile. Even in his black cassock—the constant reminder of his religious pledge—Francesca thought Tommy looked striking.

Stopping her car in front of St. Elizabeth's, Francesca shifted to park and watched Tommy come down the steps. "I hope you haven't been waiting long."

"Six on the nose." Father Matthew slid his six-foot frame into the passenger seat. "You're punctual. If I may say, and this is in no way meant as a sexist remark, but that's a rarity for a woman."

Turning on Rutherford, she said, "Maybe, I'm a rare woman."

Tommy's smiling eyes flicked to Francesca's. "I hope Nick's Burgers is as good as you say. I've been craving a burger since I called you this afternoon."

"Then, you're in for a treat." Francesca pointed out the window. "Over there is Scott's Garden Center. The best greenhouse for miles."

The new owners had updated the sign. It was more colorful and larger now, but it still bore the SCOTT'S GARDEN CENTER name. Francesca gauged Tommy's reaction when he aimed eyes out the window. Nothing.

"Good to know. I enjoy gardening. I'll go as far as tooting my own horn and saying that I have quite the green thumb."

"I know."

"You do?" Father Matthew's brows drew together, and that vertical crease between them she'd seen so many times before formed.

"You, ah, gave yourself away when you named, by their Latin names no less, many of the plants in my garden."

"Are you telling me I need to stop showing off?" Father Matthew breathed the scent of her Chanel perfume flowing in the car. Sweet, memorable, he thought. It set off that nagging sense of familiarity he'd had since arriving in the city.

"I'm a pious girl. I'd never do that."

His grin flashing Father Matthew took in the signs rolling by. Sidewalks teemed with crowds looking for good food and entertainment. There was a lineup at the Main Street Theater for the seven o'clock showing of Road to Rio with Bob Hope. Mamma's Pizza and The Cave brimmed with diners. Tommy watched Mel's Cleaners and The Shoe Repair shop roll by. It triggered that familiar nagging feeling in him.

"Do you dabble in gardening?"

"I mainly puttered with a friend of mine. He was a whizz in the garden. He owned Scott's Garden Center." Francesca gave each word separate weight but got no reaction from him. Francesca breathed in for calm as she turned onto Steeles. Traffic was heavy, and as much as she could have gone through the side streets, she insisted on following the same route she and Tommy often took. "He's the one who introduced me to Nick's Burgers."

Father Matthew saw Francesca's eyes turn melancholy. "He sounds like someone important to you."

It's you, she screamed in her head, but I can't tell you because I'm afraid of scaring you away, and I can't deal with that. Not right now. I need you, Tommy. I need you more than ever right now. "He was."

"Was?"

"He enlisted and went overseas, and he ... changed. Everything changed." Was the best way she could put it.

"So much changed when he did. You know, after the war, nothing's the same anymore."

Father Matthew heard the bitterness in her tone and vowed to smooth those rough edges causing her so much pain. "I'm sorry, Francesca."

"My friends call me Frankie, and you have nothing to be sorry about. It's like you say, life is full of interruptions and complications."

"It is, and I like Francesca."

Francesca sounds exotic, European, sexy, Tommy had told her.

"What's your friend's name?"

"Tommy."

"You called me Tommy the first time we met."

"You look like him. And here we are," Francesca said before he could get another word out.

"This looks and smells interesting," he said, taking in the cool evening air painted with the scents of grilled meat and everything that was Nick's Burgers. Above him, the awning with the string of colorful lights looked cheerily bright under the night sky. In the background, Nick, in his thick, Greek accent, called out orders to his cooks.

"Does it remind you of anything?" Francesca asked when she thought she saw a flash of recognition in his eyes.

When he said, "Yes, it does," Francesca's face flushed with excitement. "It reminds me of how much I've missed a good hamburger."

Disappointment reached up and grabbed Francesca by the throat, but she forged on. "You grab us a table, and I'll go put our order in."

Several of the diners, parishioners of St. Elizabeth's, waved at Father Matthew. He stopped at their tables, exchange sociable words. A young couple offered him their table as they rose to leave.

"Hamburger, onion rings, and a chocolate milkshake." Father Matthew reached for an onion ring. "All favorites of mine."

I know. "Mine too." Francesca spread the food before them, set the tray aside. "How's your hamburger?"

"It's as good as you said it would be." Father Matthew stared at her when a soft wind fluttered through her hair. A quick, flash of recall came at him but swiftly faded.

"Is something wrong?" Francesca asked when she thought she saw the same spark of recognition in his eyes she'd seen earlier.

"May I ask you something?" Father Matthew watched Francesca set her hamburger down and focus her attention on him. "Why did you come to see me on Thursday? I can't help but think there was an underlying reason for your visit." Tommy watched Francesca stiffen. "You know you can talk to me about anything."

When he rested his hand on hers, Francesca's brain staggered under his touch, and the flashing images burned into her memory came fast. She saw them watching the stars, digging her garden. She remembered their first kiss under the pouring rain. All the stuff that made her fall in love with him, blazed thought her mind. Why couldn't he remember? Why couldn't he summon up those same memories that to her were as vivid as if they happened yesterday?

Why couldn't Tommy be there for her when she needed him most?

When Father Matthew saw Francesca's eyes drifting, he said, "Francesca, please talk to me. You know whatever you say to me remains between us."

"I, um, think I need to get you back to the church for your eight o'clock wedding rehearsal."

MISSY WALKED INTO THE LIVING ROOM, stopped in her tracks when she found Francesca in the same position she'd left her two hours ago. There, stretched out on the sofa, with Bear at her feet, the book on her lap opened. Her hair was tied into a messy ponytail, and her feet clad in furry, bunny slippers. She wore a faded sweatshirt twice too big and stonewashed jeans that had seen better days. It was as if she'd stop caring about herself and everything, Missy thought.

Francesca had been drifting aimlessly for the last couple of days, and Missy believed only divine intervention was going to get her back to the Francesca she knew. Missy hoped her mother's plan did the trick.

"Mum wants you to join us in the kitchen for lunch, Frankie." Missy smiled at Bear, who on hearing the word "lunch" sat on his haunches and pasted a goofy smile on his face. "Yes, you're invited too. Just don't get under Mum's feet, or she'll chase you out of the kitchen with her wooden spoon."

"I'm not hungry."

"Mum's not taking no for an answer." Missy set to straightening the living room. "No, buts, and I say this will love, get your butt off the sofa and into the kitchen now," Missy said, deciding tough love was what Francesca needed.

Francesca angled a look toward Missy. "I can see going to Sunday mass is doing a wealth of good for your manners."

Missy's smile turned sly. "I said it with much love, and Mum's worried about you. As am I. All you've been doing since you got here is mope, brood, and feel sorry for yourself. It's not like you to give up so easily, Frankie." Missy set the discarded coffee, and untouched croissant on the tray wiped the coffee table clean.

"I have so much going around in my head right now, and I'm..."

"You're what, Frankie?" Missy prodded when Francesca went silent.

"I'm scared, Missy."

"Oh, Jesus! That bastard has you running scared." Pity and anger swam into Missy's eyes, and she rushed to chain arms around her.

"Don't tell anyone. Especially not your mum. I couldn't deal with the pitiful looks." Francesca took a moment to steady her voice. "I'm scared, Missy, of what James will one day do to me."

Missy took Francesca's hand, noting the way it trembled. "I won't say a word, but you need to go to the police, Frankie."

"I can't. They don't deal with probability."

"Yeah, you're right, but, Frankie, you need to talk this out, get it off your chest. You need to figure out how you're going to deal with that loser, sonofabitch, fucker of a husband. Again, all said with much love."

"I know, and you know it isn't so much that I can't talk to you."

"We've been over this. It doesn't matter why. You need to talk to someone, Frankie. Promise me you will," Missy said understanding Francesca's reason for not opening up, came down to the self-inflicted shame, blame, embarrassment, and guilt battered women inflicted on themselves.

Missy understood Francesca's refusal to admit what was happening to her wasn't her fault. She'd faced the same form of denial from her mother until the day she gathered the strength to do what she should have done years ago, pack up the both of them to escape her father's abusive hand and emotional control. Even now, years later, the guilt and shame her mother lived with was so ingrained in her psyche, she couldn't bring herself to share her story with Francesca.

"I promise."

"And as long as you're here with us, you're safe. Now, come to have lunch with the help. Some food in your tummy will make everything look sunny." Missy held hands up in the air. "Mum's words. Well, come on."

Arguing reaching futile level, Francesca rose to follow Missy to the kitchen. Her heart slammed into her throat when she saw Father Matthew sitting at the table.

"It's her lounging around look," Missy said, gripping Francesca's arm when she swirled to make her exit.

"It's a good look on you." Father Matthew's lips curved slowly when he rose.

She must have looked a fright in the rumpled clothes and untidy hair, Francesca thought and rolled eyes with just enough temper at Missy. "No one told me we had a lunch guest."

"It's Father Matthew. He loves everyone, no matter their pitiable appearance. Isn't that right, Father?" Missy shoved Francesca toward the table.

Father Matthew let out a hearty laugh. "I wouldn't put it that way, Missy, but no, I'm concerned about your soul, heart, and mind, not your appearance, Francesca."

Father Matthew was as charming and as entertaining as Francesca knew him to be. Minutes into the lunch, Francesca stopped feeling self-conscious about her appearance—one James wouldn't approve of—and enjoyed the great food and excellent company.

"That was a wonderful meal," Father Matthew said, finishing off his third helping of lasagna. A man could eat canned soups and ham sandwiches for only so long. He had to get himself a cook, Father Matthew decided.

"It's our pleasure, Father. You're welcome at our table anytime." Mrs. Richards gathered the dirty dishes off the table, set them in soapy water. "Frankie, you and Father Matthew head into the living room. Missy will bring in a coffee and dessert tray."

"Would you like something stronger than coffee?" Francesca motioned Father Matthew to the sofa, as she walked to the bar. "I'm having a brandy myself. I have a feeling I'm going to need it."

"Why?" Father Matthew eased himself into the buttery-soft cushions of the sofa.

"You tell me." Francesca reached for a snifter, poured brandy.

"I don't know what you're referring to."

"I saw Mrs. Richards exchange a coded eye message with you."

"On second thought, I'll take that drink."

"I thought so. So, are you going to tell me what that eye exchange with Mrs. Richards in the kitchen was about?"

Reaching for the handed glass, Father Matthew drank. "Missy and Mrs. Richards are worried about you. They didn't say why, but they want me to speak to you."

"There's nothing to talk about. Nothing to worry about." Francesca drained her glass.

"Sit down, Francesca. Please." Father Matthew walked the bottle of brandy to the sofa, refreshed her glass. "Drink, all of it." He encouraged, hoping to loosen her up. No one better than him knew people talked when their reserve was down, and noticing the marks of violence on Francesca's face, she'd tried to hide under layers of makeup he wanted to get her talking.

"I want you to tell me about the cut on your cheek."

Francesca's eyes flicked out the terrace doors. A bold afternoon sun shone out of a dreamy blue sky. Rust, gold, and copper leaves fluttered in the crisp fall wind laced with a touch of the incoming winter. On the terrace, chrysanthemums popped from stone planters in rioting colors.

"How did you know?"

Father Matthew refilled. "Drink more." Francesca started to object, but changed her mind and drank deep. "Is he all right?" He kept his eyes on Bear, who sat by the terrace door, staring up as if trying to communicate his thoughts.

"He wants to be let out. To do his business." When she started to push to her feet, Father Matthew waved her down.

"I'll do it." Opening the door, he watched Bear hurtle across the terrace and disappear behind an elm tree.

"Did Missy tell you about my ... injury?" Francesca studied Father Matthew over the rim of her glass.

He shook his head. "I was in the war. Gashes, cuts, and injuries were par for the course and simple to spot." Father Matthew's mind unexpectedly flashed back to the man in his arms, the recognizable fear of death in the eyes that stared up at him.

"You remember being in the war?" Francesca jumped in to raise the subject she hadn't known how to broach until then.

Francesca's words shocked Father Matthew out of his thoughts. "We're here to talk about you. Tell me about that cut, and don't tell me you ran into a door."

Francesca closed her eyes. For a long while, he waited for her to brush pride aside and open up. "My husband did it." The moment she said the words, the heavy burden of guilt, fear, and anger, weighing her down, slid off her shoulders. "Do you want to know why?"

Father Matthew shook his head.

Eyes bright with the stimulation of alcohol, Francesca snapped, "First, you want me to talk openly, and when I finally do, you have no interest to know why?"

Blue eyes steady on heated eyes, Father Matthew, sat next to her. "I don't need to know because there's never a good enough reason to justify anyone, particularly your husband, the man who professed to love you 'till death do us part,' to lay a hand on you in harm."

Tears sprang to her eyes. "I'm sorry."

"You don't have to apologize—for anything." Father Matthew handed her a tissue. "Was this the first time he's laid a hand on you?"

Francesca shook her head. She was through denying and protecting James, through feeling small, scared, and trapped. It felt liberating.

"What are you going to do about it? And I want you to know that whatever it is, I want to help you."

"I don't know." Francesca thought of her father, his plans for James, of the people at Thompson and Associates, depending on her. She thought of Noah Mulligan. "It's complicated."

"Situations like these often are, but I believe there's a solution to every problem and we, you and I, will find the right one because no one is laying a hand on you again. Not on my watch." Father Matthew firmed his lips in steely determination.

It was Father Matthew before her, but it was Tommy who spoke the words because that was precisely what he'd say to her. If anyone could help her out of the toxic relationship, Tommy could. Feeling the surge of courage, Francesca went on to tell him everything.

She told him about Bora Bora—a restrained version. She told him about the Noah Mulligan case, and the anger that spewed from James the day he found out she was going up against him. Francesca explained how she couldn't recuse herself from the case because she feared it would trigger more anger in James. All the while, she told her story he saw the flash of fear in her eyes, heard it in her voice.

"Is Mr. Mulligan innocent?"

"Yes, he is, and only I have a critical piece of information that I can't share with anyone that will exculpate him," she said without consideration for the solicitor-client privilege.

Blue compelling eyes stared blindly at Francesca. "Then, you must represent him. You must save an innocent man." A flash of a man dying in his arms flared for seconds in his mind.

"Are you all right?" Francesca said when his eyes glazed with shock.

"Yes. You'll represent Mr. Mulligan, Francesca, and you'll win the case for him. You can't in good conscience let an innocent man go to jail."

"No, I can't, but if I win, I'll feed the demon in James, and God only knows what he'll do." The impetus that had brought on her confidence faded.

"The demon is my specialty."

"I can't win the case. I just can't."

Father Matthew read the terror in her eyes, and still, he said, "You can, and you will. It's what you're supposed to do as Mr. Mulligan's attorney."

"You don't understand." Francesca paced the room with nervous energy. "James is capable of killing. I've seen it in his eyes," Francesca said, the talons of fear clawing through her gut.

Twenty-Five

FRANCESCA'S HEART POUNDING, she waited a
moment until she was sure she was strong enough to
respond. "I'm not coming home, James. I'll be staying at
the estate for a while," she said over Bear's throaty snarls
directed at James.

"Please come home, Frankie. I'm sorry. I didn't mean to
hurt you. I love you." James went silent when Missy burst
into the living room without knocking, chock full of
attitude. Only Francesca would allow a subordinate, a maid
nonetheless, to blatantly disrespect her employer, he
thought.

Pouring tea into two cups, Missy eyed James like a
rabid raccoon, ready to pounce at any misstep. "Here," she
said, setting cup and saucer on the coffee table before him
with a thump.

"Respect your employer." The quiver of temper edged
into James' voice.

"I do respect her. Her you go, Frankie." Missy's tone
was sweet as honey when she delivered the teacup into
Francesca's hand. "He better not be staying for dinner.
Father Matthew is joining us, and I don't believe he'd be
pleased with the stench of brimstone at the dinner table."

James' anger surging, his voice became clipped and
hard. "Why you..."

"Thank you, Missy." Francesca flicked eyes toward the
door.

"You sure, Frankie? I can stay," Missy said, and only when Francesca nodded did she leave, but not before giving James one last scorching look.

"I suppose you've polluted her mind with your bullshit."

"No, James, I didn't. I'm too humiliated and ashamed." Francesca raised a hand to her cheek. "But there's only so much concealer I can apply."

"I'm so ashamed about that, Frankie. You know that's not the man I am. I've been under a lot of stress at work. It's no excuse, but I let it get the best of me."

Her face expressionless Francesca remained silent. The only sound in the room then was Bear's growls, which stopped the moment James shot him a fiery stare, and he ran out of the room.

"Please, Frankie, I need you home. I need you next to me in bed. I haven't been able to sleep well since you left."

I, I, I, Francesca thought. "I'm sorry, James, but I need time for myself."

"I miss you, Frankie." James closed the distance between them. In a lunge, Francesca rounded the sofa to put it between them. "What do I tell your father?"

"Why would you need to tell him anything?"

"I'm having breakfast with him this Friday, and he's bound to ask about you."

And there it was. James wanted her back home to make the case to her father that he was the perfect husband, son-in-law, and the optimal choice to sit on the board.

"What am I to tell Peter if he asks about you?"

Tell him, you raped me on our honeymoon and that you've physically and mentally abused me because deep down, you're a bully and a coward. But James wouldn't utter those words. Even if he did, they'd be wasted on her father, who believed James Templeton III walked on water. Clean him up, dress him up with fancy manners, a fancy education, and a family lineage that traced back to some puffed-up pedigree, but underneath it all, James was as common as they came. And worse, a cowardly bully, pure and simple. Peter, however, would never see James Templeton III to the foundation of who he really was.

"Tell Daddy what you want, James. Right now, I want you to leave my home," she said with the confidence she garnered when she saw Father Matthew arched at the living room door. Today, she was in control and wasn't going to allow James the upper hand.

James followed Francesca's smiling gaze. "Who are you?"

"I figured my stylish cassock would give me away. I'm Father Matthew, a friend of the family."

James' eyes followed Father Matthew to the console table, where he poured himself a cup of tea. No Priest he'd ever seen looked like he'd stepped out of the centerfold of a magazine as he did. He was tall. The brilliant Viking blue eyes were sultry. Even under the flowing cassock, James made out the sinewy arms and broad shoulders.

Eyes flicking to Francesca, James thought he saw her eyes deepen with emotions as they scanned the priest's face. "Friend of the family?"

Father Matthew rounded the sofa, sank into it in a fluid motion, and Francesca joined him. "More like a spiritual advisor."

"I see. And what has Frankie been asking you to advise on?" James shot Francesca a warning look.

Father Matthew saw Francesca pale, the lick of fear flashing in her eyes and was overcome with the need to protect her. "Nothing much, and even if she had, much like a lawyer, I couldn't break the seal of disclosed information. Under any circumstances."

"Good to know." James eyed Francesca with a cautionary stare. "Still, I wouldn't put too much weight on whatever Frankie may say. She tends to overreact. Women are weak in that respect."

"Funny, I find men to be the weaker sex and to overreact to excess," Father Matthew said in a mild tone that was in contrast to the fire burning eyes James aimed at him.

The bitch told the pretty-padre everything. Her version, no doubt, James concluded. And Francesca was so obtuse she didn't see the play celibate-padre was making to bag her. James imagined the delusional ideas of self-worth, strength, and the many platitudes the padre was pumping her ego with. Well, the padre was in for a rude awakening. Francesca was a Templeton. She was his, and no one laid claim to what was his.

"May I top up your tea?" Father Matthew offered when James fury laced eyes lingered on him. "I'm sorry I never got your name."

"I never gave it," James spat out.

Eager to smooth James' boorish behavior, Francesca stepped in. "Father Matthew, this is…"

"James Templeton III. I can introduce myself. I'm Frankie's husband," he snapped with barely restrained fury. "And no on the tea. I'm not staying."

"I was looking forward to getting to know you, James."

James heard what he thought was sarcasm drip from Father Matthew's tone and lobbed it right back. "So was I, but I have more important things to do with my time." Reaching into his jacket pocket for his car key, James turned to Francesca. "We're not done with our conversation."

With Father Matthew sitting inches from her, Francesca's confidence pulsed fierce. "We are, James. I won't be coming home. I'm staying here." She saw James' jaw set tightly and was sure were it not for Father Matthew's presence, he'd have raised a hand to her then.

It felt good to have the upper hand on James Templeton III, and at that very moment, Francesca determined to stop running from herself or allowing James control over her. She wouldn't allow him to terrorize her anymore. James' dominance over her wouldn't exist without her passivity.

Francesca decided then she was going to fight James to the death in court. She was going to humiliate him. She was going to win the Mulligan case—for herself.

She told Father Matthew precisely that when they sat down for dinner and talked it out with him when they took Bear for his walk on the estate.

He didn't talk her into it or out of it. Father Matthew merely pointed out the pros and cons, which was what she needed to hear because, in the end, it was her decision to make.

Pros and cons laid out and talked out led her to decide to press on with the case. Fighting James was what she had to do for herself. Taking James on was what she had to do to regain her self-dignity.

"You're sure it's what you want to do?" Father Matthew said when they walked past the gardens and gazebo. The perfumes of fall floated in the cool night air, and a bright moon cast the land in a blue wash and shadows.

"I'm as sure as that moon is round and white tonight that it's exactly what I want to do." Francesca looked up to the starred night sky. "Not for Noah Mulligan, not for my father, not for the people at work, but for me." She was tired of running, of being afraid.

"I'm proud of you, Francesca, and be sure I'll be right by your side with spiritual and emotional support through it all. 'So do not fear, for I am with you … I will strengthen you and help you; I will uphold you with my righteous right hand.'"

"Isaiah 41:10," Francesca quoted, and aside from being surprised, he was impressed. "I guess the catechism classes paid off," she said with a shy smile playing across her face. "Anyway, I am going to need your support. I'm not as strong as I appear." Francesca walked toward the nurse log, sat, and Father Matthew followed suit. She could hear the sound of the creek's gurgling water splashing over rocks.

"Don't underestimate yourself. You're a strong, resilient woman." Father Matthew watched Bear raise his leg to the elm, then run ahead and disappear into the tall grass. "He's not going to get lost, is he?"

Francesca shook her head. "He knows this property like the back of his paw. Anyway, we'll find out just how strong I am because I'm in for a nasty fight."

After meeting James, there was no doubt in Father Matthew's mind Francesca was right, but he said nothing. Visiting the challenges the case brought on her personal life wasn't going to help Francesca's nerves. For a long, while they sat in silence listening to the murmuring creek, owl's hoots, crickets, and cicadas serenading their prospective mates.

"It's beautiful out here this time of night." Father Matthew watched Bear reappear, sniff his way around them until he settled down at their feet.

"I love this spot. I used to come here often with Tommy. We'd sit here for hours talking and watching the stars. He was a star watcher." Francesca hoped to stir memories, but all it did was stir her emotions.

Sitting next to the man she loved and he not remembering her or their past made Francesca feel immensely sad. To have found the kindness, strength, and the protection she needed in him and not be able to be close to him—maybe forever—was tearing Francesca apart.

"He sounds like a romantic sort." Father Matthew glanced up to see Francesca staring at him with tender eyes. The tightening in his gut, raw and intense, was unexpected and one he hadn't felt before. It made him nervous. Confusion turning into concern, he said, "We should start heading back. It's getting a chilly out here."

Twenty-Six

PETER WATCHED FRANCESCA pace her office. From time to time, she'd stop mid-pace, studied the papers in her hand, crossed out words with a flourish, and scribbled new notes. She'd talk to herself while animatedly waving her hand in a poignant flare. To anyone else, Francesca appeared foolish, but Peter recognized the pattern. Expression for expression, pace for pace, hand wave for hand wave, it was the routine he'd adopted years ago when rehearsing his opening statements.

Peter was flabbergasted when he offered Francesca a pair of fresh ears, and without hesitation, she accepted, telling him she'd appreciate his expert advice. Peter's chest puffed with pride at his little girl's willingness to recognize her weakness and that he was the best legal mind she knew.

Francesca waited for Peter to sit before reciting her statement with poise and confidence. She didn't flinch, didn't think of James. She thought of Tommy the entire ten-minute speech, and it flowed from her as fluid as water. Peter couldn't have been more proud of his daughter. Francesca had a sharp legal mind and was becoming as brilliant a litigant as he was. A plus in their business because optics was everything. She was a Thompson through and through.

If Francesca won, she'd elevate the firm's standing in the legal world, not to mention the invaluable publicity she'd garner. They'd be the talk of the town. Peter had already put a projection in place for contending with the excess cases that would undoubtedly come their way. He expected every one of his departments, from criminal to family, corporate to tax law to experience a significant rise in business. Win-win.

After pouring himself a whiskey, Peter walked to the window. The corner office he'd persuaded Francesca to move into had a much better view. She'd insisted she was fine in the smaller office, but Peter decided Francesca deserved it.

"You sound pumped about the case, Frankie. James certainly is. He's looking forward to going up against you."

"He said that?" Francesca suddenly felt the need for alcohol.

"Yes, at breakfast today." Peter watched her face, gauged for her reaction.

"It's the third breakfast this week. You, too, have certainly become chummy." Francesca poured herself a snifter of brandy, drank deep.

"It's business. He also told me you're staying at the estate and that you now have a spiritual advisor. A Father Matthew."

Francesca's gaze came to him, held from above the rim of her glass. She wondered how he'd react if he knew the truth. "He was certainly the chatty one this morning. What else did he tell you?"

"What else is there to tell? All I know is you're not by your husband's side, and a wife needs to be."

"Daddy, don't interfere in my married life. I won't have it anymore. What goes on between James and me is our business, not yours." Francesca spoke coolly, but heat flashed in the brown eyes.

She'd never spoken to him with such a sharp tone, and Peter's stunned look came with shock. "Frankie, I…"

"What goes on between James and me is none of your business. Especially when all you do is favor him, a stranger over your flesh and blood." Feeling strong and fierce, Francesca rounded her desk, sank to the depths of her leather chair. "Now, unless you have business to discuss, I need you to leave. My two o'clock meeting is waiting outside." Francesca's words delivered with a cold, steely glint sliced at Peter.

There was a breathless hush in the room before Peter, in stunned silence, left Francesca's office.

MEETING OVER, EVERYONE GATHERED THEIR PAPERWORK off the table and rose to leave Francesca's office. Lamont was halfway out of his chair when Francesca gestured him back down, and he sat his imposing six-foot, two hundred pounds of pure muscle back down.

As intimidating as Lamont was, he was a teddy bear with ebony eyes as dark as his skin and a broad smile that lit up any room he walked into. There was a time when Francesca had been smitten with him and thought every knight in shining armor should look like Lamont.

Francesca slid the sealed envelope across the table. "I'd like you to help me track down a Mr. and Mrs. Harry Scott. Last I heard they were in Ireland. The old address and telephone number where I've tried to reach them, with no luck and the necessary details are in the envelope. This work is for me, so bill me directly for your time, and I'd appreciate it if you kept it between us."

Lamont gave her a subtle nod. "That goes without saying. Any work I do for the partners and the firm is confidential."

For one second, Francesca was tempted to ask Lamont if he'd vetted James for her father. When it came to his business, Peter wasn't one to leave any stone unturned. But she said nothing. Lamont was not only the best in the business, but he was a professional through and through, and he wouldn't betray her father's confidences. It was why he'd been with the firm for fifteen years.

"I'd also like you personally to set a tail." Francesca slipped him a second envelope with the inked name.

If Lamont was surprised when he read the name, his eyes and tone betrayed nothing. "What am I looking for?"

"Anything you deem questionable. Regardless of the parties involved, I want you to report it back to me."

"How soon do you need feedback?" Lamont stuffed the envelope in his jacket pocket and tore the piece of paper with the inked name into tiny pieces. He'd flush it down the toilet. He'd been in the investigating business long enough to have seen shredded paper resurrected to evidential value.

"In the next few weeks is fine. I don't want it taking over any of the Thompson and Associates business you're working on."

"It never would. I'll get to work on it personally right away." Lamont took the last of his coffee, flashed Francesca an all-perfect-teeth smile as he left her office.

Twenty-Seven

PETER WAS PLEASED to see Francesca come barreling down the curving stairs with a smile, and a quick, swinging gait. He hoped that cheeriness came with forgiveness, which was what he'd come in search of. Much like Katherine had often made him feel after their arguments, his conversation with Francesca had left him feeling sheepish. Katherine had a fiery temper he'd respected, and he'd seen so much of her in Francesca's angry eyes yesterday.

"Hi, Frankie." Peter's gaze rose to Francesca, held.

At the sound of Peter's voice, Francesca came to a screeching halt. His dark eyes smiled up from beneath a wide-brimmed Stetson. He wore cowhide chaps over jeans, brown, leather boots, a fringed vest, and a plaid shirt beneath it. He made a handsome cowboy, Francesca thought.

"What are you doing here? Missy was just up, and she never told me you were here." Knowing Tommy was on the other side of the closed living room door, Francesca shot Peter a flustered look.

"I just got here." Peter gave Bear a stern stare that stopped him yapping. "I'd like to have a word with you, Frankie," he said, turning toward the living room.

"I'm glad you stopped by, Dad. There's something about the Mulligan case I'd like to run by you." Francesca steered Peter toward the study.

She felt seventeen again. When was she going to feel like her own woman around him? She wondered if every daughter felt as inadequate as she did around their father.

"I'm not stopping for long. Tiffani and I are on our way to the club's Halloween dance. She's fixing her face." Peter hesitated for a moment. "I wanted to apologize for yesterday, Frankie. You were right. I shouldn't be interfering in your personal life."

Peter's apology caught Francesca off guard. Peter Thompson apologized to no one, and it felt like a monumental achievement, a rite of passage. For a moment, Francesca relished in the magical feeling. But the moment was short-lived. Right now, she had to get Peter out of the house. She couldn't risk him running into Tommy.

"Apology accepted. Now, go get the car started, and I'll get Tiffani." Francesca bent down to pick up Bear when he started scratching the living room door.

Peter caught a whiff of Francesca's perfume, noticed the touch of rouge on her cheeks, the glossy lips. Although casually dressed in jeans and a cashmere sweater, Francesca looked overdressed for a night in. "Are you planning to go out?"

Francesca cleared her throat as she searched for the lie in her head. "Missy and I were going to a bar in town."

"Shut up," Peter snapped at Bear when he started barking at the living room door. "While your husband is at home pining for you, you're off to a bar?"

"James? Pine?" Francesca rolled her eyes. "That'll be the day."

"Don't get smart with me, young lady."

"You promised not to interfere, Dad."

"That was before I knew you were painting the town and with Missy, nonetheless. The help. Really, Frankie?"

Francesca's eyes flared. "For one, Missy is my friend and two..."

The tapping of heels on wood cut into the heated conversation, and Francesca and Peter turned to Tiffani. Her blonde hair was knotted into two braids. Her breasts spilled over a low buttoned plaid shirt tied high above her flat belly. She wore a thigh-high pleated skirt with knee-high, suede boots, and her face was overly painted. She looked like a cheap, tart, and Francesca wondered what her father saw in the woman.

"Hi, Frankie," Tiffani said, in her feigned honeyed voice. "Hello, Lion." She scratched Bear's head, who watched her with confused eyes. "Baby, my face is fixed. Let's go."

"Yes, go. You shouldn't keep Tiffani from making her grand entrance. Especially when she looks so," sluttish, "great." Francesca subtly steered them toward the front door.

"Thank you, Frankie. I do love my grand entrances, and I do look great."

"Have a great time." Francesca opened the door.

Tiffani and Peter were inches from stepping out when Tiffani turned to Francesca. "By the way, Frankie, that priest of yours is way too yummy for words."

Shit! Shit, shit. So close. The contrived smile died out from Francesca's face.

A frown creased Peter's brow. "How do you know what he looks like?"

"He's right there in the living room, looking all fatherly and delicious. To think he's celibate. What a waste."

"Father Matthew is here?" Peter turned to Francesca, eyes sharpening as he realized her blatant deception.

"I don't know his name, baby, but there's a hunky man dressed as a priest in the living room. Not as hunky as you," Brittani said, at Peter's annoyed gaze skimming fingers down his chest.

Batting Tiffani's hand away, Peter turned narrowed eyes to Francesca. "I want to meet this priest you're hiding away."

Francesca felt her skin prickled at the base of her neck when Peter turned toward the living room. The thought that Peter would make Tommy disappear from her life again made Francesca's heart sink deep in her chest. She couldn't deal with losing Tommy all over again when she'd just found him.

She needed Tommy in her life. He gave her the strength she needed to believe in herself, to stand up to James. Tommy instilled the confidence in her James had stolen from her. Tommy was the man who understood her, the man she loved, and her father wasn't going to push him away—not this time.

Francesca maintained her self-control, and leaning into Tiffani, whispered, "It would be a shame for you not to make your grand entrance. Especially when you look so stunning, Tiffani. You know, once they start serving dinner, everyone will be too focused on their meal to appreciate..."

"Me." Tossing the intolerable notion around her vacant head, Tiffani curled a hand around Peter's arm as he was about to open the living room door. "Baby, we gotta go. Now."

"We have time. I need to find out what this Father Matthew is doing here with my daughter, late on a Saturday night, without her husband present." Peter flicked eyes darkened with suspicion at Francesca.

"Jesus, Peter, it's only seven o'clock, and it's a goddamn priest. What could he possibly be up to? And, baby, if we go now I'll," she dropped her voice to a whisper in Peter's ear.

Whatever Tiffani said, had Peter swirling away from the living room door faster than a tornado, and hurrying them to the car.

FRANCESCA FINGER COMBED HER HAIR AND, taking a deep breath, stepped into the living room as Father Matthew added a log to the fire.

"Good evening." He set the screen in front of the crackling fire, turned to Francesca. "Hello, Bear." Father Matthew scratched Bear's head when he rose on his hind legs to greet him, "I'm sorry to drop in unannounced and to have caused such a ruckus."

"How much did you hear?"

"Enough." Father Matthew watched Bear flop and sprawl on the carpet by the crackling fire.

"I'm sorry." Francesca nodded slowly as she watched the flames in the fireplace burn amber. The crackle of wood, its woody scent, made the room a calming oasis. Just what she needed then.

"I would have come out and introduced myself, but it seemed like a family situation."

"It was. That was my dad and his second wife." Francesca took a decanter of brandy from the bar, poured into two Baccarat snifters.

"Next time, I'll make sure to call ahead. My choir practice got canceled at the last minute. Some kids came down with a cold, and I thought you might want to talk, seeing as your case starts Monday." Tommy sat at the sofa, took the offered glass.

"Calling would be good. Especially now that Daddy has these crazy thoughts in his head." Francesca walked to the window, slid the drapes open. A half-moon shaded the city under a silver haze lending a romantic feel to the night. "Thank you for thinking of me, but I'm feeling good and ready to kick ass. Umm, butt."

Tommy grinned. "I'm glad you're going to kick ass, and I'm proud of you, Francesca. I'm glad you're happy that you're taking control of your life. You're a good person, and you shouldn't allow a bully, husband or not, to demoralize you."

"Thank you for always saying what I need to hear." Pushing to her feet, Francesca walked to the record player. "I haven't seen you in a few days. God keeping you busy?"

"I've had an overwhelming demand for christenings and weddings."

"Post-war nuptials and babies. People have a few years of catching up to do." Francesca's dropped the needle on the record she chose. "Do you mind?"

"I'm a fan of Ernie Birchill's *Dream a Little Dream of Me*."

"You know your music. This is a favorite of mine. It reminds me of a wonderful time in my life." Walking back to the sofa, Francesca brought her scent with her and reached deep into Father Matthew.

The music, the sweet notes of her perfume, felt intimately familiar and touched him in ways he never expected. For the first time since knowing Francesca, Father Matthew looked at her. Really looked at her. Concentrating on the delicate lines of her face, the seductive, brown eyes, the spill of luxuriously dark hair, and the full mouth meant for kissing, he felt something stir in him.

Father Matthew put distance between them when he felt his heart begin to pound in his chest, when urges he'd tamed for so long, stirred hot in him. He'd made vows to God and the church that had taken him in when he was injured and lost, and healed him back to life.

TOMMY'S EYES BLINKED OPEN TO THE three strange faces by his bedside staring down at him. He watched them exchange words in a language he didn't understand. Afterward, the oldest of the three men walked out of the room. The remaining two took a seat on opposite sides of his bed.

When Tommy attempted to sit up in bed, the pounding headache kept him down. The younger of the two rose to help him. Tommy swept a confused gaze over the man who fluffed the pillow and set it behind his head. He, like the other two men, wore a brown linen tunic with a capuche, and a rope belt. Around his neck hung a wooden cross, and he was cleanly shaven.

"Thank you, but who are you and where am I?" Tommy's voice was groggy, his eye dazed.

"Prego." The young man bowed sat on the straw chair.

Massaging the ache at his temple, Tommy struggled to hold a conversation with both men but gave up when all he got were silent nods. "Where the hell am I?" Tommy scanned the small, austere room.

There was a bed, a night table, and a three-drawer dresser. Brick walls were whitewashed, and the only window in the room was curtained in simple white linen. There were candles in ancient candleholders, which cast shadows on the ceilings and walls. A small earthen jug and basin stood on a wooden table, and next to it were two neatly folded towels. The smell of incense hung heavy in the air.

All eyes flicked to the door when it swung open, and the bearded man carrying a tray walked in. "Buon Giorno. I bring you some food."

"You speak English." Tommy sighed happily.

"Yes. A little." He set the tray down at Tommy's lap. "The coffee is hot. The bread is fresh, so is the butter. Made by Signora Capitano."

"Where am I?" Tommy sipped on the steaming espresso, winced at the pungent taste.

"I'm sorry, sugar does not come easy since the war."

"Where am I?"

"You are in the Benedictine Monastery. We are Sicilian monks. I am Father Pio. This is Lay Brother Enzo and Lay Brother Vincenzo. They have been by your side since your accident." Gray eyes turned to the sitting men who bowed their heads.

"Accident? Jesus, that smarts." Tommy yelped when the headache and dizziness circled back to his eyes. "Sorry, Father," he said when the spinning stopped.

Father Pio slid his hand from the wide sleeve and waved it in dismissal. "You don't remember the accident?"

Tommy dug into his memory but came up empty. "No, I can't seem to remember much."

"How about your name?"

Digging into his fuzzy brain, Tommy came up empty, and he shook his head.

"You were hit on the head and left for dead. We deduced you were a soldier with the allied forces. Does any of that sound familiar?"

Tommy's confused eyes flashed to the sitting men, back to Father Pio. "No, I can't seem to remember anything."

"Do not panic. It will take time for your memory to return."

"What do you mean?" Tommy struggled to remember, but he kept on coming up blank. "How long will it take?"

"Maybe days, months, possibly years." Father Pio sat on the chair. Lay Brother Enzo vacated for him. "Signora Capitano and her sister found you amid the rubble and bodies. They took you back to their home. Took care of you until they realized you needed more serious medical care they couldn't give you and came to me for help. I was a medic in the war of nineteen fourteen. I never thought I'd see another world war in my lifetime." Father Pio reflectively ran fingers over his peppered beard. "You've been unconscious for seven weeks. We weren't sure if you were going to come out of it."

"Jesus! Sorry, again, Father. You say I was a soldier," Tommy said, and Father Pio nodded. "Where's my uniform, my dog tags? Seeing them may trigger my memory."

"Signora Capitano and her sister burned your uniform. And you had no tags."

"Why would they burn my uniform?" Tommy jolted up in bed, sending his head spinning.

"You must not agitate yourself." Father Pio tilted his chin to Lay Brother Vincenzo, who immediately rose to pour water from the pitcher on the night table into a tin cup. "You drink. They had to get rid of any evidence you were a soldier in case the Germans raided our town again.

They did it for your safety and theirs." Father Pio explained.

"Yes, of course. Do they remember the insignia on my uniform? It would tell me which country I fought for."

Father Pio shook his head. "But they did keep one thing for you. They found it in your ripped haversack. Unfortunately, it was partially torn." Father Pio tilted his chin up at Lay Brother Vincenzo, who crossed to the brick wall, and pulling the loose brick, retrieved the letter.

Tommy read, his eyes welling up in tears by the time he finished it. "There's no name on the letter, and I can't remember who she is."

FRANCESCA CLOSED THE GAP BETWEEN HER and Father Matthew. The subtle scent of her perfume nagged at him. The silence and their closeness caused emotions long-buried to stir.

Francesca met the lake-blue eyes overflowing with emotion. "What are you thinking?"

His breath fluttering unevenly, he looked down at her. "So, so many things," he said, absently running a hand over her hair in a casual intimate way that made her pulse race.

"Is one of those things to kiss me?" Francesca stepped closer,

There was shame, so much shame when he felt the burn in his belly when his mind raced to forbidden thoughts, and his body responded. The guilt went deep in him when all he wanted to do was reach out to touch Francesca, to kiss her. "Yes."

"Then kiss me." Francesca laid her hand against his cheek.

He leaned into her hand. There was a sense of familiarity in her touch, her voice, and it sent his mind floating. He felt the jolt of a staggering kiss, the feel of tender lips on his. He felt a sharp edge of passion and the love of a woman deep inside him. For a moment, he felt an absolute bond with Francesca, a tangible link to her that spanned for years. He felt it deep in his bones.

Reaching for Francesca's hand, Father Matthew brought it to his lips and brushed them over her palm. His moist lips on her skin sent her head spinning, touched the dozens of nerve endings in her body he'd once brought alive. Pulsing with the wonderful sensations only Tommy could spark in her, Francesca drew her mouth close to his.

Tossing aside logic and caution, Father Matthew said, "I want to."

"I very much want you to too."

Francesca's mouth was a whisper from his, her hot breath on him, the next wave of memory hit him then. He didn't know how, but he knew how her mouth fit with his and God, he wanted the taste of her in him. No one made him feel as she did just then, but vows, commitment, guilt had him pulling back.

"I can't. I'm so sorry. I need to go." Darting out of the room, his face raw with guilt and remorse was the last thing she saw.

Twenty-Eight

IT HAD BEEN weeks since their almost kiss and since Francesca had seen Tommy. Maybe, just maybe if they'd kissed, Tommy would have remembered her—everything. Then, Tommy would have come back to her. Now, guilt and self-blame had him distancing himself as she feared he would if she pushed him. Now, Tommy may never come back to her.

The knock at her office door had Francesca lifting eyes to Lamont. In a gray pinstripe suit, white, silk shirt, and blue tie, he looked elegant and handsome, Francesca thought. "Come in."

"I heard your first few weeks in court have gone well." Lamont sat across Francesca at the meeting table stacked with law books and files on Noah Mulligan.

"Yes, it has."

"Good. Because you've been right all along."

"Usually, am, but what about this time?" Francesca returned a dimpled smile.

"Noah, Mulligan. He's innocent." Lamont handed her the folder, stretched out his legs, his feet comfortably crossed at the ankles.

Francesca's eyes went wide when she saw the file's contents. "You're a miracle worker. How did you get your hands on this without a warrant?"

"You really wanna know?"

Lamont's reply caused Francesca to lift a brow. "Guess not. Well done, Lamont," she said, flipping through the rest of the photographs and documents with a brimming smile.

"Let's leak these two photos one week before Dr. Sampson takes the stand? I think the media and the public will be keen to see our good doctor with the wealthy Mrs. Marguerite Tremblay dining in a third rate restaurant."

"Can do. Do you want the headlines to read corruption, bribery, or affair?" Lamont watched Francesca pour them both a cup of coffee.

"I say we let the media run with it. They'll lead with an affair and come up with the perfect headline. Although I don't believe there is anything there, the media loves the attention a scandalous, illicit affair arouses. It's more salacious and sells more newspapers and gets better ratings. Two days before Dr. Sampson takes the stand, leak copies of the signed document. In the meantime, have the signature authenticated as Dr. Sampson's." Francesca handed Lamont the cup of coffee.

"Can do." Lamont tilted eyes up to Francesca over the rim of his coffee cup. Francesca might be Peter Thompson's beautiful daughter, neatly wrapped in designer suits and good manners, but instinct and a laser-sharp mind, traits inherently part of Francesca's makeup, made her a formidable prosecutor. She knew how to control the news cycles to her advantage, assemble the information and experts, to give her the winning edge. "You're all sweetness and innocence on the outside, but a real badass on the inside."

"I'll take that as a compliment."

Lamont flashed Francesca, a dimpled smile. "It wasn't meant as anything but." He reached into his jacket pocket and retrieving the envelope. "I got you a new telephone number for Mrs. Scott and her new address."

When Lamont hesitated, Francesca became wary. Still, she said, "Don't hold back, Lamont. Tell me everything you've uncovered."

"Mr. Scott passed away a few months ago, a heart attack. The cousin I spoke to believes he died of a broken heart. He couldn't seem to get over the fact his son went missing in action, and so many years later was still missing. I'm sorry, Frankie."

A cold chill raced through Francesca. Her head swimming in a fog, she choked back the tears.

AS SOON AS LAMONT LEFT, FRANCESCA reached for the telephone and dialed Mrs. Scott's number. The moment they heard one another's voices, tears and emotions burst like a geyser, unstoppable for minutes.

"I'm sorry I wasn't there for you, Mrs. Scott." Francesca's tone was drenched in sadness.

"I'm sorry, I didn't call you Frankie, but you'd just gotten married when Harry passed, and I didn't want to hang a dark cloud over such a happy time in your life. You deserved to be happy, Frankie."

"I should have been there for you."

"No, love. You need to live your life. It's what Harry wanted for you. It's what I want." Affection came through in her voice. "Harry called out for Tommy before he took his last breath. He'd caused his father a lot of grief and a lot of gray hairs, but he loved that boy."

Francesca heard the strain of anguish in Mrs. Scott's voice. "I know."

"I should have called to let you know my new telephone number sooner, but it got crazy fast, and I didn't have the time."

"I understand. I've been swamped myself with work and life." Francesca sat in the leather chair behind her desk when Mrs. Scott proceeded to catch her up. Hearing the hurt that throbbed in Mrs. Scott's voice when she spoke of Mr. Scott and how much he missed Tommy, Francesca jumped in. "I have something to tell you."

"Sounds serious. What is it, Frankie?" Mrs. Scott prodded when Francesca slipped into silence.

"It's about Tommy." Francesca closed her eyes, took several quiet breaths. "Tommy, is, ah, he's alive, Mrs. S.

He's here. He's the priest at St. Elizabeth's." Francesca heard Mrs. Scott's breath catch in a gasp of shock followed by a loud thud. She wasn't sure whether Mrs. Scott fainted or if she'd dropped the handset. She hoped for the latter.

When Mrs. Scott finally came back on the line, Francesca went on to tell her about running into Tommy, his memory loss, and her failed attempts to recover it in the past few weeks.

"We almost kissed," Francesca said, after some deliberation. The thump at the end of the line was louder this time. Francesca pictured Mrs. Scott dropping the phone to cross herself several times and say a silent prayer to save her sinful soul.

"Jesus, Joseph, and Mary, Frankie. Did you trick a holy man into kissing you? That's sacrosanct," Mrs. Scott said when she came back on the line.

"I figured if Tommy kissed me, he'd remember me, and all his memories would surface."

"Mmm-hmm, that's why you, a married woman, tempted a man of the cloth to kiss you? Sweet Jesus, did you hear how wrong all that sounded?"

"Yes, but I honestly did it to stir Tommy's memories."

"It's Father Matthew, and don't lie to me. It's me you're talking to. We may be speaking over the telephone, but I can hear the lie in your stutter," Mrs. Scott said, hopeful no immoral acts of turpitude were committed.

"Well, we didn't kiss, and I haven't seen Tommy since that night."

"Father Matthew," Mrs. Scott reminded. "And good. At least one of you has an iota of sense." There was a moment's hesitation as Mrs. Scott fell deep in thought. "I'm packing my bags and catching the first flight out. I need to keep you on the straight and narrow, and I'd like to see Tommy. Aside from you, he's the only family I have left."

"I don't want you to unsettle your life, Mrs. S." Francesca's tone was contrite, but there was a brimming smile on her face.

FRANCESCA'S DAY AT THE OFFICE OVER for the day, she drove home with the idea of soaking in a luxurious, lilac scented bath. Once home, feeling too restless for such a sedentary activity, Francesca wandered into her home office. What she needed was girlfriend-time. Tossing her purse and briefcase onto her home office desk, Francesca reached for the telephone and dialed Lily's number.

After hearing Tommy's story, Lily said, "Jesus! I can always count on you to have an incredible story to share whenever you call, Frankie."

"If I'm able to impress a psychiatrist whose father is running for president, and who ministers to politicians, Washington isn't as dysfunctional as I thought." Francesca drew the vertical blinds open to a moon, painting the evening sky crimson red.

"Oh they're dysfunctional, you're just more so than they are." Lily snorted a giggle, and Francesca joined in. "So those past few conversations we had about a friend named Tomlin were about Tommy?"

"Yes. I'm sorry, I didn't mean to lie, but I wasn't ready to tell you everything." Francesca heard the glug glug of water pouring from jug into glass over the telephone.

"You're forgiven. In my line of work lying is an occupational hazard. I've often wondered why that is when I'm here to help. That's one of the questions I'm addressing in the book I'm planning on writing. I'm working on taking a sabbatical from my practice to get it written."

"And it will become a bestseller, but for now, tell me what you think about telling Tommy about his dad's passing. I feel an obligation to do so. Up until now, I've been following your advice. I've tried to trigger Tommy's memories by showing not telling, but…"

"But nothing, Frankie. You can't shock Tommy's memories out. Memory loss caused by a traumatic event has to be carefully handled. We're not certain if he has brain damage as a result of a sustained injury or if it's an emotional or psychological defense mechanism he's developed due to Battle Fatigue or Combat Stress Reaction. Many of the returning soldiers have been diagnosed with it. You need to get him to see a professional. Can you do that?"

"I'm not quite there yet. I don't even know if he's aware there's a past he can't remember. It's killing me, Lily." The constant, dull headache no amount of Tylenol seemed to help flared up, and Francesca raised a hand to massage her temple. "What's worse is that by trying to get him to kiss me, I've alienated him. I wanted too much, too fast, but I believed we'd reached the point of familiarity to attempt the kiss."

"Maybe, but don't you think it was your longing to have Tommy remember you that made you push the process along. You feel as if you're a reversed version of snow white and the prince that brings her to life. Subconsciously, you feel your kiss will resurrect all of Tommy's memories."

Francesca wasn't sure if Lily's observation came from knowing her as well as she did or because she was good at her job. "It's so hard to have him so close and yet so far from me."

"I know, but you have to give it time, sugar. You have to give Tommy time. He's been through a traumatic life-changing event."

Francesca gave an acquiescent nod. "I know."

"Give Father Matthew time to come around to Tommy on his own time. He will, Frankie. I've seen it many times over. As for the kiss incident, he's embarrassed, remorseful, and feeling ashamed. Not of you. He thinks he's compromised himself and his vows."

"Is that your professional opinion?"

"No, that's my expert opinion of men. I've dated enough to know the signs," Lily said with a grin Francesca visualized. "By the way, my plan to come to visit you for Christmas is looking good. Daddy will be too busy with his campaign and his fourth—or is it fifth?—wife. No matter, this one will be around until he's elected. Maybe. She's a thirty-year-old aide and perfect arm candy, and she does play the role well. What is it about sexagenarians needing to relive their youth?" There was a long deep sigh at the end of the line.

"But I digress. Anyway, I'll be seeing you in a month. Set up a dinner with Tommy, you and me. I'd rather not have James there. It's better not to have a male presence while I conduct my observation and analysis of Tommy. Men are more vulnerable without rival testosterone in the room."

"James won't be there." Francesca recoiled at the thought she'd have to tell Lily on her visit about her failed marriage and abusive husband.

Lily would understand and be supportive. Still, it wasn't an easy conversation for Francesca. Her self-esteem and confidence were still precarious enough that, at some level, she blamed herself for James' attacks. The horror and the shame were too raw in her to open up to anyone—even Lily.

"Hopefully, once I spend some time with Tommy, I'll come up with a better plan on how to deal with his memory loss. I'll do everything I can to make him better, Frankie. I promise."

The assurance and the thought of having Tommy back made Francesca want to smile and weep at the same time. "Thanks, Lily. I'm so looking forward to seeing you."

"Ditto." Lily's buzzing intercom had her putting Francesca on hold. "My next patient is here. I'll talk to you soon. Kisses and love," Lily said, leaving Francesca hopeful that Tommy soon enough would remember everything. Remember her.

Twenty-Nine

THE ORDINARY YOUNG man she'd come to accept as her son, in a clerics robe, looked anything but ordinary. He looked divine, Mrs. Scott thought with pride. There were a couple of new scars, a few more lines on Tommy's face than Mrs. Scott remembered. The blue eyes looked cautiously wiser, and his hair didn't flow wildly. Aside from that, he looked like the Tommy Mrs. Scott had come to love as a son.

Coming face to face with Tommy, Mrs. Scott couldn't help but hug him tight and for longer than she should have, but it felt like she was touching the past and newfound future. Mrs. Scott was relieved when she drew away, and Tommy didn't question her emotional release, but helped her out of her flannel coat, and proceeded to get to know her better.

Mrs. Scott told Tommy what she could about herself and his father without crossing the line. Francesca asked her not to. Mrs. Scott told him about owning Scott's Garden Center and the son who used to manage it, hoping to stir a reaction. Nothing. She told him about Harry and leaving when their son was reported MIA. She didn't see recognition in Tommy's eyes.

Mrs. Scott nearly told Tommy how his father died broken-hearted thinking he'd lost his son to the war before she caught herself. Going deeper into his history would trip her up, and exposed Tommy to too many life stories too quickly, which may cause Tommy to withdraw further from the reality of his life. That's what Francesca had told her that psychiatrist friend had said.

Scanning the office, Mrs. Scott noted Tommy had gotten rid of the clutter and disorder Father Albert was fond of. The once brown walls were painted white, his desk was neatly arranged. A Christmas tree, blinking with colorful lights, was propped up in the corner next to the window. It sat on a white skirt, simulating snow. A vibrantly red poinsettia sat atop the gray, metal filing cabinet.

It was an orderly office. It was Tommy's office.

"Will I be seeing you in church this Sunday?" Father Matthew said.

"You most certainly will. I'm a devout catholic."

"Good to know."

On seeing the potted aloe, spider plant, and the English ivy sitting on the window ledge, Mrs. Scott said, "You like plants."

"I do. I seem to have the ability to make them thrive. At the monastery, I was the designated gardener. I started with a small patch of land, enjoyed it so much, I tripled the garden size and grew all of our vegetables."

Mrs. Scott's eyes flashed with hope. Francesca had told her not to push his memory along too much, but now that he'd opened the door, she couldn't let it pass. "That was where?" she asked with a tone of innocence.

"Sicily. I was a member of the Benedictine Monastery. They were my salvation," Father Matthew said contemplatively, and Mrs. Scott made a mental note to pass the information on to Francesca. "I was sorry to leave it behind, but when Father Albert was offered a teaching position in Madagascar, and they were looking for his replacement St. Elizabeth's called to me. And here I am."

"The Lord does work in mysterious ways," Mrs. Scott said, taking inventory of the fantastic story, which took Tommy across an ocean, changed him, and brought him back to the place of his birth as Father Matthew. He had no idea who she was, didn't know Francesca or St. Elizabeth's, his church until his teens when he'd strayed. He was lost amid his own life.

"He does." Father Matthew nodded in chorus with Mrs. Scott. "Can I offer you something to drink? I'm afraid it will have to be water or tea. I can boil water." He gestured toward the kettle on the filing cabinet. "I'm in between cooks, and it's all I can offer you."

Mrs. Scott smiled broadly. "I'm a great cook. You loved … you'll love my cooking."

"I don't want to impose."

"Nonsense. I believe God sent me across an ocean to look after you."

"He just may have." Father Matthew's voice was rich and jovial. "The church pays a modest stipend."

"You put that stipend to better use. My husband, Harry Scott," she spaced the words out for effect. When Father Matthew didn't react, she went on, "May he rest in peace, left me comfortable. I'll be telling you all about him in the coming days. He was a man you'd want to know."

"He sounds like a good man."

"He was." Struck by thoughts of him, Mrs. Scott paused for a moment to collect herself. "I'm staying at the Thompson estate. I believe you've met Frankie."

Guilt and shame played into Father Matthew's eyes, and he turned to give Mrs. Scott his back. "Yes, I know Francesca," he said, contemplating the kiss he almost made happen.

"She told me you're a good friend and that you helped her get through a difficult time in her life. I don't know what that was, but I do know you lifted her spirits when she needed it most. I'm grateful to you. She's always been like a daughter to me, and if I couldn't be there for her when she needed someone, I'm glad you were."

Father Matthew turned to face Mrs. Scott. "She's a wonderful woman."

Mrs. Scott's eyes stayed on him. "Good friends are hard to come by, needed. I know she cherishes your friendship and needs you." She rose, picked up her purse and her coat off the rack. "Now, show me the way to the kitchen, and I'll get busy making you lunch, which by the way, is served at noon on the nose. Not five past. On the stroke of twelve. You'll eat dinner at six, and breakfast at…"

Thirty

OUTSIDE THE COURTROOM, Francesca avoided James when possible, but in front of the clicking cameras capturing their every move, she was cordial, feigning smiles and exchanging friendly hellos. Francesca wouldn't give anyone reason to believe she and James hadn't shared a bed or lived under the same roof in three months.

James wasn't as affable. In and out of the courtroom, he made it a point to assert his imposing presence on Francesca. In the courtroom, James aimed threatening glares Francesca's way to unsteady and instill fear. Particularly so, since one week ago, when the scandalous headlines along with photographs of Dr. Sampson and Mrs. Tremblay dining together at the Noodle House restaurant made front-page news.

James knew it was one of Francesca's lackeys—at her direction—who'd leaked the photographs to the media. Then there was the copy of a false, unsigned rape report from the MEs office that miraculously appeared in the papers, which James suspected was also Francesca's doing. It was a well-played hand, but one Francesca would pay for because James wouldn't allow her to make a fool of him.

"I have no further questions for Dr. Sampson. Your witness." James strutted past Francesca's chest puffed, feathers spread out like a cocky peacock, to intimidate. Although Francesca held her head high, James knew he instilled the intended fear in her.

Francesca closed her eyes, searched for calm. She could only imagine how James was going to react when her questioning of Dr. Sampson was likely to lead to Noah Mulligan's acquittal. James had been intimidating enough throughout the trial to lead Francesca to believe he'd act on his anger if she won. And Tommy wasn't in her life to give her the strength she needed.

Panic and fear had Francesca turning eyes to the door, contemplating her escape from the courtroom. When she abandoned that as an option, she thought of throwing the case. She could do it without raising suspicion, but a risk nonetheless, which could destroy her reputation, derail the career she'd worked hard to establish, and send an innocent man to jail.

The notion had a dozen tight knots twisting in her stomach.

How had she gotten to this point?

"You'll do fine, Frankie," Nicholas said when he saw Francesca's shaking hands. Francesca's eyes said yes, but her knotted stomach told her she wouldn't, not without Tommy by her side. She needed him, his support, and his strength, but he wasn't there for her. "Let Dr. Sampson thump his chest before you go in for the kill, Frankie. You got this." Nicholas reassured.

"Are you planning to question the witness, Mrs. Templeton?" the judged asked.

"Yes, Your Lordship." Francesca took a moment to settle her nerves. "Dr. Sampson, you claim the only reason you and Mrs. Tremblay were at the out-of-the-way restaurant was out of convenience. That it was close to your office."

Dr. Sampson's blue eyes flicked from Francesca to the jury. "That's right. I'm aware Mrs. Tremblay is accustomed to fine dining, but after seeing her daughter in the morgue, she was distraught, and I thought to calm her down I'd take her out for a drink. The Noodle House is within walking distance."

Francesca turned to face the jury. Five men and seven women all had their eyes on her. "Very thoughtful of you,

Dr. Sampson. Have you done that before? Have you taken a distraught family member out for a drink to calm them down?"

Dr. Sampson mulled the question over searching his brain for the optimal answer. In the end, he opted for the truth. "No, I haven't, but as you can appreciate, Mrs. Tremblay and her husband are big philanthropists, and their contribution to this city has been extensive. I felt an obligation to go the extra mile."

Francesca caught the pleased smile on Mrs. Tremblay's face in the gallery. "Yes, the Tremblay's are a very wealthy couple who have been very generous with their money."

James shot to his feet. "It's well known how generous the Tremblay's are, Your Lordship. Do we need to waste the court's time with repetition?"

"Mr. Templeton is correct, Mrs. Templeton. Please move along," the judge said.

"Yes, of course, Your Lordship." Eyes on James, Francesca, considered her next comment deciding whether to make it or not.

"Does the defense have another question for this witness?" James' tone was berating.

"Mrs. Templeton, do you?" The judge pressed.

Francesca turned to Noah Mulligan, his eyes holding trustingly to fate, she had no choice but to proceed with her questioning. And here it goes, the point of no return, she thought, and taking a deep breath said, "In fact, Mr. and Mrs. Tremblay are so charitable they generously paid off your twin sons Harvard tuition to the tune of twenty thousand dollars."

The hushed room instantly turned raucous. Reporters got to their feet and lobbed questions. Photographers snapped their cameras at a shocked Dr. Sampson while spectators in the gallery exchanged comments and expressions of disgust.

"I offer exhibit I, your honor," Francesca said when the judge managed to get control of his court again. "This is proof of a payment issued from a numbered account from the Cayman Islands traced back to Marguerite Tremblay to Harvard University for Justin and Jared Sampson." Francesca turned to a flushed Dr. Sampson. "Isn't it true, Dr. Sampson, that this payment was made to get you to retract your findings of rape on Elsie Mulligan during your autopsy?"

Dr. Sampson took out his handkerchief to wipe the sheen of sweat already pearled on his flushed face.

"Your lunch at the Noodle House was to negotiate with Mrs. Tremblay your terms for tossing out the original autopsy report not to comfort her."

"She's reaching, Your Lordship." James huffed.

"We've tracked down Donny Lam, the waiter from the Noodle House, who overheard your conversation with Mrs. Tremblay and who you paid five hundred dollars to wipe his memory. He had a lot to say when we told him he could be charged as an accessory. A lot, Dr. Sampson."

James scrambled to his feet. "I object."

"To what, Mr. Templeton?" His Lordship eyed James over the rim of the tiny reading glasses on his hooked nose.

"We were not made aware of Donny Lam as a witness," James' voice boomed.

"Mr. Templeton, Mrs. Templeton, was merely making a statement not calling Donny Lam to the stand."

"It's a, umm, a legal maneuver. She's raising the argument to open to the possibility." James' voice sounded awkward.

His Lordship cocked a bushy brow. "Now who's reaching, Mr. Templeton?"

"With all due respect, Your Lordship, I want you to question Mrs. Templeton," James said as anger piled over arrogance.

"Very well. Mrs. Templeton, are you making a play to call on Donny Lam, who is not on the witness list, to the stand?" His Lordship asked.

"I wasn't planning to, Your Lordship, unless Dr. Sampson believes I should." Francesca turned to Dr. Sampson.

"No. No, there's no need for that." Panic dripped from Dr. Sampson's voice.

"Satisfied, Mr. Templeton. Now sit down and stop wasting the court's time." The judge's voice firm, James limply dropped to his seat.

Francesca saw the rage radiating in James' eyes, and she thought she saw him mouth, "You'll pay for this, you bitch."

Panic leaped at Francesca's throat, churned in her stomach, as the fear, raw and real, sprinted up her spine. Francesca concentrated on moving air in and out of her lungs to keep from fainting. She'd come too far for Noah Mulligan, and there was no turning back now.

Taking a long, steadying breath, Francesca said, "I submit exhibit J. An original signed copy of Dr. Sampson's initial report of Elsie Mulligan's autopsy stating she was raped. My office has authenticated the signature as Dr. Sampson's."

James bolted to his feet faster than the speed of light. "The prosecution hasn't been provided copies of the document by the defense, your honor. I've only seen the unsigned document Mrs. Templeton leaked to the media," James said with an impatient hiss.

"Your Lordship, I object to the implied accusation." Nicholas shot out when Francesca said nothing.

"Mr. Templeton, keep the editorial comments to yourself." His Lordship gestured James down to his seat.

"Our apologies, but my office only came across the signed document yesterday, via anonymous delivery, and we needed time to authenticate the signature." Francesca kept her voice leveled.

"I'm sure you did." James sent Francesca a look designed to wither.

"Is that your signature, Dr. Sampson?" the judge asked directly, and Dr. Sampson gave a half nod. "Please verbalize your response, Dr. Sampson."

The doctor cleared his throat. "Yes, it is."

Dr. Sampson's acknowledgment sent shocking ripples through the gallery, and His Lordship to bang his gavel. "Silence."

"Isn't it true, Dr. Sampson, your drinking session with Mrs. Tremblay at the Noodle House was to discuss payment for the retraction of your rape finding from the report?" Francesca said.

From James came a desperate, "That's supposition and proves nothing."

"Actually, it proves a lot," Francesca said. "Mrs. Tremblay's goal was to pin the murder on Noah Mulligan. You see, if Noah were found guilty, his prenuptial agreement disqualifies him from inheriting his wife's ten million dollars and their Victorian mansion and turned over to Mrs. Tremblay."

From James again. "That's ridiculous and absurd."

"I wish it were. I present exhibit K, a signed copy of the prenuptial agreement."

"The defense is wasting the court's time, Your Lordship. I've reviewed that document, and there's no such clause," James tone sounded frustrated.

Francesca looked over at Noah. At his nod said, "This is a second prenuptial agreement, which only Mrs. Tremblay, Elsie, and Noah know bout. It was done in confidence shortly after Mrs. Tremblay found out Noah Mulligan was a…" the light of battle in Francesca's eyes melted into compassion, "homosexual."

The gallery burst out with shocked oohs, ahhs. Wide eyed, the members of the jury turned to one. Reporters made notes, and cameras clicked to capture it all.

"Elsie married Noah to spare him the shame society bestows on people like him out of ignorance and fear. When Mrs. Tremblay found out of their arrangement, she threatened to expose Noah's homosexuality unless Elsie, and he signed the document." Francesca, along with the jury, turned to gauge Mrs. Tremblay's reaction to the statement. The indignant look on her face spoke volumes.

"Noah is innocent of your daughter's murder, Mrs. Tremblay," Francesca said firmly. "He was never intimate with Elsie, and you knew that. It's why you paid Dr. Sampson to conceal the rape. Noah loved Elsie as a true friend does their best friend. He tried to get Elsie cleaned of her drug dependency when you gave up on your daughter. Noah supported Elsie, spent nights by her side, encouraging, helping her give up her drug habit. He offered her a crying shoulder when she needed it, when her family, you Mrs. Tremblay, deserted her. Noah was never interested in Elsie's money, and he would have never hurt her. Their marriage was one of convenience that worked for both of them, but not so much for you. Their marriage shook that strict moral code of yours right down to the foundation of your self-important life. Your close-minded arrogance has prevented the authorities from finding your daughter's true killer."

When Francesca finished delivering the heartfelt speech, the courtroom broke into frenzied mayhem. Journalists ran out of the room to file their reports, some shed tears, while others remained stunned in their seats.

In the front row of the gallery, a wide-eyed Peter murmured, "Jesus Christ! Frankie just won the case against James."

Mrs. Tremblay rose and stomped out while Mr. Tremblay eyeing her with disdain, refused to join his wife in her dramatic exit.

With tears streaming from his eyes, Noah Mulligan gave Francesca an appreciative nod.

At the defense table, Nicholas pumped his fists in victory.

Lamont sat back in his gallery chair with a satisfied smile. "And that's how it's done."

From the back of the room, tucked away in a corner, Father Matthew watched Francesca with pride before sneaking out the side door.

Thirty-One

MRS. SCOTT DRANK the last of her tea and tucking her hair under the knit hat, shrugged into her coat. "I have to get to the rectory to make Father Matthew his breakfast."

"You fuss over that man too much." Mrs. Richards set the steaming cup of coffee on Francesca's breakfast tray.

"It's my job to cook and take care of the rectory." Mrs. Scott slid stubby fingers into black, leather gloves.

"If you're his employee, why aren't you being paid for the work you do, or are there ulterior motives."

Mrs. Scott cut Mrs. Richards off. "What are you trying to insinuate you old battleax? This is a man of the cloth and me you're talking about."

When Mrs. Richards started to respond, Missy cut her off. "What Mum means to say, Mrs. Scott is that our Frankie's hurting. She's been hiding away in her room for days. She looks like hell and refuses to eat or say anything. You're our last resort." Missy set fork and knife on the tray.

Mrs. Scott's lips formed a tight line. "I'm sure that's what she means. I've tried talking to Frankie. She won't talk to me either."

"Father Matthew got her talking last time she shut us out, but for whatever reason, he hasn't been around. So, you'll need to get her talking, or she'll wither away. I'll go to the rectory this morning for you, Mrs. Scott. You get Frankie to eat something and get her to tell you what's got her running so scared she won't leave her room." Missy reached into the refrigerator for the butter.

"How exactly am I to do that? That girl is as stubborn as her mother was. May she rest in peace," Mrs. Scott said, and all crossed themselves in unison.

"Be as forceful as you are with me when you see me in my—what is it you call them?—sin-seeking dresses."

"You look like a harlot in them." Mrs. Scott looked over at Mrs. Richards, who set the anger derived from the battleax comment aside and nodded in agreement. "Squeezing your body into a tiny, short, tight dress, which leaves nothing to the imagination."

"That's the opinionated, forceful woman Frankie needs right now," Missy said, handing Mrs. Scott the tray.

THE VICTORY GLOW FROM THE NOAH Mulligan "not guilty" verdict, lasted minutes for Francesca. The calm, leveled look James aimed her way had an underlying coldness that sent a chill that went bone-deep and skirting reporter's questions, photographer's cameras, and spectators, Francesca made a quick exit from the courthouse. Heading straight for home, with Bear trailing, she ran up the stairs and locked herself in her bedroom. It was where she'd been for the past week.

Francesca snatched the bottle of brandy off the night table and poured a shot. She drank from nerves rather than want, although it hardly mattered to Francesca why. The alcohol calmed her, at times, allowed her the only couple of hours of relaxed sleep she got at night.

Francesca did what she had to do, what she loved to do. In the process, she saved a man from ending up in prison. She should be celebrating her accomplishment. Instead, she was cowering in her room out of fear. This feeling was never going away, Francesca thought pouring herself another shot of brandy.

Mrs. Scott startled Francesca when she walked into the bedroom, and she stopped her drinking mid-sip. "Drinking at seven in the morning, Frankie. Really." Francesca looked exhausted, there were dark circles under her eyes, and her hair was a knotted mess. It broke Mrs. Scott's to see her like that, but now wasn't the time for gentle love. "This is going to stop now." Mrs. Scott took the glass from Francesca's hand, set it on the dresser next to the three empty brandy bottles. "Missy has been letting you get away with murder," she said, scanning the bedroom.

Clothes and shoes were strewn throughout the room. The dresser was stocked with bottles and dirty glasses. In one corner of the bedroom, Bear's food and water bowls sat on a spread-out towel. That and the dog would be the first thing to go from the room, Mrs. Scott decided.

"Why are there so many clothes about when you haven't slipped out of those pajamas in days?"

Francesca wouldn't tell Mrs. Scott she'd attempted to get dressed several times only to give up.

"I want you out of bed, Frankie." Mrs. Scott slid the curtains open to a flash of white snow falling out a blue sky. As far as the eye could see, trees and the green rolling hills of the estate were blanketed in white. "Go take a shower, and afterward, you're going to eat what that old battleax calls a breakfast," she said, coking a brow toward the untouched food tray.

"I'm not hungry, Mrs. S, and I'm perfectly fine right where I am. And you need to stop calling Mrs. Richards an old battleax and getting along with her now that you're living under the same roof." Francesca sat up in bed, and Bear followed suit.

"You will not be eating people food or eating in this room anymore. Get off this bed and get yourself downstairs." Mrs. Scott waved Bear down, and in a full doggy snit, he jumped off the bed and left the room. "Mrs. Richards knows she's an old battleax, and she and I are best of friends. But never mind about us. Hungry or not, you're going to eat then, you're going to pack up and go home to your husband. The trial is over, and the sad excuse you needed to keep your distance from James while you fought it out in court doesn't wash anymore." Mrs. Scott gathered clothes and tossed them into the hamper. "Not that it did before, but now it makes even less sense. You need to be with your husband now."

Francesca idly ran her fork through the scrambled eggs. "I'm not going home—ever."

Mrs. Scott stopped dead in her tracks. "Of course you are. You need to be with your husband." At hearing Francesca's sigh run deep, Mrs. Scott set the shoes in her hands down and sat at the edge of the bed. "It's not like you. What's wrong, Frankie? Talk to me."

Francesca's bleary eyes fell on Mrs. Scott. "I can't. It's so ... demoralizing."

Mrs. Scott slid fingers under Francesca's chin, raised her face to meet hers. The amber eyes shimmered behind a sheen of tears and carried an air of fear and shame.

"What is it, love? What's bothering you?"

Francesca passed a weary hand through her messy hair. "James is not the man he appears to be."

"What do you mean by that?" Mrs. Scott pressed when she heard the angst in Francesca's voice. "Frankie, you know you can tell me anything."

Francesca went on to tell Mrs. Scott everything. Francesca told Mrs. Scott about Bora Bora and the violent rape. She told Mrs. Scott about James' ongoing psychological and verbal abuse, the threats he'd lobbed when he found out she'd taken the Mulligan case. The words flowing as easily as when she'd spoken them to Tommy, Francesca went on to tell Mrs. Scott what Lamont had uncovered on Jasmine White.

"Jasmine was his high school sweetheart. He proposed to her on prom night, but she turned him down." Francesca brought up her knees, circled them with her arms. "She's been missing since that night."

"She could have left the city, the country," Mrs. Scott said, trying to wrap her head around what Francesca was suggesting.

"Lamont checked. The police have no record of her leaving the country."

"She could be living in another province."

"It's doubtful. There are no bank accounts or credit cards registered under her name, no tax returns. Her parents have been looking for her ever since. I know James killed her, Mrs. S, and I think he wants to do the same to me."

"Jesus, Joseph, and Mary." Mrs. Scott's mouth was dry, her palms moist.

"Are you all right, Mrs. Scott?"

There was a moment of stunned silence before Mrs. Scott recovered. "I'm trying to process all of this. I'm sorry I wasn't here for you, Frankie. I'm sorry you've had to go through this alone. I should have never left you, love." Mrs. Scott chained loving arms around Francesca.

"Mrs. Scott, don't. You had to get on with your life, and I wasn't alone. I had Tommy or Father Matthew to talk to. He gave me the strength I needed to face James. It was because of Father Matthew I didn't give up on the Mulligan case. I wanted to throw the case. I told him as much, but he … It's because of him I won the case, and now I'm so scared, Mrs. Scott."

Mrs. Scott held Francesca when the tears started flowing. It suddenly became clear to Mrs. Scott why Francesca needed Tommy so much.

It wasn't as much to revive their romantic relationship, but for protection.

MRS. SCOTT SET THE PLATE OF lasagna she'd made for lunch and a glass of merlot in front of Father Matthew.

"Although I'd never turn down a plate of lasagna, a sandwich and salad for lunch would be sufficient. At this rate, I'm going to start rolling to the altar," Father Matthew said even as he picked up a forkful of lasagna.

"You have a demanding job, which requires you to eat well." Mrs. Scott covered the lasagna pan with foil and walked it to the refrigerator. "Father Matthew, you know

I'm not the type to meddle in other's business." She closed the refrigerator door.

"No, you're not." Father Matthew bit back the grin.

"I think you need to set aside your shame and guilt and talk to Frankie." Mrs. Scott turned to Father Matthew after setting the last of the washed pots on the dishrack.

Rigid with shock and embarrassment, Father Matthew's eyes lowered to the wine in his glass. "Why would you think I feel shame or guilt?"

"Because I know about the almost kiss." Mrs. Scott overlooked the flush of pink riding on Father Matthew's cheeks. "I'm not saying I approve of your actions or hers, but sometimes you need to set humiliation aside for someone in need, and right now, Frankie needs you."

Father Matthew's stomach clenched. "Why what's happened? Is Francesca all right?"

The concern Mrs. Scott saw in Father Matthew's eyes went deeper than that of a priest for a parishioner. He may not remember who Francesca was, but from the look in his eyes, Mrs. Scott saw clear as day he'd fallen in love with her all over again. It was why he'd put distance between them, Mrs. Scott thought.

Mrs. Scott rubbed at her temples. She was pushing a confused, vulnerable man into circumstances that would test his faith, his entire belief system. But Francesca needed him, and her safety outweighed sound judgment.

"Frankie's fine, but she's running scared as terrified as I've ever seen her. She's locked herself up in her bedroom and refuses to leave. After what she told me, I don't think her actions are exaggerated. She can't go to the police with suspicion. She can't turn to her father for help. She needs you."

Father Matthew left his fingers to run up and down the stem of his glass. "I can't, Mrs. Scott."

Mrs. Scott clasped a hand over Father Matthew's. "Whatever happens, it's God's will. It's the direction He wants your life to take. You need to go to her. You need to protect her."

Father Matthew took a healthy swallow of wine. "You're asking for too much."

"I know." Mrs. Scott looked into the troubled eyes and told him of Lamont's findings. "There's no concrete proof, but I trust Frankie's gut feeling. I wouldn't ask you to do this if I had anyone else to turn to. Please. Will you protect her?"

Thirty-Two

ARCHED IN THE living room door, for a brief moment, Father Matthew hesitated. The room was under the magic charm of Christmas. Next to the fireplace where wood crackled, and flames curled and swayed, stood a tall fir decked with twinkling lights, tinsel, and ornaments. Garland hung from the mantel along with five stockings, one for each member of the household—including Bear. The lingering scent of burning maple and fir came at him.

With a cheerful rush, Bear leaped at Father Matthew. "I've missed you too little guy," he said, kneeling to let Bear lick his face.

The sound of his voice had Francesca shifting her eyes to him. For a long silent moment, their eyes held. His pulse jumped as the emotions he'd desperately tried to suppress in the past weeks stormed through him like a gale wind. Reckless thoughts, he'd locked away of pulling her into him, running his fingers through her hair, and kissing her arose in him all at once.

Father Matthew thought of leaving, but Francesca's pale face, her shadowed eyes, and Mrs. Scott's words "you need to protect her" circling his head wouldn't allow him.

Father Matthew stuffed his hands in his pockets. As warm as the room was, his hands were damp. Sensing his presence, Francesca swirled, met his gaze. Her smile made his heart stutter. What was she doing to him?

"May I come in?"

Francesca nodded. "He's missed you," she said when Bear hopped onto the sofa to sprawl himself over his lap.

Understanding Francesca's veiled meaning Father Matthew said, "I've missed him too."

As much as Father Matthew had tried to shake the thoughts of Francesca flooding his mind, not a day went by when her face hadn't flashed in his mind. Francesca was his first thought when he opened his eyes in the morning and his last before sleep. He'd tried to disengage from those feelings, but like a drug, Francesca took hold of him, controlled him, made him weak, defenseless. Francesca had Father Matthew doubting himself, questioning his entire belief system—and she was winning. It was why he'd distanced himself from her.

Francesca moved him in ways he'd never expected emotionally, romantically, and sexually. New emotions he didn't know how to deal with. He'd prayed, asked for guidance and forgiveness from Him, but she was too deep in him, and not even He could help him now.

Being as close as he was to Francesca, Father Matthew's emotions were surfacing again, working their way through him, raising doubts and questions he had no answers for. Holding on to his own control, Father Matthew fought the thought of taking her in his arms and crushing his mouth to hers coming over him.

"Can I get you a drink?" Francesca crossed to the bar, poured herself a glass of wine.

"Beer, please." Father Matthew waited until she walked back the uncapped bottle. "I was in court on your final day."

"I know." Francesca handed Father Matthew the bottle. "I saw you."

"I was very proud of you. In awe, really, of the way you spoke and addressed Mrs. Tremblay. You saved Mr. Mulligan's reputation and saved him from spending the rest of his life in prison."

"I had help. I had a great team, and you. Because of you, I went through with the case." At the patio doors, Francesca looked over the snow-covered terrace. She could see Bear's paw prints coming and going from when she'd let him out earlier in the day. "For a moment, just before I started questioning Dr. Sampson, I thought of throwing the case. Then I saw you hiding away in the corner, and I gained the courage to push on."

"I didn't think you saw me, but knowing that I'm glad you did." Father Matthew took a long swig of his beer.

"Your white clerical collar was hard to miss." Francesca crossed to the sofa, and with her came the scent of her lilac soap and musky shampoo. It was heady and intoxicating. Father Matthew's breath caught. What was this woman doing to him? "Did Mrs. Scott ask you to come to see me?"

"She's worried about you."

"And you're here to protect me?" Francesca picked up her drink, swirled, drank.

"She told me what your private investigator uncovered." Father Matthew watched Francesca take another good gulp of wine.

"She shouldn't have, and you needn't worry about me."

"I am."

Brown eyes from under winged brows gazed at him. "Out of guilt or concern."

Anger sprang hot in Francesca's words, but Father Matthew brushed over it. "I'm sorry I didn't come sooner, but I…"

"You don't owe me an apology. You don't owe me anything." Francesca's mouth clamped in a thin line.

"I do need to apologize. I let you down."

Francesca laughed bitterly. "You're not the first, and you won't be the last."

Father Matthew's hand whipped up to snag her hand when she started to rise. "I know you're upset, but I want to explain."

Francesca jerked back, but he tightened his grip. "Let go of me."

He could let Francesca's hand go, but he didn't. The glints of memory that unexpectedly came at him made him feel as if he'd touched his past. The nagging feeling of familiarity was rearing its head again and making him feel as if this wasn't the first time he'd held Francesca's hand.

Contemplatively, Father Matthew sensed this wasn't the first time he ached to kiss Francesca, or the thought to hold her in his arms assailed him. At that moment, the same rush of need hit him like a wrecking ball. The panic came fast, pressing down on his chest like a giant boulder. Father Matthew chastised himself for allowing the unfitting thoughts to fill him.

He'd made vows, sworn his allegiance to God. A devout man of the cloth wasn't meant to harbor feelings for a woman, Father Matthew screamed in his head. But he was harboring feelings, and Francesca's hold on him was making him cast aside the vows he'd made for her.

The thought weighing on his conscience like lead, Father Matthew said, "I haven't come to see you because I can't trust myself around you. I've been grappling with my conscience since the night I was tempted to kiss you. You have me questioning my life, testing my faith. I've spent many nights wide awake in bed thinking of you, feeling shame, and guilt that I was. Even now, holding your hand, you set off sensations in me I haven't experienced before—or maybe I have." He took a deep breath, then another. "It's all confusing. I have so many thoughts rushing at me, and it all feels chaotic in my head. And you add another layer to that chaos." He slid fingers over the nape of his neck. "I don't mean that in a bad way. I ... I never told you, but I have no memory of my life before the war."

Francesca felt the clutch in her belly. He was opening up just as Lily said he would. She did her best to tuck the excited nerves away. "I'm sorry. How far back before the war?" Francesca asked, hopeful.

Father Matthew went on to tell Francesca about being left for dead and being rescued by two sisters who tried to nurse him back to health. He told her of the sisters turning to Father Pio for help when they realized how serious his injuries were. "It's how I ended up at the monastery. If it weren't for them, I wouldn't be here today."

There was a fist around her heart, squeezing tight at the idea of him lying on a pile of rubble, surrounded by dead bodies, gasping for breath, not knowing whether it was his last.

"Father Pio and the brothers nursed me to health, gave me a home at the monastery when I had no memory of who I was or where home was. It's why I decided to devote my life to the church, and now you have me questioning everything."

"I'm sorry. I never meant to unsettle your life."

"It's not just my thoughts of you that have me questioning everything. I've listened to you tell me about your friend Tommy. Each time you've mentioned him, it's triggered something in me, but as deep as I've reached, no memories surfaced." Contemplatively, Father Matthew stroked a sleeping Bear. "You mentioned he was in Europe."

"He fought with the First Canadian Infantry Division," Francesca said, telling him what little she'd uncovered during her years of searching for him.

"Did he...?"

"He was reported MIA," Francesca finished, anticipating his thought. "They've never found his body."

"Where was he fighting when he went missing?"

"Sicily, at the base of Mount Aetna. It took me five years to find that out."

His heart lodged in his throat. "It's where I was found. It's where I did my convalescing and where I called home until I came here." Father Matthew let that sink in for a moment then turned to Francesca. "You persevered for five years?"

"I did."

"And you found him, didn't you? But he was lost and damaged like many of the soldiers that returned home from the war."

Francesca tilted her head to look into the eyes of the man she'd lost. There were tears in her eyes and so much sadness. She eyed her wedding ring, rolled it on her finger along with the mounting wave of regret. "I found him too late. I'd already married James when I did. Had I found him sooner, lost or not, I wouldn't have married James," she said in between sobs.

Father Matthew felt something inside of him break. He raised a hand to her wet cheeks, and she leaned her face into it to fill herself with his touch. It was as warm and as gentle as she remembered.

Their faces inches from one another, he held Francesca's gaze. "Am I Tommy?"

That he asked made Francesca's heart ache. "Yes," she said, and for a long while, watched him struggle as he dug deep into his memories.

"All you've been telling me about him, it's my life." When she nodded, Father Matthew shot to his feet in one fluid motion, almost knocking Bear off the sofa. Sorrowful eyes rolling to the window, he saw the bone-white moon that lent a silver wash to the land blanketed in snow stretching to the grove of majestic trees. Father Matthew sensed there was something in those shadows that had meaning, but he couldn't figure out what. "I don't remember anything. I have no memory of you or anything about my life. I see things, and they feel familiar, but no matter how hard I try to remember, I come up blank."

"What happened over there?"

"I don't know." Father Matthew dug out his wallet, pulled the letter. "It's the only thing I have left from my past."

Francesca took the letter, wrinkled and brittle, from years of handling. The bottom half was missing. When she read it, her throat constricted, and big silent tears coursed down her face. "I wrote this to you."

"What's my full name?" He sat beside her.

"Thomas Scott. Everyone called you Tommy."

"Scott? Is Mrs. Scott related to me?"

"She's your mother, step-mother," Francesca told him about his father and of his passing. As she spoke, his eyes welled up in tears. "He was a wonderful, kind, and loving man. He was very proud of you and loved you to bits."

"Goddamn war. It's taken so much from me." Tommy's voice cracked with anger and emotion, and Francesca felt the flutter of guilt and panic in her throat.

In time she'd have to tell Tommy she was the reason he'd enlisted. She was the reason he'd gone overseas to a foreign country and gambled with his life. How was she to explain to him she was the reason his father died a broken heart? She was the reason for his memory loss, for who he was today—or who he wasn't. How was she to justify everything that had happened to him was because of her?

Tommy had always protected her, always defended her, and all she'd done was to cause him pain. Had she been stronger, she would have stood up to her father and not allow Peter's arrogance to mark Tommy's life, and hers, in the worst possible way. When Francesca thought how different Tommy's life would be if her father had been a better person, she couldn't help but hate him.

Francesca laid a hand on Tommy's arm. "I'm so sorry, Tommy, for all the pain in your life. More than that, I'm sorry you had to go through it alone."

Steadier now, Tommy turned to her, met her gaze. There was love in her eyes, so much love—for him. "I know you love Tommy, but I'm not the Tommy you knew anymore, and I'm not sure if he's ever coming back."

Francesca's eyes swam when she lifted them to his face. Who lived behind those eyes? "I know."

"Mrs. Scott said earlier today that whatever happens, it's God's will that it was probably His plan for me all along. She says it was Him who steered me to you. We can't change what's happened, and we have to accept those events changed us forever. Even if my memory was to return, we're not the same people we were all those years ago."

"I know."

"The only thing I'm certain about, and God forgive me, is that," he framed her face, slowly combing her hair back with his fingers, "I've fallen in love with you all over again."

Nothing had ever felt so good or so perfect and taking Tommy's hand, Francesca laid it on her heart. "My heart has always been yours. I never stopped loving you," she said, resting her brow against his. "I've missed you, Tommy."

He lifted his hand to cover the one resting on his heart and felt the bond, the connection, the absolute rightness he'd felt each time he'd been with her in the past weeks. This time, however, being this close, linking fingers with hers felt magical, and his heart filled with a wonderful peace.

"If this is how wonderful it felt when we were together all those years ago, I've missed you too."

"It did feel this wonderful, and it will again."

Tommy nuzzled to her hair, breathed her scent in as he'd dreamed of doing for days. "I know it will."

"The first time you kissed me was under the pouring rain. Grant it, it was after I threw a few potted plants at you."

"I always figured you were a spirited woman. Did you get me?"

Francesca's lips ripe with a smile she ran a finger over the tiny scar on his forehead. "I caused it."

"I always wondered where it came from." The only thought circling his head now was the sweet longing to kiss her. "I know it's so very wrong. You're a married woman, and I'm a man of the cloth, but right now, all I want to do is kiss you." The shy, sweet smile that played in Tommy's eyes made Francesca's insides liquefy. She felt like the seventeen-year-old girl getting a taste of love for the first time.

"Then kiss me."

"I, umm, haven't had much practice with umm, kissing a woman."

"It's like riding a bicycle. It'll come to you." Francesca lifted her mouth to his.

Tommy's breath caught in a gasp of shock when Francesca moved in closer, letting her lips hover so close to tasting. He wanted, needed the taste of her in him. Intuitively, Tommy wrapped his hands around Francesca's waist and leaning in, brushed his lips to hers. Tommy kissed her slowly, ever so tenderly, as dreamily as she remembered.

His kiss filled Francesca's heart with the love she'd wanted for so long. Tommy kindled the long-dormant fire in Francesca, and she floated in the glorious sensation, the feeling she hadn't felt in a long, long time. He was still the man she'd fallen headlong in love with since forever.

"How was that?"

Francesca swallowed. Hard. "I think we need to try again."

Tommy brushed the hair from her face, gazed into her eyes. "I think you're right."

And with that, Tommy's mouth was on Francesca's again. Clinging to her mouth, the kiss grew longer, deeper, more passionate when her mouth became more demanding. Feeling the quick intake of her breath, the tremble of her body Francesca shocked his system, in the best way possible.

When Francesca bit lightly on Tommy's bottom lip, he wanted to devour. Tommy's breath shuddered when Francesca parted his lips with her wet tongue and, in one instant, became intimate with his. The sharp, taste of her flooded through him and roused the best possible feelings in him. Like a geyser coming to life, Tommy's emotions burst from their long slumber.

Tommy matched Francesca's urgency, her need, and want. He was drowning in her. Something was frightening and exciting in the emotions Francesca unleashed in him, in the way she made his nerves tangle and twist.

"Father Pio is not going to be well pleased with me," Tommy said, resting his forehead on hers.

"I'm sorry I've disrupted your life as much as I have."

"I'm not." Tommy brushed a finger up and down Francesca's cheek. It scared him to think he needed her as much as the oxygen he breathed. "No one has made me feel as complete or as alive as you do."

A yawn from Bear had them both turning to him. They watched Bear rise from his slumber, stretch, shake himself and walk to the French doors where he looked over with a chop-chop-I-need-to-be-walked-out stare.

Tommy's eyes lit with laughter. "Well, we've been told."

"I'll take him out. I don't like him roaming around by himself when he goes out this late. His name may be Bear, but he's a pussy cat when he comes face to face with a coyote or a raccoon."

"I'll take him, and when I come back, you're going to tell me all about my past."

"All right." Francesca handed him the lead. "I'll light a fire and make us some hot chocolate."

Tommy touched her lips with his. "I'll rush back."

Sometimes, fate hands you the death you deserve.

—M.L. Lexi

Thirty-Three

FRANCESCA'S LIPS RIPE with a smile, she added a couple of logs onto the fire glowing in the hearth. She was looking forward to spending the night telling Tommy everything she knew. She couldn't wait to recount the story of how they'd met, revisiting their first date and their first kiss.

How right Lily was—about everything. She'd projected Tommy's recovery, shown Francesca how to navigate her way around him to help uproot his repressed memories. There was still much more to Tommy's recovery than repressed memories, but Francesca trusted Lily to help him heal. Lily had graduated top of her class not because, as the daughter of a wealthy oil magnate-slash-politician, she'd had everything handed to her, but because she was smart.

Lily would use her honed medical skills to find out what had caused Tommy to shut off his memories. Regardless, having Tommy ask Francesca to tell him everything she knew was a great start. Better than that was Tommy telling her he loved her with no memory of their past. What were the chances of falling in love all over again with your first love? Francesca let that sink in and a moment of complete understanding of how much Tommy truly loved her made her heart bloom inside her like a red rose in spring.

As warm as the living room was, Francesca suddenly felt a shiver creep up her spine. Wrapping arms around herself, she turned to head to the kitchen to make the hot chocolate. Francesca saw him then. Arched in the doorway, heat flashed in James' eyes. Francesca's breath caught, and her throat constricted. She dug her fingers into the back of the chair to keep herself steady.

Recognizing the shock and fear in Francesca's eyes, James' lips curved. "Hello, Frankie."

At his long, slow stare, a look of utter horror paled Francesca's face. "How did you get in?"

James held up the key. "You change the locks, but leave a key beneath the planter. How stupid is that?"

"What are you doing here, James?" Francesca's voice, in direct contrast to the river of fear flowing through her, was calm.

"I came to collect you."

Francesca swallowed hard. "Collect me? I'm not furniture, James."

James spurned the comment. "And to my surprise, I find you locking lips with your priest. I'm sure the archbishop will be pleased to know how he's been spiritually advising you." The muscles in James' jaws quivered when her eyes darted away. "Look at me, goddamnit. Look at me, you whore," he repeated when she didn't. "Has he gotten you into bed already? He does have a lot of catching up to do."

"I don't know what you're talking about." Francesca reached for the poker to push logs around the fire.

"Is he a better fuck than I am?"

You can clean it up, dress it up, but rubbish was always rubbish, Francesca thought. "Don't be so crude."

"You're a whore who gets it on with a priest."

Francesca found her courage and set hard, unwavering eyes on James. "I want you to leave. Tom ... Father Matthew will be back soon."

"You can call him Tommy, and I'm not leaving you with your lover to make a bigger idiot of me than you already have in court." Crossing to the bar, James' gaze whipped up, two heated dark points that managed to infuse fear in Francesca.

"He's ... he's not my lover." The muscles of her stomach clutched into a tight knot of nerves. If she could make it to the patio doors, she could outrun James and catch up with Tommy.

"Don't even think about it," James warned when he saw her plotting. "You do take me for a fool." Pouring himself a whiskey, he took it in in one swallow.

"I don't," Francesca said, doing her best to tuck away the sharp claws of angst tearing at her stomach.

"I heard your entire conversation. 'I've fallen in love with you all over again.' 'I never stopped loving you. 'I've missed you so much.'" James mimicked, flinging his glass into the fireplace. "You fucking slut. Your father told me he was dead, but you've fooled everyone, haven't you? You've kept him hidden away as sideline entertainment. He's been fucking you the entire time we've been married, hasn't he?"

Francesca tightened her grip on the poker. "I want you to leave. Now, James."

"You spread your legs for a priest, and suddenly, you think you can tell me what to do." James drained a second whiskey, flung the empty glass into the fire with more force. The half-empty bottle of Crown Royal followed, scattering a shower of glass and whiskey everywhere.

A wave of panic sweeping through Francesca, she gripped the poker tighter and rounded the chair to put it between James and her. The cutting smile creasing one corner of James' mouth made the hair prickle on Francesca's neck, and fear had her feet cemented to the floor.

"He can't help you. We're alone, my dear wife," James said when Francesca's eyes darted to the patio doors.

Before Francesca knew, James came at her. Francesca swung the poker with all her strength, aiming for James' head, but she was inches shorter, and she struck his upper arm.

"You fucking bitch." The dizzying pain shot through James' shoulder.

Francesca took a blind step back and fell into the chair. Fighting back the panic, Francesca pulled herself to her feet in an attempt to get away from James, but he snagged her arm, gripped hard enough, his fingers dug to the bone. She tried to free her arm, but James was too strong.

"You fucking bitch, you leak information to make me look like a fool during the trial." The back of James' hand came at her fast and hard across her face. "You whore around behind my back with your lover." His fisted hand landed a punch on her face, splitting her lip and making her taste blood.

Francesca cried out in shock, and her lungs hitched for breath. "I would never leak information or cheat on you." She blinked to clear her vision back.

"You're like all of them, a lying, whoring bitch." Cold fury burnt in James. "I should kill you right now."

"Is that what you did to Jasmine?" The words, which burst out of Francesca, caught him off guard. For a long moment, poker-faced, he stared at her, but Francesca saw the admission of guilt in his eyes. "Oh, my God! You killed her."

James gave Francesca a hard push, and she fell back into the chair. Clamping his hands on the arms of the chair, he pushed the weight of his body to cage her in. "The bitch deserved it. She dates me for years, then when I propose, she tells me I deserved better than her. As if I'm going to fall for that lame-ass excuse. What she meant was that she deserved better than me. The whore thought she deserved better than me, James Templeton III." His blood raging, he punched Francesca over and over. She lifted hands to block him, but all she managed to do was make him angrier. "You're all the same. Teasing, lying, whores." Landing punches where they fell, James berated, called Francesca Jasmine as his fists became more forceful with each blow.

Francesca was sure she was going to die tonight.

WALKING UP THE TERRACE STEPS BEAR'S ears pricked. The flash in his eyes, the throaty snarls, was a clear reaction to impending danger. In reaction to Bear, Tommy listened, intently. Through the cold blowing wind, he heard the man's menacing shouts and Francesca's curdling pleas for him to stop hurting her.

Bear lunged toward the door, and Tommy propelled himself across the slippery, snow-covered slate. Flinging the patio door open, in one long stride, he and Bear were in the living room. The smell of alcohol and blood slapped Tommy. Shards of crystal scattered around the hearth and floor glinted like diamonds under the dancing flames from the fireplace.

Then Tommy saw Francesca. Her face was streaked red with blood, and one eye was shut closed. There was a cut on her cheek, and her lip was split open. Crouching over Francesca, James' eyes looked wild like a rabid dog's. Shouting oaths, insults, and threats, James spat in her face.

Tommy's heart bumped, and anger, so much anger pressed down against his chest as if someone had taken a hammer to it when Francesca's head shot up, pleading for help. Adrenalin, along with his military training kicked in when Tommy saw James swinging a fisted hand toward Francesca's face, and he charged at him.

Latching onto James' arm mid-air, Tommy's voice roared, "Take your hands off her, you bastard." The fury simmering, the adrenalin pumping, Tommy pulled James off Francesca and tossed him aside like a rag doll.

"You're going to pay for that." James pushed himself off the floor to his feet.

It was then Bear who leaped at James, fangs gleaming, to latch onto his arm. As James fought Bear, Tommy bent down to scoop Francesca into his arms. The blood on her face looked bright against the pale skin that seemed almost translucent. Anger melted into compassion. "I'm getting you out of here?"

"Get off me, you flea-infested beast." James snarled punching at Bear, but a growling Bear dug his fangs deeper, latched on harder. With his free hand, James reached for the silver candleholder on the coffee table to strike Bear. "I should have run you over when I had the chance," James barked, raising the candleholder over Bear's head.

"He's going to hurt Bear," Francesca screamed.

Tommy whirled around in one quick motion, lunged at James, and knocked the candleholder out of his hand. The thump of silver on wood followed.

"Release, Bear, go to the kitchen," Tommy ordered, but it wasn't until Francesca's weak voice repeated the command that Bear let go of James' arm. With one last fierce growl, Bear scrambled out the room.

Wincing in pain, James dragged himself off the floor. "You too can be on your way. My wife will not be entertaining you anymore, and you can be sure I'll be calling the archbishop."

"I'm not going anywhere." Standing tall and fierce, Tommy shielded Francesca's limp body on the chair. "I'm not leaving Francesca alone with you." Tommy's eyes glared in defiance straight into James' eyes.

"This doesn't concern you. She's my wife." James spat.

"It does when you lay a hand on Francesca. And it stops now." The cold, withering look Tommy aimed at James could have extinguished the fires of hell.

James saw past the temper in Tommy's eyes to love, deep and strong for Francesca. "You sonofabitch. How long have you been screwing my wife?" James snapped. Refusing to dignify the question with a response, Tommy set hard, unwavering eyes on James. "That long, eh?"

"You need to leave now." Tommy's eyes hard, lethal, mingled with posturing.

"Who the fuck do you think you are to tell me what to do in my home?" The resentment at being barked at by the man screwing his wife smothered James, and he lunged a tight-fisted punch at Tommy.

Tommy dodged the blow aimed to his face, but he wasn't expecting the head-butt to the stomach that knocked him back and off his feet. Tommy's head bounced against the edge of the coffee table, blurring his vision and knocking him out.

Tommy out of the way, James turned to Francesca. Snatching her breath, she sprang up, tried to escape. Before she could run away, James latched onto the end of her ponytail and yanked hard. Francesca's head snapped back, and for a moment, the clutch of death clawed at her.

Francesca's pulse drummed to the beat of fear. Kicking and screaming, she called out for Tommy, but her cries went unheard. All they did was cut the smothering silence in the room.

James brought his face within inches from Francesca's. "Your priest is a pussy. He's out cold. There's no one here to help you."

"Tommy. Tommy." Francesca called out.

"Call out for him all you want. Your lover's unconscious. That little boo-boo on his head did it." James taunted, shoving her face inches from a passed out Tommy. "Where's your boyfriend when you need him, eh?" James drove a fist into her ribs that made Francesca's lungs chock up.

The air searing in and out of Francesca's lungs, she fell to her knees next to Tommy. On all fours, Francesca gulped air to fill her lungs. Her lungs filled, she moaned out Tommy's name one last time.

Nothing.

Francesca raised her arms to block James's next blows. "Please stop, James. I'll do whatever you want."

That time, Francesca's petrified voice pierced Tommy's ears, and her face swam into his eyes. Through blurred vision, Tommy saw Francesca fighting for air as James' hands closed around her throat. With one blind burst of adrenalin, Tommy pushed himself off the floor.

"Let her go," Tommy shouted. When James refused, Tommy reached for the candleholder on the floor, brought it down on James' back.

The pain radiating down his spine, James' eyes gleamed with fury. Releasing his chokehold on Francesca, James turned, charged at Tommy, and mowed him to the floor. Both men rolled on the ground, but James outweighed Tommy by thirty pounds, and he pinned him under him. As James drove his fists into Tommy's face, Tommy struggled to reach the candleholder inches from him.

The punches to Tommy's head came for what felt like an eternity. The vicious roaring in her ears became louder, and his lungs snatched what air it could. His vision dimmed to a hazy blur, with some effort, Tommy felt his way around for the candleholder.

The candleholder was the only thing between salvation and death.

Next thing Tommy heard was James taking one last struggled breath that to James felt like jagged knives slicing his throat on the inhale before he collapsed on the floor.

Thirty-Four

THE DRIVEWAY WAS teeming with police cars, red lights flashing brightly in the night. Inside, a forensic team had sealed the living room and were busy gathering evidence as the Medical Examiner zipped James' body in a black bag. The smell of blood and death permeated the air.

"What's going on here? What's happened?"

The uniformed officer blocked Peter from entering the house. "Sorry, buddy, this is a secured murder scene. You're not allowed in there."

"Murder? Jesus! I'm Peter Thompson. This is my house. Whose body is in there?" Peter demanded. "Who did this? I want answers."

"Of course, Mr. Thompson. Mark, you're needed out here." The officer called out over the din of first responders. After a brief exchange with the officer, the man in a wrinkled, gray suit, scuffed tan loafers, and brown Fedora waved Peter in.

"Mr. Thompson, I'm Mark Mill, the head detective." Mark tipped his hat back to expose dark, bushy eyebrows and sharp cop's eyes.

"What's happened here?"

"Not sure yet exactly. We're still trying to piece everything together. What I can tell you is we've identified the single male body in the living room as James Templeton III."

Peter ran fingers through snow-wet hair. "Jesus! James."

"You know him?" Mark Mill retrieved the notebook and pen from his jacket pocket.

"He's my son-in-law and an associate at my firm." Peter drew a deep breath. "Jesus! James? Are you sure? How?"

Mark flipped his pad open, scribbled notes. "ID on him says so. The monogrammed shirt, cufflinks, and tie clip confirm it. The medical examiner's educated guess is blunt force trauma to the head. The fact we found a bloody, candleholder near the body confirms it. A visual examination of the body tells us your son-in-law was struck several times on the head with it. We'll know more when the medical examiner files his official report."

"Jesus Christ." Peter slanted a look over the detective's shoulder, watched the plastic bag wheeled out on a stretcher. His stomach turned when he caught sight of the room. There was blood everywhere. Sofas and walls were splattered with it. Pools of it coagulated on the floor.

"You all right, Mr. Thompson?"

Peter nodded. "Fine. Who did this to James? Who killed my son-in-law?"

"We have a suspect in custody, being held in the kitchen." Mark offered Peter a stick of juicy fruit. "Sometimes, it helps settle the stomach."

"No, thanks. Why would you be holding them in my kitchen? Shouldn't you be hauling their ass off to jail?"

Mark unwrapped the stick of gum, folded it, and tossed it into his mouth. The fruity smell instantly painted the air, temporarily masked the smell of death. "We should be, but your daughter says she's his legal counsel and refused to let us take him in."

"Christ, Frankie," Peter murmured, making a mad dash toward the kitchen where he found Missy, Mrs. Richards, and Scott, sitting on one side of the table. On the opposite side, with their backs to Peter, were Francesca and the priest. Two officers guarded the room exits. The coffee-maker on the counter gurgled a fresh pot, its scent painting the air. The somber silence matched the mood in the room. "Are you all right, Frankie?" Peter's voice drew everyone's attention.

Gesturing Bear to jump off her lap, Francesca took a shallow breath, and slowly—so as not to trigger more pain from the broken ribs to shoot through her—turned to face Peter.

Peter's breath staggered when he saw Francesca's face. Her left eye was swollen shut, and her right was barely open. Her face was black and blue, her nose was taped, and her lips looked twice their size. Her right arm was set in a sling. There were red marks on her neck. Peter didn't want to venture to guess what they were.

"Jesus, Frankie, what happened?"

"I'm fine, Daddy. I need to talk to you. In private." Francesca spoke from the left corner of her mouth.

"How did James end up dead, in our home, on our living room floor?" Peter couldn't imagine any plausible explanation for James' death, let alone for it to have occurred in his home.

That Peter was more concerned about James than his battered daughter, didn't surprise Francesca. It should have, but it didn't. Nothing Peter did surprised Francesca anymore, and she'd stopped letting his self-centered, heartless ways eat away at her long ago. You couldn't drive sense into someone with tunnel vision, and she needed to take refuge in normality.

She'd felt alone for the longest time, but soon enough realized she had great friends in Missy, Mrs. Richards and Scott, Jennifer, and although thousands of miles away, Lily. The women in her life gave her the support, friendship, strength, and the love she needed—everything her father didn't.

To Francesca's surprise, it didn't take long to accept the direction her life was taking without a father. Not that Peter had been the type of father she'd needed. It had been a long time since she'd turned to Peter for support or love, and eventually, she'd come to accept the notion of going through life fatherless. At least her heart wouldn't break again, and although it still stung, the wound of Peter choosing James over her wasn't as raw anymore.

"Daddy, let's go to the study." Francesca urged limping toward the door.

They'd made it to the door when Peter whirled around. "Why's the priest here?" he asked, recalling the detective's statement: Your daughter says she's his legal counsel. The priest was the only man in the kitchen. Peter flicked eyes to the table, watched Missy, Mrs. Richards, and Scott's gaze drop to their folded hands. "Did the priest kill James? He did, didn't he? You did this to my daughter. Who the hell are you?"

"Daddy, please. I need to talk to you. Stay here with Missy, Bear," Francesca told Bear when he refused to leave her side.

"Your father's going to find out sooner or later, Francesca. I may as well confess now." Tommy rose, turned to face Peter. "Yes, Mr. Thompson, it was me who killed James."

The shock caused the breath to back up in Peter's lungs. His eyes fixed wide in disbelief. For a long time, Peter stared at the man in the cassock. The shock of dark hair, the determined glint in the steel-blue eyes, were Tommy Scott's.

The night couldn't get any stranger, Peter thought, falling into a chair and looking up to meet Tommy's eyes. "How? When? You're supposed to be dead."

"MIA." Tommy corrected.

Peter's eyes turned from Tommy to Francesca. "How long have you known?"

"You're my family, and you deserve to hear this," Francesca told Missy, Mrs. Richards, and Scott when they rose to leave the kitchen. To the policemen, Francesca said, "Can you give us a few minutes? We need some privacy." Francesca waited until they left the room to say, "Tommy's been back in my life a few months."

"I see." Peter gave Tommy a long, hard look then turned to Francesca. "Only a few months and your husband is viciously bludgeoned to death. Once a criminal, always a criminal, even if he is dressed in priests clothing. Will you never learn, Frankie? Missy, get me a drink?"

"Stop, Dad, before you embarrass yourself. Look at me, Dad. Look at me." Francesca pressed until Peter flicked eyes to her. "James, the man you chose over me, did this to me, and it wasn't the first time. He raped me, Dad. Your golden boy, with the pedigree and name you so admire, viciously raped me on our honeymoon. When he found out I'd taken the Mulligan case, he beat me, threatened to kill me if I won."

"That's not possible. You never said anything until he," Peter's head spun to Tommy, "Came into the picture. And James is a Templeton."

"Do you hear yourself, Dad? How could I tell you anything when this is the reaction I get when it comes to James? You believe what you want, Dad. I'm not going to make an effort to change the way you think because it would be wasted on you." Francesca stood next to Tommy. "I will tell you that were it not for Tommy, James would have killed me tonight. If it weren't for Tommy, I'd be the one being carried out in the body bag instead of James."

Mrs. Richards turned to Mrs. Scott. "Why does she keep calling Father Matthew, Tommy?"

"Shhh, I'll tell you later. It's a long story."

"I want to hear it too," Missy whispered after handing Peter the tumbler of whiskey and the bottle she figured he was going to need.

"How is the fact that he's been in the picture all this time, only coming out now?" Peter took the whiskey too quickly for pleasure, then poured himself a double shot. "I forbid you to represent the man who killed your husband."

The anger Francesca hadn't let herself feel for her father flared hot in her now. "Listen to you, Dad. Your snobbery makes you such a narrow-minded fool with such limited vision you can't see what I look like right now or accept that my husband, your golden boy, did this to me. Most days, I've wondered what mom saw in you. I'd never want the man I spend the rest of my life to be anything like you.

Tommy is twice the man you could ever be. I'm not done." She winced in pain when she held a finger up to Peter to silence him when he started to speak.

"Tommy has no memory of his past. Until tonight, he didn't know who I was. He didn't recognize this house or Mrs. Scott. Until tonight he didn't know what we once meant to each other." Francesca reached for Tommy's hand. The gesture made eyes go wide and sent minds racing. "He doesn't know that had it not been for your interference in our lives, your insistence on keeping us apart, our lives would be very different today. I'll never forgive you for that, Dad. Mom wouldn't either. You coerced me into a marriage with an abuser because he suited your purpose and because his name would help your business. I want nothing to do with you anymore. I will be representing Tommy, and you can consider yourself out of my life." She tugged at Tommy's hand. "Let's go talk to Detective Mill. We need to tell him what happened here tonight. Then I need to get to the hospital." She turned on her heel and headed out of the kitchen.

"By the way." Francesca stopped at the kitchen door, turned to her father. "James was sleeping with Tiffani since the night of our wedding reception—that I know of. He slept with her hours before we consummated our marriage. I have a witness, but I know you won't believe me unless you see proof. You'll find all the proof you need in the manila envelope in the safe." Francesca slammed the door behind her.

Thirty-Five

FRANCESCA LIMPED HER way to the driveway when she saw the taxi stop in front of the house.

"God, I've missed you." Francesca's smile came with a wince as she threw her arms around Lily.

Lily looked like Hollywood royalty in a white cashmere cape and red knee-high boots that stood out amid the white snow-covered ground. Gold columns danced at her ears. Diamonds on her neck and fingers gleamed under the afternoon sunlight.

"I've missed you more." Lily's voice was edged with her Texan drawl. "Hello, Bear. I've missed you too, little guy." She bent down to scratch Bear behind the ears when he gave her a couple of cheerful yaps. "Let me look at you, sugar." Although Francesca wore a cowl neck sweater to hide the choking marks, her bruised face, swollen eye, mending lip, and slung arm was visible. "Christ, Frankie, you look terrible."

"You sure know how to flatter a girl." Francesca flinched when she attempted to curve her lips into a smile.

"I'm glad that sonofabitch is dead. If Tommy hadn't killed him, I would have." The fury in Lily's tone made the taxi driver freeze mid-air with the suitcases. "Do you have cucumbers? If not, I can get the driver to pick some up."

Francesca would have frowned if she could maneuver it without inducing pain. "I think we can dig some up."

"Good. I'm going to give you a cucumber facial. It won't get rid of the bruises, but it will make you feel great. Now, enough talk of murder and facials. Sugar, would you take all this luggage into the house?" Lily handed a crisp fifty-dollar bill to the driver, who returned a toothless grin.

"Travelling puts a thirst on you, and I need to get me a large glass of peach schnapps. I hope you stocked up."

"Will one case do for your two-week stay?"

"The liquor store is not too far, is it?"

Francesca snorted a giggle. "You haven't changed one bit."

"Why would I change perfection? Now lead the way," Lily said, linking arms with her best friend's.

Settled into the study sofa, Lily took a satisfying sip of schnapps. "The living room is still out of bounds?"

"Not because it's still a crime scene. The police and forensic investigators are done poking around. I'm renovating the entire room, replacing all the furniture and rugs. All reminders of that night need to go." A good sign, Lily thought. Francesca had accepted and understood death happened here, and she was getting on with her life—like ripping a Band-Aid off. What had happened to her was shocking, and devastating, but what had happened under her roof, in a disturbing way, was empowering. "Although, and I'll only admit this to you, there are times I walk past that room and picture James face down in a pool of his blood, and I feel an infusion of pleasure. Is that morbid of me?"

"No. It's your way of dealing with the anger and the hate you've bottled up all this time. More importantly, it's your way of refuting blame for his actions against you and his death. And that's how it should be because none of what happened, his death, your assaults, and the beatings was your fault. Abusers do their best to ensnare their victims in a cycle of self-blame and you're recognising you neither asked nor deserved any of it. I wish you would have told me about what you were going through, Frankie. Not for my professional help, but because I'm your friend. I would have hopped on the first flight out to be with you."

"I know you would have, and it wasn't that I didn't want to tell you. It was because I was ashamed. James made me feel as if I deserved every beating. He made me feel worthless, and eventually, I believed it because I couldn't get Tommy off my mind. I felt James was justified in doing what he did to me because he'd often say I was thinking of

Tommy when we made love, or he kissed me, and it was true." Francesca sipped on brandy to wet her sand-dry throat. "I only told Tommy because he guessed what was going on."

"I'm glad Tommy came into your life when he did. I'm glad you had him to turn to." Lily coaxed Bear onto the sofa and delighted him with head scratches when he did.

"I wish I hadn't told him anything. By getting him involved, my worst fears came true. Look at the mess I got him into. I managed to get him out on parole, but now he's facing life in prison. He's lost his church pending the investigation, and he's the talk of his parishioners, of the country." Francesca handed Lily a handful of newspapers from the stack.

The headlines read: PRIEST KILLS RENOWNED ATTORNEY. JAMES TEMPLETON III BLUDGEONED IN HIS HOME BY PRIEST. JAMES TEMPLETON THE III, WIFE ABUSER, BLUDGEONED TO DEATH BY WIFE'S PRIEST. PRIEST HAILED AS HERO FOR KILLING WIFE ABUSER JAMES TEMPLETON III.

"You have to stop reading this trash. And if I learned anything from being a governor's daughter is that people's memories are short. This will blow over after the trial is done." Lily tucked her legs beneath her as she stirred her drink with a manicured finger. "And the last headline and article praise his action."

"I know, but those are far and few. In the meantime, Tommy has to endure this because of me. Although he doesn't say anything, I know he spends his days wondering if he's going to end up in jail." Francesca flicked eyes to the fir Missy, Mrs. Richards, and Scott set up in the study, hoping to infuse Christmas cheer at a somber time.

"Your father won't allow that. He's the best criminal lawyer there is. Tommy couldn't get better representation than Peter Thompson." Lily laid a reassuring hand over Francesca's. "He'll get Tommy his freedom."

"I pray to God he will. I was shocked and thrilled when daddy stepped in to defend Tommy when I had to recuse myself. Not so much because he's an excellent attorney, but because it's made me believe we can mend our frayed relationship. He's finally acknowledged how wrong he was about Tommy." Francesca's gaze was focused on some distant point as she dug into memories of Peter and her. "Our relationship is a work in progress, but my mom would be happy to see how much closer we've become."

"She'd also be thrilled your father finally came to his senses and sent that two-timing, floozy on her way and without as much as cab fare." Lily stroked Bear's tummy when he flipped, paws up, for her.

"A personal triumph of mine. Tiffani won't be getting a dime from Daddy, nor will she contest the divorce. Not after my father threatened to hand out the photos I gave him to the wives of the men she was sleeping with. I only had the stomach to look at the top four or five when Lamont handed me the package. It turns out the remaining ones weren't of James and Tiffani. They were of Tiffani and a litany of married men she'd met at the country club." Francesca walked to the bar cart, picked up the peach schnapps and brandy bottle, walked them to the sofa. "I'm glad Lamont pursued that angle after he was done with James."

"It's too bad that your dad won't be able to release the photographs. Those poor women should be told what their husbands were up to, if not still, because once a bimbo always a bimbo." Lily held her glass out to Francesca for a top-up of schnapps.

"My father can't, but I can." Francesca fished for the envelope from the desk drawer. "I kept copies of the photographs. Once daddy finalizes his divorce and turns over his photographs and negatives to Tiffani's lawyers, these copies will mysteriously make their way to each wife."

"I always knew that beneath that sweet-as-sugar girl, there was a devious bitch." Lily flashed Francesca, a wicked grin. "I have to say, Frankie, no one would ever know you used to steer clear of conflict."

"Trouble seems to go out of its way to find me nowadays."

"When do I get to meet Tommy? I'm dying to get to work on helping him get his full memory back." Lily yawned, stretched across the sofa next to a snoring Bear.

"He's joining us tonight for Christmas eve dinner. As will Daddy, Missy, Mrs. Richards, and Scott. It's going to be the best Christmas ever." Francesca spread the throw over Lily as she dozed off in sleep.

Thirty-Six

THE MAY AIR was sweet with the hints of spring. Trees capped with the fresh greenness of the new season danced under a warm breeze, and birds flitted in celebration. The spring-like bliss didn't carry into the courtroom where the verdict on the murdering priest was about to be rendered after what felt like five long, excruciating months to Tommy.

In courtroom two, the atmosphere was ripe with anticipation, the silence stifling as every eye in the room, spectators, reporters, photographers, Francesca, and Lily—who'd flown in to support Francesca and Tommy—was on the foreman. At the defendant's table, Tommy stood, his head bowed in prayer. Beside him, Peter inhaled deeply.

"Mr. Foreman, has the jury reached a verdict?" The judge asked.

"We have, Your Lordship."

Every eye followed the clerk who took the verdict form from the foreperson and walked it to the judge. Eyes locked on the judge, they tried to read the expression on his face as he unfolded and read, but his face gave nothing away. In unison, everyone's eyes swiveled from the clerk to the foreman when he handed the verdict form back.

"How does the jury find Thomas Scott in the murder of James Templeton III?" the judge asked.

"We find Thomas Scott." There was a moment's hesitation and whether the foreman did it for effect or to savor the power he wielded at that moment, was anyone's guess. "Not guilty in the murder of James Templeton III."

Tommy's legs buckled, and he fell into his chair, his hands locked in thankful prayer. A triumphant Peter slapped a congratulatory hand on Tommy's back. Francesca's head dropped limply onto Lily's shoulder and let the tears of joy flow. Mr. and Mrs. White, who'd traveled across the country to be in the courtroom in support of the man who'd killed their daughter's murderer, hugged and cried.

"Mr. Scott, you are a free man," His Lordship slammed his gavel in the finality of the sensational case that had gripped the nation and headlined the front page of every newspaper and the nightly news for months.

On the courthouse steps, when the commotion from the cheering crowd, the reporters' questions stopped coming, and the flashes from snapping cameras died, Peter watched Francesca and Tommy. In her eyes, Peter saw happiness, something he hadn't seen for a long time. For the rest of his life, he'd regret discounting how happy Tommy made Francesca to put his interests above hers.

Peter blamed himself for every horrible experience Francesca endured with James. The hell she'd lived through with James was on him. He'd put her through all of it for no reason other than to satisfy his ego. He'd carry the guilt for the scars, the psychological trauma, Francesca would carry for the rest of his life. Peter hoped Francesca would let him make it up to her, allow him to become the father she deserved.

It had been five months since the night of Francesca's brutal attack, and aside for the scar above her right eye, her face showed no signs of the injuries James inflicted. Lily being a great friend, had devoted the past months to help Francesca work through her mental anguish. Those scars would take a lot longer to heal, but Lily was confident Francesca would one day be able to put the ugliness in her life behind.

"If you don't mind, honey, I'll drive Tommy back to the estate." Peter turned to Tommy. "I want to speak to you. All right with you, Son?"

"Of course, Mr. Thompson."

"It's Peter, Son."

Francesca smiled at that. Seeing the two most important men in her life coming together touched her deeply. "Thank you for what you did for Tommy, Daddy. I knew you wouldn't lose. You're a Thompson after all." Francesca pecked her father on the cheek. "I love you."

"I love you too, Frankie." Emotion choked Peter's voice. It had been too long since they'd said the words to one another.

"My car's here," Peter said to Tommy when his chauffeur pulled the town car up to the curb. Settled into the backseat, Peter offered Tommy a glass of champagne, touched crystal to crystal. "To your freedom."

"Thank you, sir, Peter."

Peter sipped champagne contemplatively. "You probably don't remember, but you and I haven't had a smooth relationship—ever. Mainly because of me. I was, as Frankie put it, a narrow-minded snob with tunnel vision. Let me finish, Son," he said when Tommy started to speak. "It's not easy for a man to admit his mistakes, but I was wrong about you. I'm sorry for not seeing the honorable man you are sooner."

Tilting back his glass, Peter drained champagne. "I'm also very grateful to you for giving my daughter back to me. Frankie and I haven't always had the type of father-daughter relationship we should since my wife died. Again, mainly because of me. That has now been rectified, and I have you to thank for that. I will forever be grateful to you for saving my daughter and for stepping in to take the blame for the murder she committed." In the silence that hung in the car, Peter topped up glasses with champagne.

"You knew?"

"I did. A few weeks after the night of the incident, when a cooler head prevailed, I went to see Frankie. She confessed she was the one who'd killed James, not you. In all honesty, I suspected it. I've defended enough murderers to know the difference between a passionate killing and a fortuitous one. James' murder was personal. It was indicative in the number of blows to the head. And yet you took the blame for a murder charge that could have sent you to jail for life. Why, Tommy? Why would you risk your life like that? There was a high probability you would have been found guilty. Was it because you thought as a priest, albeit an excommunicated one, you'd have emotional leverage on the jury? Was it to protect Frankie's reputation, her name?"

Tommy's eyes calm and level on Peter's he said, "It wasn't as strategic or as noble as all that. I did it because I love her, and she'd had enough hurt to last her a lifetime. I did it because Francesca didn't deserve to be labeled 'The Guilty Woman' by anyone."

Peter lifted a brow. Francesca was right, he thought. He wasn't half the man Tommy was. He'd been so wrong about Tommy, misjudged him all because he couldn't put his past behind. He'd talked himself into believing he knew what was best for Francesca and along the way convinced himself everything he did, every decision he made was in her best interest.

But it wasn't. What he wanted to do was control her, so she'd never leave him as Katherine had. It took Tommy Scott to make him realize how wrong he'd been and that everything he'd done was for himself to maintain control of a life gone off the rails after Katherine's death.

Marrying Tiffani was impulsive and stupid. She was a brainless bimbo, but he could control her—or so he'd thought. Peter had never been able to do that with Katherine. Katherine Thompson was a woman to be reckoned with. Katherine had been his equal, and she wouldn't allow him to forget it. And Francesca was as strong-willed as her mother, but he was losing her to Tommy, and he couldn't have that.

If Katherine were alive, she'd have seen through James' puffed up ego down to the skeleton of who he was the minute he'd set foot in their lives. If Katherine was alive, she'd allowed Francesca and Tommy to come together. The past few years would have been filled with happiness rather than horror.

Peter would never forgive himself for that.

"I'm sure you would have done the same for your wife, Katherine."

Without hesitation, Peter said, "Yes, I would."

"I love Francesca. I love her with all my heart. She makes me happy." Tommy smiled when he said that. "And isn't that our quest in life. To be happy."

Peter nodded. "But you're still leaving tomorrow?" he asked, looking out the window at the rain that was beginning to come down from a sky that had gone dark.

"I have to. I can't stay here with Francesca and pursue a relationship with her. They'll crucify her. She'll be forced to endure undeserved backlash, gossip, and innuendo. Not to mention the repercussion you and your firm will have to deal with. I can already see the headlines. ACQUITTED PRIEST MOVES IN ON HIS VICTIMS WIFE or PRIEST KILLS JAMES TEMPLETON III FOR HER. It's not going to benefit anyone if I stay."

"I suppose you're right, but you don't have to worry about me. I've weathered worse. Look at the headlines in the tabloids about Tiffani and me," Peter said, rolling eyes to the sky as the limousine pulled into the estate's driveway. "I want you to take this, Son. This will help you get settled wherever you're going."

Tommy opened the envelope. "I can't accept this."

"Sure, you can. It's the least I can do to help you get started on your new life. This is my way of saying thank you for giving my daughter back to me, and it'll help ease my guilt. I feel responsible for everything that's happened to you, son." Peter waved a finger in the air. "Do not insult me by giving it back. Now, go to Frankie. I understand Missy, Mrs. Richards, and Scott, have planned a celebratory dinner for the two of you. Make her happy for tonight. She deserves happiness." Peter held out a hand, and Tommy clamped it.

FRANCESCA AND TOMMY TRADED THEIR ROMANTIC dinner for a family celebration. With Lily, Missy, Mrs. Richards, and Scott, Francesca and Tommy enjoyed the lobsters, filet mignon and asparagus risotto the misses had prepared, along with the Pepperoni pizzas Missy ordered. They listened to Mrs. Scott's stories of Francesca and Tommy's youthful antics while Bear milled about for pizza scraps—his favorite. Eventually, Lily lifted her glass of wine, and everyone followed. Together, they toasted Tommy's freedom.

After dinner, tired from the long day, Lily went straight to bed. Mrs. Richards and Scott busied themselves cleaning up in the kitchen. After serving Francesca and Tommy, a warm cognac in the living room, Missy, along with Bear, disappeared for the night.

In comfortable silence, from the sofa, Francesca and Tommy watched lightning flash on the roar of thunder and split the sky. The patter of rain against the living room windows lent a romantic feel to the moment.

Francesca's head dropped limply onto Tommy's shoulder. "This is nice."

"It is." Tommy gathered Francesca to him, held her tight "Did you and Daddy have a good talk?"

"We did." Casually he wound her hair around his finger. "We agreed to let bygones be bygones."

"I thought I'd never see this day." Francesca rolled the idea of having two guardians in her life. It made her feel safe and protected. "I'm so glad because I need both of you in my life."

Tommy could smell her hair, fresh clean. "I don't know how I'll ever repay him."

"You don't owe him anything. It's me who owes him for keeping you from going to prison. I couldn't stand to lose you again." Francesca watched lightning as it slashed and flashed over the rise, lancing it white like fireworks on New Year's Day. "Thank you for what you did for me, Tommy. If I'd admitted guilt, I would have been disbarred. Lawyering, saving people from the injustices this life wreaks on them is all I know. It's what I love to do."

"I know." Tommy touched his lips to hers when she started to speak again. "There are only three of us who know the truth."

"Four." Francesca corrected. "I told Lily in one of our sessions."

"And your secret's safe with her. As I was saying, there are four of us who know the truth of what happened that night, and neither Lily, your father, you, or I will discuss this again. Understood?"

"Understood."

"You're meant to do good, to fight injustice for those who can't do it for themselves, Francesca. For you, it's not about money or prestige. It's about being a good person, using your God-given talent to help right the wrongs in this world."

Francesca's lips quivered into a smile. He understood her so well, always had. She gaped at him for five seconds, then scrambled to her feet. "I just thought of a way I can thank you," she said, then held out a hand for his.

When he took it, she led him up the stairs to her bedroom.

They made love all night, celebrated life, and their newfound love in the shadows of candlelight. When Francesca woke in the morning, she reached out for Tommy, but in his place found the note on his pillow.

> *My beautiful Francesca,*
>
> *By the time you read this, I'll be on a flight out of the country.*
>
> *Last night was the most wonderful night of my life. Being with you, making love with you, having you nestled in my arms made me feel complete and loved.*
>
> *I've felt a void in my life for a long time, and I thought it was my lost memories causing it. That may have been part of it, but Last night you filled a huge part of that void. After last night, I realized the emptiness I've felt all these years was from not having you in my life. I'm so blessed to have found you again.*
>
> *I love you, Francesca Thompson. I love you so very much.*
>
> *It's why I left this morning without saying goodbye. I couldn't face you. I couldn't look into your eyes and say*

goodbye. It's cowardice of me, and I'm sorry, but I couldn't do it.

You will be in my dreams and my thoughts every hour of every day. When I'm missing you, I'll look up to the stars and search for your face in them. I hope you do too.
Love Tommy

His words struck like fists in her heart, and she broke down in tears.

Epilogue

IT WAS NEARING noon when Francesca steered the car off the main road onto the driveway. The crackle of gravel on the tires of her rental car as she drove up to the ornate wrought iron gate felt oddly comforting.

In the horizon, the quiet undeniable beauty of the snow-covered peak rising majestically into floating white clouds in the distance caught Francesca's eye. Rolling green hills where sheep and goats grazed spread out like a beautiful oil painting.

It was November, harvesting season on the Mediterranean island. Dozens of pickers were busy filling their baskets with olives from the hundreds of trees lined in perfect rows, heavy with fruit.

Stepping out of the car, Francesca waved Bear out. Leaping out, Bear darted to the manna tree, sniffed, then lift his leg. That taken care of, Bear's ears pricked at the sound of bleating goats and baaing sheep, and off he went to explore.

Tipping back the wide brim of her sunhat, Francesca watched Bear run down the sloping hill. "Don't go too far, Bear. I don't want you getting lost," she called out as he yapped at his new friends in introduction.

"He's always made friends easily." The woman's voice came at Francesca over her shoulder.

"Lily." Francesca went in for a fierce hug. "It's so great to see you. You look great," she said, stepping back to study her. Her skin was bronze against the white, flowing sundress. Her hair was uncharacteristically tied into a braid behind her, and her pretty face was unpainted.

"You too." There were more hugs, kisses, and tears. "I wasn't expecting you."

"I wanted to surprise you. And yes, I know we agreed I wouldn't come to visit you for one year, but six months is long enough."

"You don't have to sell me. I'm thrilled you're here. Let's get you something to drink. This hot sun can dehydrate an ocean."

"I love this place. It looks so Mediterranean-ish."

The home was a Spanish style villa with golden stone walls, large picture windows, and a terracotta roof. A large wooden door, ornate and medieval-looking, was flanked with terracotta vases spearing colors from daisies and violas. Red, white, and pink bougainvillea tumbled from balconies encased in wrought iron.

With a grin, Lily nodded. "It is beautiful. And it's been perfect for my intended purpose."

"I'm so glad." Francesca's eyes filled with a mound of delight. "How's your book coming along?"

"Swimmingly. This place has been inspirational. I'm so glad I listened to your father and took an earlier sabbatical." Lily hugged an arm around Francesca's shoulders. "I hope you're hungry. Paolo cooks up a true Italian feast for lunch every day."

Francesca caught the smile that lit Lily's face. "Paolo, is it?"

"It is. I met him up at the local winery, which by the way, he owns. He's a vintner, he's gorgeous, and a fantastic lover. The man tires me out. Can you believe it? Me?"

"That's way more information than I need." Francesca breathed in the fragrance of the flowers in bloom mixed with the scent of the sea.

Lily broke into a brilliant smile. "You're such a prude, Frankie. How you could be my best friend boggles my mind."

"How a nympho could be my best friend boggles my mind." Francesca wiped the sheen of sweat that had already pearled on her face. "Is it always so hot here?"

"It's actually a coolish eighty today. And there he is," Lily said when they rounded the side of the house. "I could watch him all day."

Francesca's eyes darted to the man setting the picnic table under a pergola swathed in colorful bougainvillea.

Large steel-gray were set in a roman face with an olive complexion and a fashionable dark stubble. A bounce of ash-brown hair flitted in the wind. The fit of his blue jeans against the tight behind was as admirable, as the white, cotton shirt that traced broad shoulders and thick arms.

"Jesus, he's gorgeous."

"And great in bed." Lily bit on her bottom lip.

"So I've heard," Francesca said on a long sigh.

"Paolo, amore. That's my love in Italian." Lily explained to Francesca. "I want you to meet my dearest friend, Frankie."

"Ah, you are Francesca. Lily tell me all about you." Paolo took Francesca's hand, pressed it to his lips then, launched into an Italian exchange that flowed like sweet music. Neither woman understood a word, but both listened intently sighing in unison.

"I'm not Italian. The only thing Italian about me is my name," Francesca said when he stopped speaking.

"No worry. I teach you. I already teach Lily a few choice words in Italian. Right, amore?" A wicked grin spread slowly across Paolo's face eliciting a mirror response from Lily. "You excuse me now, Francesca. I must finish making lunch. You come to help me, Lily." Paolo said with a wink.

Coded message understood Lily glanced over at Francesca. "I really should go to help him. He does things with fruit," she whispered in Francesca's ear.

"I'm sure he does."

"Will you be okay by yourself?" When Francesca nodded, Lily pointed the way. "Follow the path. It will lead you to the olive grove."

"YOU LOOK WONDERFUL." THE VOICE CAME at Francesca from between the trees.

"So do you. The Sicilian sun agrees with you." Francesca's gaze locked on his. He wore jeans, and the white T-shirt smudged with dirt, hugged tanned arms. His dark hair now long, crowned the face golden brown from his days in the sun. "I've missed you so much." Francesca fell into Tommy's arms.

His mouth was on hers quick and hard. Her taste floating in him the memories came—all of them. In his mind, Tommy saw the beautiful girl in the tiny bikini sun tanning by the pool now a woman, wiser, more sophisticated, but as striking as the first day he laid eyes on her.

"I've missed you too. God, have I missed you." This time. Tommy slowly kissed her neck. His scent, sweat, and man made every bone in Francesca's body go limp. "I thought we agreed to keep our distance for twelve months to let the sensationalistic media become distracted and off me, off you, and the case."

"We did, but I couldn't wait any longer to see you. Besides, I've decided I'm staying here with you. Lily said this place been your salvation."

"It has been, but how are you going to practice law here. You don't speak the language?"

"Daddy wants me to open offices in Europe, and you and Paolo can teach me."

"I'm not letting you near that Italian Casanova. Besides, he's too busy chasing after Lily most days he won't have time to teach." Tommy pulled her in closer. "I've put up with him because Lily has been great. Your father talking her into coming out here with me to work on getting my memory back has been a Godsend. She's a damn good shrink."

"The best."

Tommy knelt to Bear's level when he appeared out of nowhere and rushed at Tommy. "Hey, little guy. Have you been exploring?"

"He has. He's already made friends," Francesca said when Bear's ears shot up at the bleating call and got on his way. "I'm sorry about your friend, Tommy."

He sat under the shade of the olive tree. "His name was Mike. I couldn't save him, and he died in my arms. He was just a kid, Francesca." His eyes sheened at the memory.

"I'm so sorry." Francesca sat next to him.

"Lily concluded Mikes' death, shell-shocked me, and caused the memory loss. She explained the guilt I felt for his death made me want to forget the event and everything leading to that moment. She, of course, said it in more medical terms, but the bottom line is I erased everything from my mind not to trigger the memory of Mike's death. Once she figured it all out, she made me call Mike's parents."

Francesca's hand clamped around Tommy's. "How did it go?"

"It was the hardest thing I've done, but Mike's mother was grateful. I called to share my story with her." Tommy went silent for a moment to bottle the emotions churning in him. "She thanked me for being there for her son when he took his last breath."

The ravages of war had far-reaching tentacles, Francesca thought. "Watching someone you love die in your arms is traumatic enough without having to deal with the additional stresses of death and destruction all around you, which is what you had to do. It's enough to break anyone." Francesca's face radiated sympathy.

Tommy buried his face in her neck and let long-held tears flow. Chaining her arms around him, Francesca cried with him.

"We're planting a tree in Mike's honor with a plaque dedicated to him. We'll make sure the tree lives forever, and the fruit will be given to Father Pio and the Benedictine Monastery in perpetuity in Mike's memory."

Tommy ran a finger over Francesca's wet cheeks. "Mike would like that," he said, casting eyes to the grove of trees and the grazing sheep and goats where Bear was running circles around his new friends.

"I remember everything, Francesca. It took Lily months to help me work through it, but it all came flooding back. I remember sitting with you on the hood of my truck and watching the stars on our first date. I remember making love with you next to the creek. I remember my father, Mrs. Scott, and your father. I remember Scott's Garden Center. I remember it all, and although the memories are wonderful, they don't matter as much anymore. I fell in love with you all over again without them. And it has to mean something. A lot, I think." Tommy got down on one knee. "You and I were meant to be together. Our destiny was written in the stars years ago, and I don't want to lose you ever again.

Will you make new memories with me? Will you marry me, Francesca?"

She felt the quick intake of her breath before she said, "Yes, yes, triple, yes."

Tommy's arms wrapped tight around her waist; he urged her up to her toes to glide his lips over her. "I don't have a ring to give you. I may not for some time. All my money is invested in the farm."

Hazel eyes steady on blue eyes she said, "I don't need a ring."

"Every woman needs a ring." Tommy reached for a blade of tall grass and wound it around her finger. There was a pause as she eyeballed the blade tied around her finger. "It's only until I can afford a real one."

Tears glistening in her eyes, Francesca took Tommy's face in her hands, "This is beautiful and perfect."

If you liked *The Guilty Woman*, look for M.L. Lexi's other novel: *The Unfaithful Woman*, available as eBook and paperback.

Special Excerpt from
THE UNFAITHFUL WOMAN

One

FROM BEHIND THE damask curtains of her living room, Anastasia watched the fire-red Ferrari race up the curved driveway. The unique famed roar of its engine pulsed, then went silent when it came to an abrupt stop next to the flowing fountain. A smile played across Anastasia's face. Only one person could be behind the wheel of the high-powered sports car.

How Tristan had come to be there when Anastasia hadn't worked up the nerve to call him to tell him about Minnie's funeral was anyone's guess. The last time they'd spoken, Tristan told her they should go their separate ways and disappeared from her life. In the past three decades, except for their two-week encounter and the dutiful attendance to her parents' funerals, Tristan slipped out of Anastasia's life as quickly as he came into it.

Anastasia felt a pressure in her chest, heavy and tight when the tangles of emotions long buried rushed at her. Tristan always managed to stir her insides without much effort.

The cold, steely glint in Anastasia's hazel eyes softened the moment she saw Tristan squeeze his six-foot frame out of the tight-fitting Ferrari. It felt like an eternity since she'd last seen him, yet the moment she did, the memories unspooled in her mind as if they'd happened yesterday.

Tristan Ferguson was her first love, the boy she'd shared her first kiss with. Tristan was the idealistic teenager who'd asked for her hand in marriage then disappeared from her life. Now here he was, after all these years looking tall, tanned, and as gorgeous as she remembered. D&G sunglasses perched on his nose the wind blowing through the long, honey-brown hair, Tristan looked like the subject in one of his famous paintings.

Anastasia watched Tristan slide the dark sunglasses off and flick blue eyes over the green rolling hills that stretched for acres to woods celebrating summer. The gardens that wound around the house were a rainbow of colors from lilac, roses, bleeding hearts, and rhododendrons in full bloom.

Tristan smelled it now, the familiar scents of horse and manure, and he looked over to the paddocks. His lips slowly curved when the mare whickered, big brown eyes aimed at him. His pulse picked up at the muffled thunder of hooves lifting off the earth as they raced around. There was no sound like it on earth, he thought. It had been a long time since he'd been around horses. God, he missed it.

Tristan's smile widened as the memories came flooding back. Stillbrook Estate was where he grew up, the place of his boyhood, and even after steering clear for decades, Tristan still considered it home.

On the stretch of grassed land, in the turn-of-the-century home, with its large picture windows and tall column entrance, was where Tristan had spent many memorable days. He and Anastasia had played and spent every waking minute together on that land. They'd mucked stalls in the stables, spent summer days swimming in the pool. Mill Pond was where they'd fished for trout. On sunny days, alongside Anastasia at the reins of her horse Bandit and he on Sparky, they'd ridden over the roll of land. Afterward, under the shade of the willow tree, he'd read to her.

In his artistic leaning phase, under the willow tree, with Anastasia watching on, Tristan flipped through the art books he frequently checked out from the local library. Tristan read about oils, impressionism, expressionism, and every ism there was. He absorbed the information like a sponge does water. Those books had steered him to the canvas, and in time, art became his passion and his chosen career.

Stillbrook always brought back good memories, but in the decades passed, Tristan had set foot on the land he considered home twice. The first time was for James' funeral when, at the young age of seventy-two, the unexpected heart attack took him in his sleep. The second time was one year later, for Caroline's funeral, who, after her thirty-seven years of marriage to James, Tristan believed she died of a broken heart. Now, he was here for Minnie's funeral.

Filling his lungs with air scented with earth and pine, Tristan rounded the car and picked up his overnight bag from the passenger seat. The tote was all he needed on this visit. He wasn't planning an extended stay this time, either. He was scheduled to fly out the day after the Minnie-bration—leave it up to Anastasia to come up with the cookie idea—to make an appearance at his art exhibit in Florence.

Bag in hand, Tristan walked up the stone walkway flanked with tulips dripping with color. At the tall, mahogany doors, Tristan hesitated for a beat, debating whether to use his key. In the end, he decided to ring the doorbell. Stillbrook hadn't been his home for too long. It was now Anastasia's, Colin's, and the twin's home.

On the second bell chime, the door swung open, and there she stood as if frozen in time.

ANASTASIA STUDIED THE TIMID EIGHT-YEAR-OLD boy with eyes as blue as the sky. He was way tall, Anastasia thought, and the short, sandy-blonde hair was way neat. He had long eyelashes above the large eyes and rosy cheeks. His T-shirt and blue jeans were way too clean. He wasn't anything like the messy, dirty boys from school.

The tall woman holding his hand tilted her eyes down to Anastasia. Her smiling eyes looked like luminous black pools in a flawless face that might have been carved out of polished onyx. Her hair, dark as her skin, was rolled into a bun, making her look taller. She had an exceptionally long, thin neck, like a giraffes Anastasia thought where a canary-yellow bauble necklace that matched her summer dress hung. Her arms and wrists were slim but elegant. She looked like the Nubian Queen Anastasia had seen in a book in her father's library.

"Who are you?" Anastasia studied Minnie, a frank and cagey stare out of brown eyes.

"This here is Tristan Ferguson, and I'm Minnie Williams, your new maid. "And you must be Anastasia," Minnie said.

"How do you know my name?" Anastasia blew a bubble of gum as pink as her lips.

"I'm a friend of your father's," Minnie told the petite girl with the delicately upturned nose dotted with freckles.

Anastasia brushed the cloud of chestnut hair around the pretty, heart-shaped face back. "Daddy has a lot of friends. He says that when you own a large law firm, everyone wants to be your friend."

"Is that so?" Minnie stifled a chuckle. "I like your dress. It's frilly and flowy, and yellow like mine."

"I like yours too. Daddy never told me about a new maid with a shy boy. You going to live here?" Anastasia eyed the suitcases.

"You are an inquisitive one." Minnie smiled a quick flash that deepened the lines time had etched on her face. "Yes, I'm going to live here."

"Him too?" Anastasia's eyes latched onto Tristan.

"He is." Minnie slung an arm around the young boy entrusted to her through death. "We travel together. You could say we're a package deal."

Anastasia shrugged her shoulders. "Did the cat get his tongue? That's what Mama says when I don't answer her back."

"He's just a bit shy. Aren't you, Tristan? But something tells me, Anastasia, that in time, you'll draw all that shyness out of him." Minnie gave Anastasia a wink.

"I can do that. I'm six and three-quarters years old. How old are you?"

"Well, go on, boy tell Anastasia."

"I'm eight." Tristan's voice was quiet and flat.

"I bet you can't pronounce my name." Anastasia's defying tone prodded.

"Can too." Tristan shot back indignantly.

"Prove it. Go on, say it."

"Ana ... Anas ... ummm ... Tassie."

Anastasia's giggle sounded remarkably girlish. *"I told you."*

"I can't say it because it's a stupid name."

Anastasia crossed her arms. *"Nuh-uh, it's a princess's name."*

"Sure, it is. Anyway, you look like a Tassie to me," Tristan's lips proudly spread when she smiled.

"I like it. You can call me Tassie. Do you want to play? I have lots of toys in my bedroom. I'll share them with you."

Tristan lifted his eyes to Minnie. *"Can I go play with Tassie, Auntie Minnie?"*

Minnie smiled at the pleading eyes, staring up at her. It was the first time since his parent's death he'd expressed an interest in anything. *"Of course you can, honey."*

"Well, come on, follow me," Anastasia said, and Tristan did.

Since that day, Tristan followed Anastasia everywhere, becoming inseparable best friends, sharing everything.

"HI," TRISTAN'S EYES HELD ONTO ANASTASIA'S.

She wore jeans, tight and faded, a flowing teal blouse, tucked at the waist, and patent ballet flats at her feet. Her long, chestnut hair spilled around the unpainted face seemingly untouched by time. It had been years since he last saw her, but she was as beautiful as the picture he'd taken and carried with him all this time.

"Hi." Anastasia stepped back and let him in. "Nice ride. It suits you."

Tristan's lips curved into a smug grin. "The fiery-red is me," he said, setting his carry-on down on polished tiled.

"I was leaning more toward the midlife crises message it screams out." Anastasia let out a quick smirk.

"If I recall, you're only two years younger than me." Following her into the living room, Tristan headed straight for the bar. "And by the way, I'm three years away from fifty, which is the official mid-life crisis age."

"There's an official age?" Anastasia fell back into the soft leather of the long sectional, which had replaced the Victorian couch.

"There is for me. I see you've remodeled. I like the modern look. It's very ... you." Tristan eyed the glass, leather, and chrome that filled the room. "Brandy, still your drink?" Rounding the bar, he caught sight of the large vase filled with freshly picked roses. He remembered how, at first bloom, she'd fill every vase in the house with fresh daisies from the gardens.

"Yes, but we only have cognac." Brandy's not a woman's drink. From now on, you drink cognac, Colin told her when they'd married and replaced brandy bottles with Remy Martin. "Isn't it too early for a drink? It's only ten in the morning."

"It's four in the afternoon where I'm from." Tristan poured two glasses and walked them, and the bottle, to the sofa. "You look great, Tassie." He shook off the pain he felt in his heart when she reached for the handed glass, and her wedding band doused him in reality.

"You do too, but as a painter, shouldn't you espouse the poor starving artist look?" Over the sexy soccer player one, she held back saying.

"Why should I? I'm neither starving nor poor. I sold my last painting to Oprah for half a million dollars. Before that, the Clintons bought my The Art of Politics for as much."

"You've come a long way." Anastasia watched Tristan walk to the baby grand when he caught sight of the collection of photographs. "Olivia and Jimmy are eighteen now."

"I know." Tristan cast an eye over the framed photographs, and the ache went into him fast.

Aside from the black-framed glasses, Olivia was the spitting image of her mother. Dark, intelligent eyes, long, chestnut hair, ivory skin, and a daintily upturned nose. As her twin, Jimmy looked much like Olivia, with a masculine allure. Seeing the photographs stung deeply, and Tristan downed the cognac in one swallow to soothe the pain.

Tristan imagined the joy of being a father. Marriage and fatherhood hadn't been in the cards for him. The only woman he loved slipped through his fingers, and he'd never married and made a family. It wasn't by design. It was just how things had worked out for him. So instead, Tristan had focused his time and energy on his career. Just as well, becoming a worldwide renowned artist had taken a lot of time and energy.

"You haven't seen the twins since Mama's funeral." Anastasia crossed one leg beneath her.

Tristan's eyes never left the photograph as he refilled his glass with a double shot. "It's best that way."

"In case you were wondering, they're in London right now, getting themselves settled into their residence at Oxford."

"Oxford?" Tristan arched a brow. "Impressive."

"Jimmy is planning to study law. Olivia is also, with a minor in art. Although I have a feeling, it will in time become her major." Anastasia studied Tristan over the rim of her glass. She was pleased to see the smile of approval on his face. That Olivia had a proclivity for something, he was so passionate about undoubtedly pleased Tristan.

"Good genes in those kids."

The comment made her smile. "They take after their parents."

"Mmm-hmm." Tristan tipped the glass to his lips, drank deeply.

"They're staying at the Royal London Hotel for a couple of days before they settle into their dorms. Then they'll be off on a tour of Europe. It's their graduation gift. They left last week before Minnie left us. When they found out, they were devastated. They wanted to take the next flight out, but I told them what Minnie would want for them is to focus on making memories rather than thinking of death."

Tristan nodded. "That's exactly what she'd have said."

"Colin's with them." Anastasia crossed one slender leg over another, drawing his eyes. Those legs were still as long and as toned as he remembered. "He flew out with the twins. We were supposed to go together, but when Minnie took a turn for the worse, I stayed behind." Anastasia lied.

"THE DOCTOR SAYS HER CANCER HAS metastasized, Colin. He says Minnie has weeks, if not days left." Anastasia dabbed a tissue at her teary eyes.

A stoic Colin continued to stack folded shirts and pants into his suitcase. When Anastasia reiterated the diagnosis, Colin's only response was a succinct, "And?"

Anastasia stared at him with disbelief. When she pointed out they couldn't leave Minnie at the end of her life, and they'd need to postpone their trip, Colin angrily shot the idea down. Flinging rolled socks into his suitcase like projectiles, Colin made it clear he and the children were not putting their life on hold for a dying maid.

Anastasia shot Colin a shocked look. Minnie was family. She was a part of the family, had been an integral part of Anastasia's life since she was a child. Minnie raised her, raised the twins. But Colin was adamant. He and the children weren't sticking around for death to fetch Minnie. They were leaving in the morning—with or without her.

"I don't care if you stay behind." I prefer it if you did. "But my children and I will not lower ourselves to cater to a common maid." Colin waved a hand in Anastasia's face to silence her. "End of discussion. Now, make yourself useful and help the twins pack and, Anastasia, not a word about Minnie to them."

"COLIN'S GETTING THEM SETTLED IN. HE won't be back for a week," Anastasia added, watching Tristan dip his hand into his shirt pocket for the pack of cigarettes. "Sorry, you can't smoke in the house. Colin doesn't like the smell."

"Colin doesn't like much, does he?" Tristan tucked the pack back into his pocket. "Does he know I'm staying here?"

"Of course."

Tristan's eyebrows shot up at the blatant lie. "Really."

"Really. Will you stay the week, Tristan?" Anastasia watched him considering and assuming he was leaning toward turning her down said, "I want you to stay. I miss talking to you. I miss having you around. I miss you, Tristan."

"I fly out the day after tomorrow. I have an art exhibition to attend…"

"In Florence, at the prestigious *Le Gallerie Degli Uffizi*. Yes, I keep track of you, Tristan," she said when his brow winged.

"Yes, well, I need to be there."

"Colin's not here, Tristan. You don't need to run away. This is your home as much as it's mine. It's our home."

"It's not, Tassie. It's your home, your husband's, Jimmy, and Olivia's. It's your family's home."

Something in the way he spoke the words made Anastasia's stomach knot. She reached for his hand, tightening it to keep him from walking away. "We're your family, Tristan."

At the feel of her warm hand on his, it felt as if she touched his past.

"WHEN I GET OLD ENOUGH, AND you do too, I'm going to marry you, Tassie," Tristan looked deep into her eyes.

"Okay." Anastasia beamed.

Tristan reached into his pocket, and drawing the Cracker Jack prize ring slid it on Anastasia's finger. "As long as you wear it, Tassie, you're my girl."

Anastasia held it up to the sunlight to admire. The plastic diamond sparkled in the light, and she thought she'd never seen anything so beautiful. She promised Tristan she'd never take it off.

Anastasia was eight, and he was ten when they swore on the promise, but that wasn't how it worked out. At eighteen, Tristan went off to school in Milan to study art. Five years later, when Tristan was due to return home, he found out

Anastasia had married Colin Wilder and built a new life for herself—without him.

Something crumbled inside Tristan, but he had no one to blame but himself. He should have never left Anastasia. Absence didn't make the heart grow fonder, he thought. It drove the woman you loved to seek comfort in the arms of another man. It made the woman you wanted to spend the rest of your life with slip away and into Colin's arms.

The heartache Tristan felt was like a sharp knife cutting deep and clean, and he planned to fly back and win Anastasia back. He'd made it as far as the boarding gate when he realized disrupting Anastasia's life was selfish of him and vowed to remain in Milan.

Tristan pledged then never again to set foot at Stillbrook.

"DID YOU HEAR WHAT I SAID, Tristan?" Anastasia's voice brought him back.

"Yeah, you got my room ready for me and lunch is at noon and dinner is at six. No doubt more of Colin's rules," Tristan said, slamming his empty glass on the bar counter.

"Don't be like that."

"Well, am I lying?"

Anastasia dismissed the jab. "I'm sorry about Minnie, Tristan. I know she was like a mother to you."

Emotions swam into Tristan's eyes. Minnie had been his rock, his protector. Without a second thought, she selflessly assumed the role of mother and father when his parents died. Were it not for Minnie, Tristan would have ended up in foster care, living with strangers, bounced through an imperfect system. Tristan's life would have been much different from the caring, loving one he'd had were it not for Minnie. Minnie made him the man he was today.

And he'd repaid her by leaving, absolved himself from the guilt of deserting her with the random call home. He called Anastasia weekly, and when told she wasn't available to take the call, he'd default to speaking to Minnie, but both knew she hadn't been his primary reason for calling.

Tristan hoped Minnie understood he couldn't come back to Stillbrook because he couldn't stomach the idea of coming back to the home he no longer considered his. He'd rather die than see the only woman he'd ever loved sliding into the arms and bed of another man. No matter the reasons, the excuses Tristan made didn't justify leaving Minnie. She'd sacrificed her life for him. Minnie had given up everything for him and opened her heart to him. Everything Tristan had, who he was, he owed to Minnie, and now it was too late for him to make it up to her.

He'd carry the guilt for the rest of his life.

Anastasia drew herself off the couch, walked to Tristan. "I wish you would come back more often than for funerals. I've missed you, Tristan." Anastasia took a step forward. Tristan took one back. She always managed to draw feelings from him with few words.

"Me too."

"I want you to stay." Anastasia stirred more than old memories.

It wasn't a good idea to stay under the same roof with her. Anastasia was a married woman, a mother. She had a family, and he was an intruder now. "All right, but only for a couple of days. After the funeral, I'm leaving," Tristan said without a second thought.

Anastasia considered it a small victory. "Up to you, but you can stay for as long as you want. You must be tired from the long flight. Get settled in. Maybe take a shower to wash the day off. You know the way."

"I do." Tristan's hand on the doorknob, he stopped. "Do you want to go for a run? I'm wound up from the flight. The run will relax me. We can run to the pond and back."

Anastasia's eyes lit with a smile. "Like old times," she said, thinking it wasn't going to be an ordinary couple of days.

Coming Soon

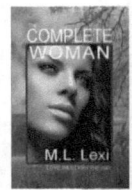   

Visit us at www.mllexi.com to read excerpts of
upcoming releases.
Author contact: mllexiauthor@gmail.com
Visit our website at mllexi.com
Visit our blog at mllexi.blog

Email us mllexiauthor@mail.com to receive emails
whenever M.L. Lexi publishes a new book. There's no
charge or obligation and your information will remain
confidential